FELL MURDER

CONTENTS

INTRODUCTION

Fell Murder, first published in 1944, was written when E.C.R. Lorac was at the height of her powers. The crucial ingredients of character, setting, and plot are so nicely balanced that it is surprising that this book has been out of print for decades. But the success of previous reprints of Lorac novels by the British Library has shown that there is an appreciative twenty-first century readership for her brand of well-made traditional detective fiction.

This was Chief Inspector Macdonald's first case in Lunesdale, Lorac's love of which is evident from the very first page. Her description of the countryside is lyrical. We are introduced to the area through the eyes of a local man, John Staple, who gazes out as far as "the blue hills of the Lake District... Scafell, the Langdale Pikes and Helvellyn. Staple had climbed them all, and he knew every ridge and notch of the blue outlines." But Staple's home is in that part of the country just to the south of the Lake District, less well-known but with a charm of its own, the valley of the River Lune. Lorac is especially interested in the close connection between the people of Lunesdale and the landscape. Although not a farmer, from start to finish she displays a deep empathy for farming folk, and the pressures (and compensatory delights) of their way of life.

Staple is surprised to encounter Richard Garth, who is making a brief trip back to Lunesdale after an absence of twenty-five years. He is the eldest son of old Robert Garth, but left after a fierce row about his decision to marry a local woman (now deceased) of whom his father disapproved. But Richard isn't in the mood to bury the hatchet. He makes clear that he has no wish to meet up with members of his own family, or indeed his late wife's father, another man with a grudge against Robert Garth. As he sets off for a hike, Richard makes Staple promise not to tell anyone of his return to the area. However, their conversation has been overheard…

Fell Murder is, therefore, an example of that interesting sub-genre of crime fiction, the "return of the prodigal" story. A returning prodigal can be a catalyst for outbursts of passion leading to murder, and over the years a great many detective novels have rung ingenious changes on this theme: Julian Symons' *The Belting Inheritance*, another British Library Crime Classic, is a case in point. Agatha Christie's *Hercule Poirot's Christmas* and *A Pocket Full of Rye* both concern the return of a prodigal son, although her two plots are quite different from each other. Highly readable crime stories in this vein include Josephine Tey's *Brat Farrar*, Mary Stewart's *The Ivy Tree*, Martha Grimes' *The Old Fox Deceiv'd*, Robert Barnard's *Unruly Son*, S.T. Haymon's *Death of a God*, Peter Robinson's *The Hanging Valley*, and Ruth Rendell's *Put on by Cunning*.

One doesn't need to be a great detective to foresee that Robert Garth is likely to fall victim to murder. Elderly, rich, and hot-tempered, he is a super-typical murderee in a detective story. But it's worth noting that Lorac's depiction of him is less simplistic than was often the case in Golden Age mysteries. As Staple says, Robert has "got some good qualities in him, for all that he can be a bitter enemy… By and large, he's been a good landlord."

And Lorac makes clear that being a good landlord is a major point in a man's favour. She takes pains to describe the hardships endured by people working on the land, and the ethos of co-operation between owners of neighbouring farms, and the people who work on them. Robert may be in his eighties, but even after a day's work he's prepared to lend a hand when someone else has need of assistance. A major strength of *Fell Murder* is the fascinating picture it paints of life in rural England during the later stages of the Second World War.

The farming community is close-knit, and when the police investigate a murder, Superintendent Layng finds that his methods are ill-suited to the task of winning the confidence of people he needs to question. The acting chief constable frets that Layng isn't ideally suited to leading the investigation at a time when the local force is stretched with other duties. These are memorably summarised: "Rural inspection, use of petrol, surveillance of aliens, registration of alien children arriving at the age of sixteen, black-out offences, licences for pig-killing, black-market offences—even bee-keepers added their quota to police work of to-day, for hives had to be officially inspected before the bee-keepers could get a certificate empowering them to get sugar for winter feed."

So Scotland Yard is called in, and although Macdonald is a Scot based in London, he feels instantly at home in Lunesdale. He doesn't waste time, but nor does he rush to judgment. As he tells Staple, "this crime is conditioned by the place. To understand the one you've got to study the other." Nor does he pour scorn on Layng, whose report he finds admirable, and with whom he develops a sound working relationship. But Macdonald's empathy with people of widely divergent types makes him a more effective investigator than the superintendent.

Lorac does a good job of shifting suspicion around her cast of suspects before Macdonald uncovers the truth. And it's in keeping with the spirit of the story that, in the novel's closing lines, one of the characters whose lives have been turned upside down by crime exclaims: "Thank goodness for the beasts and the land!... Listen! That's the calves calling already—they can hear our voices. Doesn't it smell good out here?" As Macdonald takes his leave, he says that he wishes he'd learned how to milk a cow: nothing could better illustrate his down-to-earth nature, and his lack of resemblance to those brilliant eccentrics Holmes, Poirot, and Wimsey.

E.C.R. Lorac was the principal pen-name of Edith Caroline Rivett (1894–1958), who also wrote as Carol Carnac. A Londoner born and bred, she settled in Lunesdale in her fifties, following the death of her mother. By the time this novel appeared, her books had achieved a considerable following. Sound craftsmanship and compassion for the underdog characterise her writing, and these qualities, much in evidence in *Fell Murder*, ensure that her work has an enduring appeal.

MARTIN EDWARDS
www.martinedwardsbooks.com

FELL MURDER

TO

A FREEMAN OF LANCASTER

CHAPTER ONE

WHEN HE REACHED THE CREST OF THE FELL, JOHN STAPLE halted in the lee of the stone wall which ran along the edge of the Garthmere land. He was panting a little from the long climb and he leaned with his back against the rough unmortared stones and stood gazing westwards, while his sheep dog stood beside him with waving tail, facing the wind, alert for any indication of his master's wishes. A sturdy grey-haired man, nearing sixty, with long-sighted grey eyes and weather-beaten face, John Staple seemed part of the landscape himself.

The prospect before him was one of which Staple never wearied: he had known it for over half a century, and throughout that time no change had occurred to mar the familiar loveliness of fell side, valley, and distant hills. Far below him, the River Lune wound its serpentine curves across the wide flood plane: beneath the clear September sky the water shone blue, flowing out to Morecambe Bay, whose golden sands gleamed palely in the western distance. On the opposite side of the valley the ground rose in a series of ridges, wooded in places, but in the main showing the chequered carpet of farm land: intense green of the fog grass in the rich river dales, pale gold of stubble on the higher levels, blue-green of unharvested kale and mangold crops: lighter green of pasture. The sun caught the stone farm buildings of the hamlet of Gressthwaite, half hidden among the trees mid-way up the slope across the river. Far beyond to the north, the blue hills of the Lake District stood out clear against the sky—Scafell, the Langdale Pikes and Helvellyn.

Staple had climbed them all, and he knew every ridge and notch of the blue outlines. Behind him, on the farther side of the wall, the fell was clothed in heather, its fragrance heavy with the sweetness of honey. At his feet the rough pasture, in which bracken and bramble and bilberry mingled, sloped down to the richer pasture of the lower levels.

Staple stood very still, his hands gripping his stick, enjoying the keen wind which whistled round him, in his ears the call of peewits and curlews, while his grey eyes dwelt lovingly on the rich valley and embracing hills. His mind was not given to formulating his thoughts in explicit words, and it would have been alien to him to express the facile enthusiasm of the more vocal southern Englishman, but he was conscious of some warmth of comfort which dwelt in the wide prospect, of an unchanging certainty in an unstable and changing world.

The wind in his ears prevented Staple hearing the footsteps which approached him from the westward. A man came towards him striding unheard through the heather, but Staple's sheep dog gave a short bark of warning just as the newcomer approached. Staple turned quickly to face the latter, surprised at the intrusion of a stranger in that loneliness of fell and sky.

"You've forgotten me, John, but I haven't forgotten you." The newcomer's voice had an alien note, for something of an American accent sounded in the deep tone of a voice which yet retained something of its north of England quality. John Staple stared at the other, his brows knitted in perplexity for a moment. The newcomer was a tall, hefty fellow, clad in a suit of rough navy blue pilot cloth, with a seaman's jersey rolled up to his chin. He had thick stubbly hair, greyish about the temples, and very blue eyes deep-set beneath shaggy brows. Most of his square face was concealed by a short curly beard, once fair, but greying now, like his hair. His low square forehead and cheeks were tanned and weather-beaten, and the face was heavily lined, yet the blue smiling eyes still had a boyish look.

After a long stare, the perplexity in John Staple's face gave way to recognition and his long face lightened to a welcoming smile as his hand shot out eagerly to grasp the other's.

"Richard Garth, by gum! by all that's wonderful it's yourself, Richard. Lord, it's good to see you home again!… Twenty-five years it'd be since you went away."

Richard Garth gripped the outstretched hand in his own.

"Aye—not far short of twenty-five years, John. It was in 1919 I talked to you last, up here it was too, against this same wall. Home? Yes, it seems like home up here, with you to welcome me."

He turned and looked northward across the valley to the lakeland hills. "It hasn't changed, has it? I've often thought of this—the river and the dales and the fells. I've seen a lot of the world since I was here last, and—by the Lord!—I've seen nothing to equal this, not to my way of thinking."

"Aye, it's a good country," replied Staple. "I've lived in it all my life, and I ask for nothing better. Have you come home to stay, Richard?"

The other gave a short laugh. "Home to stay? No. I haven't a home to stay in. You know that. I came back to see—this: perhaps to see you, as well. I've got a week's leave between voyages. I've been on the Atlantic convoys these past three years. Tankers most often."

"Tankers, eh? You'll have seen a bit of trouble, then?"

Richard laughed a low, deep, quiet laugh.

"Trouble?" he echoed. "You've said it. I've been torpedoed three times and bombed too often to remember. They call me a mascot, because I always win through, and the chaps with me, too. Ten days in an open boat isn't anybody's idea of fun… Lord, let's leave all that out and talk about something else. How's life with you, John? Still a bachelor?"

"Aye—and likely to be. Things are much the same as they always were, only the work gets harder and we don't grow any younger. All this ploughing has meant a lot of work, and labour's scarce. We're always at it—never get a pause as we did in the old days. Harvest follows hard on Haytime in these parts." He paused a moment, and added, "Your sister's made a good farmer, Richard. She does a man's share and does it well."

"Lucky for the old man," replied Richard Garth. "I bet he gets all the work he can out of her, unless he's changed a lot since I knew him. He was a hard old devil."

"Aye. He was a hard man, and he's not changed," admitted Staple, "but Marion—she can stand up to him. She works on the land because she wants to, not because your father drives her. Truth to tell, I think he scorns women farmers." Staple turned and studied his companion. "You'll be going home to see them, Richard?"

The other gave a laugh that held no sound of mirth.

"Not I! When the old man kicked me out, he'd done with me for good—and I with him. I haven't forgotten, John. Some hates die hard."

"Hate is a bad master, Richard."

"Maybe. You remember Mary?"

John Staple nodded his grizzled head. "Aye. I remember her—and a bonny lassie she was. I was grieved when I learnt you'd lost her, Richard. It was a sorry business."

"Yes—a sorry business. We went out to Alberta, you know, took up some government land and set to work from the word go—built our own shack and broke our own land. We didn't have a child for the first four years—not until we'd got our house built and we were safely established. Of course, I hadn't a cent, but things were going well—and Mary wanted a child. I didn't send her into hospital—and things went wrong. She died, and her child died, for lack of some of that money that damned old father of mine could have spared without missing it. There are some things one doesn't forget. He cursed me when I told him I'd married Mary. I remember..."

He broke off and stood staring out over the sunlit valley, and as he looked, his face softened.

"I didn't come back here to brood over past days, John, nor did I come to see the old folks at home. I finished with them the day I walked out of Garthmere. I came here to see all this, and to have a tramp over Ingleborough and Giggleswick, and down into the Yorkshire dales. It's land you don't forget. When I was last adrift about a thousand miles from any land at all, I thought about all this—and I could have kicked myself because I hadn't walked over the Pennines into Ribblesdale again before I died. They talk about the call of the sea. Damned nonsense—but I understand the call of the land. God! It smells good up here! I don't wonder the bees are out for the heather honey."

"Bees? Yes. They're young Malcolm's. You don't know him, do you? You heard your father had married again—twelve months after you left home, it was. Malcolm was the child of his second marriage. He's not a bad lad, but a weakling—he's lame, and often ailing."

"How does the old man like that? He wasn't one of the soft-hearted kind: hated sickness of any sort."

"Aye. He's like that. Malcolm has had a rough time, but he's got enough of his father in him to face things out, and he stands up to him in his own quiet way. He's a bit of a poet, I believe."

"Poet? God help him then, in that house. There wasn't any room for poetry in Garthmere. Is Bob Ashthwaite still alive? I wrote and told him when Mary died, but he never answered my letter."

"He was a poor hand at letter writing. Most of the farmers hereabouts get their wives to write their letters for them, and Bob's wife died before you married his daughter. He was cut up about Mary's death—he was fond of her in his own speechless way. Bob's over at Greenbeck now. He left Farfell some three years ago. He came to loggerheads with your father—some matter of arrears of rent. It'd gone on for years. They had an agreement by word of mouth about reduction of rent when farmers were working their land at a loss. When agriculture looked up again, your father claimed arrears of rent, and Bob repudiated the claim. Mr. Garth took him to court at last and won his case. It seemed to turn Bob's mind queer. He sold up most of his stock and went over to Greenbeck. He's got a small holding there, and he works it all alone, save for a boy who's weak in the head—a workhouse lad, with no kith or kin. They live together at Greenbeck—and it's said they pig it like beasts in that lonely house."

"I can imagine it. Doesn't sound too good. I'd thought of looking Bob up. I've got a few things of Mary's which he might like to have. He was a good father to her."

"You'll have to do as you think best about that. Bob's queer these days, as I've told you. He and I were good friends once, but now if I pass him on the fell he won't speak to me. I suppose he blames me as bailiff for the trouble over his rent, but it wasn't my fault. I'd no word in the arrangement he made with your father originally, and I did my best to ease things, but I couldn't move your father."

Richard Garth laughed again, the same bleak, unmirthful sound.

"No. I bet you couldn't. What's the betting my old devil of a parent just bided his time until he could get back on Bob because his daughter married *me*? It would have been typical of father to nurse a grudge for twenty years before venting his spleen."

"I don't know," said Staple slowly, chewing a straw he had picked. "After you left, Bob Ashthwaite went up to see your father, and they had it out, fair and square. Bob said he didn't want a Garth for his son-in-law—it was no fault of his that Mary had gone and made a fool of herself, and she could have done better than marry a Garth. Oddly enough, your father took that quietly, as though he understood it. I'm told they cursed one another long and strong—but Bob went back to Farfell and went on farming it, and your father never said a word about concluding the tenancy. Bob Ashthwaite was a good tenant, of course: farmed his land well and kept it clean."

"Yes. Suited the old man to keep him on—and then when he could conveniently do it, the old devil broke him: quite typical."

"Nay, lad, you're over hard. Your father's got some good qualities in him, for all that he can be a bitter enemy when he's lost his temper. By and large, he's been a good landlord. I've worked for him these thirty years and there's not much I don't know about him. He's an old man now—eighty-three come Michaelmas, and most men get difficult when they're old. Come to that, you mayn't be too easy yourself, Richard."

"Oh, I'm all right when I'm away from the subject of my own kith and kin. You can't expect me to take a charitable view of my father's dealings. As a boy, I saw him killing my mother—killing her slowly by bullying and hectoring. When I was grown to a man and stood up to him, he cursed me and kicked me out—and cursed my wife to my face. I often wonder I didn't kill him for that."

John Staple moved uneasily against the wall, and buttoned his coat up closer. "The wind's keen up here, Richard, and I get plagued with rheumatism. I'd better walk on. I was going to look at those ewes up on the fell side. Come along with me and then come back to tea. I can give you a good meal for all that I'm a bachelor—farm butter and home-cured ham, and as many eggs as you fancy. More than you'll get in a hotel these days."

Richard Garth chuckled, and his face was gentle again, his eyes affectionate. "Good old John! Many's the good meal I've had with you, and I've not forgotten them—but I won't come home with you now, thanks all the same. I want to walk, and I reckon I can get on to Ingleton before bedtime, stay the night there and carry on over Holmboro' in the morning and down into Sleydale. I've only got a couple of days to spare, and I've promised myself a good tramp. I want to see it all again—see it and smell it and listen to it."

"As you will, lad. If ever you want a bed you can have one with me and welcome. Come when you will, and stay as long as you like."

"Thanks. I'll take you at your word one day—if I live long enough. Is that inn outside Ingleton still functioning—the Wheatsheaf, wasn't it?"

"Aye. You can get a bed there if you want one. Matt Hodges is the landlord—the son of old Nathaniel. Can you see that man down in the dales there—walking towards the old barn?"

"Yes. I can see him all right—why?"

"That's your brother, Charles. He's living at home, at Garthmere, now. He was out in Malaya, and he got away to Java and then to Australia. Lost everything he possessed, and came back to England with the clothes he stood up in, and nothing else. He helps with your sister on the home farm."

"I hope he likes it. Does the old man pay him—or just let him work for nothing and curse him at intervals?"

John Staple chuckled. "That I can't tell you. I know Mr. Garth has his own ideas about the war like he has his own ideas about everything else: he says a few bitter things about letting the Japs get Singapore—but Charles puts up with it for his own convenience. He'll be surprised when he hears you've been home, will Charles."

"He needn't hear, John." Richard Garth turned and faced the older man. "I told you I didn't come home to see my family: they're nothing to me, nor I to them—less than nothing. You can forget you've seen me, John. Don't tell any of them. Promise me that, for old times' sake."

"If you ask it, I'll promise—but you're wrong in saying that you're nothing to them. You're the heir to Garthmere, Richard. The entail still holds. All this will be yours one day—and you care for the land, you've admitted it."

"Yes. I care for the land, but not in the sense of owning it—not the usual sense, anyway. I *do* own it, because I've remembered it— every wall and field, every gill and beck, every fell side and copse. I've come back to renew that ownership—to prove to myself that memory hasn't played me false. But as for living at Garthmere Hall and all that that involves—no. I've no use for it."

He paused a moment, staring out towards the Langdale Pikes, his shaggy brows knitted in thought. "The system of land tenure we've got in this country is all wrong," he said. "It's a remnant of feudalism, its usefulness outgrown. It isn't that I don't care about the land hereabouts. I care for it all the more that I've been away from it so long, but the system's all wrong. Anyway, it's a system that's passing. Maybe I'll come back here to live one day—if I don't get blown sky high on a torpedoed tanker—but I don't want to live at the Hall, and carry on the bad old tradition. My father liked owning things, whether it were land or cattle or his own family. He reckoned he owned us all—but he made a mistake."

Staple shrugged his heavy shoulders. "You've got a bee in your bonnet, lad—but I'll not argue with you. One day the land will be yours—and then we'll see. If you come back this way, remember you'll always be welcome at Lonsghyll. As long as I live you'll find me glad to see you."

"And what would my father say, if he learnt I was staying with you, John Staple?"

"That's between him and me, lad. One thing I've never been afraid of, and that's speaking my mind to him. I told him, years ago, that he was doing wrong when he quarrelled with you for marrying Mary Ashthwaite, and that, like as not, he'd rue it one day. Mayhap he *has* rued it. He's got Marion—she's never married. Then there's Charles—his wife died and he's no children. Malcolm—well, I doubt if he'll ever rear a family. No children about the place. A pity. Aye. He made a mistake."

"Perhaps: perhaps not." Richard Garth stared out across the river valley, his face furrowed in thought. "Don't you think we're all given to over-estimating our own importance?" he inquired. "We, as individuals, matter so little. All this—the land, the river, the hills—these endure, but we pass on. Our family—how I had it dinned into me when I was a kid, the importance of the Garths. A Garth does this, and a Garth does that. All damned rubbish and pretence. We're an old family—too old. We've outlived our usefulness, and it's time we were finished, time we gave place to something more in tune with the needs of the day. In that sense it may be a good thing that there isn't a rising generation to carry on the Garth tradition. As I remember it, the tradition was made up of outworn tyrannies."

"Maybe you're right, maybe you're wrong," replied Staple. "For my part I find it hard to think of Garthmere without one of the Garths living there—and because a thing is old, it's not of necessity bad, any more than it's good because it's new. One day I'll hope to see you living at the Hall, Richard—aye, and your children with you."

"You're a dyed-in-the-wool traditionalist, John," laughed the other. "I'm glad I met you. It wouldn't have seemed right to have walked over these fells without seeing you. Now I'll push on—I must hurry if I'm to get to the Wheatsheaf before dusk, and next time I happen along here I'll come and stay with you and we'll talk things out. You'll have to make some allowances for me though. A man can't live for twenty-five years in a new world and come back unchanged."

A moment later Richard Garth was striding away eastwards, his face set towards the great limestone mass of Ingleborough which closed in the valley to the east, and John Staple walked on slowly westwards looking for the ewes pasturing on the fell side. His mind was not on the business of his flocks. He was thinking of Richard Garth, and the family at Garthmere Hall, and he felt heavy-hearted. John Staple was essentially loyal, and despite the fact that he admitted that old Mr. Garth was a hard man and a stubborn man, a man moreover who set his face against reform and change, yet Staple was deeply devoted to him. It was true, as Richard Garth had said, that Staple was a traditionalist: the bailiff wanted to see a Garth living at the Hall, carrying on the traditions of landowner and farmer. He had often hoped that Richard would come home one day and enter into the heritage which should be his.

It was not until the sheep dog started rounding up the sheep and came to ask his master for instructions as clearly as a dog could that Staple brought his mind back to the business in hand. "I don't know. I don't know," he said to himself, as he whistled to the dog, directing him to round up the sheep in the sheltered corner of the stone wall.

A few minutes after Richard Garth and John Staple had gone their separate ways, another figure rose from behind the wall where they had stood. A tall lanky lad with a fine head and untidy dark hair stood and looked out over Lunesdale.

"So that was Richard," he said. "I often wondered what he was like."

CHAPTER TWO

I

GARTHMERE HALL STOOD ON THE HILLSIDE A FEW HUNDRED yards above the River Lune, the parkland and pastures sloping down to the river and the village. The latter was situated just above the river pastures, a tiny cluster of houses half hidden by trees. The Hall was mediæval in origin, but succeeding generations had altered it again and again. It was in part great house, in part farm house. Most of the mullioned windows dated from early Jacobean times, as did the great hall with its minstrels' gallery, but a new wing had been built in Queen Anne's reign, with fine large rooms facing the southern sun, and more window space than in the earlier parts of the building. It was in this south wing that the Garth family lived, leaving the gloomy mediæval main block, with its complexity of small rooms and passages, to the rats and mice and bats which had claimed it for their own.

It was in the "parlour" that the Garths assembled for a meal which was described as tea, though its time varied from five o'clock to seven, and its fare was more substantial than that of many an urban dining table. The parlour was a lofty room of Queen Anne period, its walls covered with the wide panelling of that date, its open fireplace having a richly ornate overmantel of carven stone in which the heraldic bearings of mediævalism were involved with elaborate decoration of late Renaissance tradition. Malcolm Garth described it as a nightmare in stone, but most of the Garths took it for granted as an essential part of the house, concerning which criticism simply did not arise. The room had long windows facing south, and a french window gave access to what had been a formal garden in other days. It now boasted a fine crop of onions. The furniture of the parlour was a medley of styles and periods, consistent only in the sense that every chair and table and piece was of good craftsmanship and beautiful wood. The long oak table and chairs were such as would be found in many a Lancashire farm house: there were oak dower chests of sixteenth century origin, and a huge Jacobean sideboard, richly carved. There were roomy armchairs with tall backs and winged side pieces, their tapestry covers faded to a pale monochrome which harmonised well with the worn oak floor and walls, and one or two rosewood bookcases of Chippendale design were filled with ancient leather-backed books seen through gold trellised glass-panelled doors.

On that sunny September afternoon when Richard Garth had met John Staple on the fell side, the Garths met for tea at five o'clock, and sat round the long oak table. They were a curious party—a medley, like the furniture of the room, but they also had a character in common—they had all been working on the land, and they had come in from the fields in their working clothes. Old Robert Garth sat at the head of the table, grim, silent, a grand figure of an old man with his still massive shoulders, shaggy white head, great beaked nose and deep-set smouldering blue eyes. Opposite him, at the farther end, was his daughter Marion, with a huge tea-pot of Georgian silver before her. Marion was forty-five, a tall, broad-shouldered, deep-chested woman, her white hair cropped short, and brushed back hard from her sunburnt forehead. She wore a short-sleeved shirt and whipcord breeches, in defiance of her father's outspoken disgust with such a costume. Marion looked what she was—a hard-working farmer, but neither cropped hair,

roughened hands nor a "stable boy's livery"—to quote her father—
robbed her of a dignity and poise which were ingrained, and had
the same ineffaceable quality as the beauty of the worn wood on
which her elbows rested. To her right sat a young woman in Land
Army uniform—Elizabeth Meldon. She was distantly related to the
Garths, and Marion had asked her to come to work at Garthmere
during the war. The Squire had expressed both derision and disgust
at the idea of having a girl to do farm labourer's work, but he had
found little reason to complain of Elizabeth's ability: she could
milk the cows, "muck-out" the shippon, drive a tractor and work
in the fields with skill and endurance. Tall and slim, her fair hair
curled in the modern manner, Elizabeth looked an anachronism
in that old room among the silent Garth family. She was defiantly
modern, and beautiful at that, and her freshness made a striking
contrast to Marion's worn, stubborn unyielding dignity. Opposite
Elizabeth sat Charles Garth, he who had recently returned from
Malaya, a big gaunt sun-dried fellow, whose grey hair was receding
on the temples, his face furrowed with heavy lines.

The sun streamed in through the wide windows, its beams danc-
ing on the heavy silver tea set, showing even more plainly that it was
sadly in need of polishing. The china was a medley which included
some valuable plates, a few cups of crown Derby, two of them without handles, the remainder of the china being the hideous white
"utility" stuff of wartime manufacture. There was a ham in front
of the Squire, boiled eggs, home-made butter and jam, tomatoes
and salad, and bowls of ripe pears and plums. Elizabeth Meldon was
peeling a pear, and Marion replenishing her tea cup when another
person came in and joined the party by way of the french window.
This was Malcolm, the son of Robert Garth's second marriage. He
was a tall slim lad who walked with a limp: in contrast to the tanned

skins of the others, Malcolm's face had the rather sallow pale skin which never tans. His eyes were dark, set under whimsical tilted black brows, and a lock of dark hair fell untidily over his forehead. He was dressed in grey flannel trousers, old and baggy, and a blue shirt open at the neck, with rolled-up sleeves, showing his long thin arms. He went and pulled up a chair next to Elizabeth, who smiled at him with understanding friendly grey eyes. The Squire pushed back his chair and scowled as he enquired,

"And where have you been wasting your time when everyone else has been working?"

Malcolm's face gave a slight twitch, but he replied with cool imperturbability, "In a place and manner of no interest to anybody else."

The Squire snorted. "God knows how I came by such a mannerless whelp," he grunted, and he pushed his chair back noisily and got up and stamped across to the door, walking heavily and banging the door to behind him.

"For these and all his other mercies…" murmured Malcolm, as he reached out his hand for a tomato, and Elizabeth inquired.

"How are the bees?"

"Oh, not too bad: there's lashings of honey for them to get, but it's too windy up there. Bees don't like wind."

Marion poured out another cup of tea and passed it across to Malcolm. "Oh, did you go along the river?" she asked him. "Has John Staple carted that last field of oats yet? He'd still got some uncarted yesterday—in the freshly-ploughed bit by the long holm."

"I didn't notice," replied Malcolm, and Elizabeth laughed.

"Don't you ever notice anything when you're out?" she inquired. "Staple has still got about three acres uncarted. It ought to be dry now, after this good wind to-day."

Marion looked across at her thoughtfully. "Yes. It'd be dry now—and the glass is falling. It is going to rain again, soon. What about lending Staple a hand this evening? The moon's nearly full, and if four of us went we could help him to get it in in a few hours."

Charles Garth groaned aloud. "Damn all, Marion, haven't we sweated enough this harvest? It was bad enough getting our own crops in, without doing a boy scout touch helping other people—and there'll be all those blasted potatoes and swedes to be lifted soon."

Before Marion had time to reply, Elizabeth cut in: "John Staple helped us with our hay crop," she said. "If he hadn't it would still be soaking in the dales. Of course we'll turn out and help him this evening. I'll take the lorry and Malcolm can take Jessie and the cart." (Jessie was a stout old mare.)

"Good," said Marion. "I'll ring Staple up and ask him if he'd like a hand. He'd never ask for help, but he won't refuse it, if we offer neighbour-like, so to speak. I'm sure father will come—even though Charles is too tired."

Charles scowled. "I've done a full day's work to-day, and I've no use for all this blasted altruism. Staple shouldn't have planted oats on land liable to flood. Any fool could see that holm land would flood if the river came up."

"You're a born fool, Charles," said Marion. "You've got a lot to learn before you're fit to live in the country. Put your feet up and take your ease—if you've got the nerve. You're not the only person who's done a full day's work to-day, and you know it." She turned to Elizabeth. "I'll ring through to Staple. You and Malcolm can get the lorry and cart out in about ten minutes. He's got one cart down there, and the Briggs will be helping. Staple will tell us who he'd like at the barn…"

She went out, and Elizabeth offered Charles a Woodbine from

a crumpled packet she drew out of her breeches pocket. "You'd better come too," she said. "Better sore hands than a sore head."

Charles took the cigarette with a wry grin. "All right—but this farming's a bloody business," he grumbled. "I'd rather be in the infantry and that's saying a lot."

Malcolm had gone out of the french window, and Elizabeth stopped a moment to listen to Charles' grumbling.

"It's nothing but a dog's life, sweating from morning till night," he went on, "and for whose benefit, I ask you? Marion works like a farm labourer—all to swell the old man's bank balance. He won't even let her have money to spend on the farm or to improve the stock. Take this Hereford bull she's been so keen on buying. She'll never get it, because the old man won't pay for it, and yet she's been slaving to get his harvest in for him. I'm damned if I can see why she does it. What does she get out of it?"

"She gets a satisfaction which you can't understand," said Elizabeth. "Marion's a born farmer. She really cares about the land."

Charles snorted. "She cares about her stock, too—but she'll never get the parsimonious old devil to pay for a decent bull or modernise those mediæval shippons." He got up and characteristically took the last cigarette out of Elizabeth's packet. The latter watched him quite good-humouredly: she knew Charles. He was mean, but he was also very hard up and Elizabeth was a little sorry for him, even while she despised him.

II

The project of Marion's Hereford bull was always cropping up as a subject of conversation at Garthmere. Marion was passionately interested in farming, and the war had given her her first opportunity to introduce modern methods on the home farm. Her father, an uncompromising traditionalist who resisted any innovation on principle, had been forced by wartime regulations to break with traditional methods. He had had to plough up pasture, swearing and fulminating the while; he had had to plant oats and root-crops, to make returns, to fill in forms, to submit to inspection, to use artificial fertilisers. Marion, her heart rejoicing, bought Farming papers, attended meetings organised by the War Agricultural Committee and even acquired a wireless set (paid for out of her carefully hoarded "egg-money") and listened to farming broadcasts with the most profound attention. She wanted to improve the stock on the home farm, and to do so she needed better beasts to breed from. The topic of Marion's Hereford bull had become almost a by-word at Garthmere Hall. Elizabeth had told Marion of an experiment made by an enterprising Exmoor farmer who had crossed his black Galloway grazing cattle with a Hereford strain: the consequence had been to increase greatly the weight of the beef cattle, and the crossbred calves appeared as shaggy little black beasts with white Hereford faces. Marion was greatly attracted by the originality of this idea; she wanted to get a Hereford bull to serve her black-polled cattle—"Pollies" as they were called in the north-country. She also wanted a good Friesian bull to improve her milking herd.

The let and hindrance which stood in the way of her ambitions was not now lack of means. Farming was paying better than at any time in Marion's experience: old Robert Garth had a sound bank balance for once, and no one knew it better than Marion. She had the data to assess the value of his stock and crops, but no means to induce the obstinate old man to spend money on further improving his stock.

Throughout her hard-working days Marion brooded on the same subject—how to induce her father to invest his money profitably in valuable stock.

Elizabeth Meldon studied her Garth kinsfolk with a cool dispassionate judgment. She saw the grim obstinacy of old Robert, for ever setting his face against any change: the energy and optimism of Marion, intent on learning new methods of farming and developing the land to its greatest fertility. In addition to the tug of war between Marion and her father was the constant irritation of the two ill-assorted brothers—Charles from Malaya, accustomed to native labour and as many cocktails as he cared to swallow, and Malcolm who was by nature more a poet than a farmer. "Never such a family of incompatibles," said Elizabeth.

Nevertheless, throughout the long summer days the family had toiled together, first at the hay crop, then at harvest; Marion never seemed to tire. Old Garth worked grimly, using a lifetime's skill to counterbalance his failing strength. Charles worked—sore against his will. His father saw to it that Charles did not live at home without working for his living. Finally Malcolm—physically a weakling, but with the keenest brain of the family, working in fits and starts, striving against physical incapacity with a courage which only Elizabeth realised and admired. Elizabeth Meldon was a modern young woman—but her heart often ached over Malcolm.

III

While Charles had been grumbling to Elizabeth and Marion had been having a word with John Staple about carting the oats, Malcolm had gone outside into the mellow sunshine and wandered over to the low stone wall which separated the one time formal garden from what had been park land—now used in part for grazing, in part ploughed for root-crops. To the right was the old orchard whose neglected trees had carried a heavy crop this year. Some of the apples had been picked, but many lay where they had fallen—there had been no time and no labour to harvest them. Malcolm cocked his ear and listened to Charles's querulous voice. After a moment or two Malcolm intervened and called Elizabeth.

"Lisa! Lisa! Someone's left the orchard gate open and the cows have got in."

This statement brought Elizabeth running out to join him. On one melancholy occasion the cows had got into the orchard and "swined away at the apples" as old Moffat put it, and the result had been colic in the milking herd.

"Who ever left the gate open? I do think it's too bad," cried Elizabeth as she ran to join Malcolm. A moment later she looked across at the orchard.

"Oh, Malcolm, you *are* a liar! The gate isn't open at all… Why did you say it was?"

"Because I wanted to talk to you, and the only thing which was certain to bring you was the thought of something wrong with the cows." He laughed, and took her arm for a moment and drew her towards the orchard gate. The neglected old trees were laden with fruit—plums, damsons, and apples weighing the branches almost to the ground.

"This fruit ought to be picked," said Elizabeth, her smooth brow furrowing in thought.

"Oh damn the fruit, and the farm and all of it!" he exclaimed petulantly. "Can't you forget it for one moment even? Lisa, darling, such a queer thing happened to-day. I was up on the fell yonder—I went to look at the bees, and then went to sleep in the lee of the wall. Heather's lovely stuff to sleep on. I woke up because somebody was talking just the other side of the wall. It was John Staple—I knew his voice at once—but there was another voice I didn't know. I lay and listened, too lazy to get up—and then I suddenly realised who it was who was talking. It was Richard. Do you know who Richard is?"

"Richard? Marion's brother, you mean?"

"Yes. My half-brother—you know. The eldest of us. The old man kicked him out years ago, before I was born, when he married Mary Ashthwaite. She died out in Canada, and Richard's never been home again since."

"Heavens! Is he coming here to stay?" Elizabeth's eyes were wide as she spoke.

"Not he! You should have heard him cursing the old man! It just warmed the cockles of my heart. No. Richard's not coming here. He'd got a yearning to see this part of the country again. He's doing a tramp over Ingleborough way before he goes back to sea again. He's in the Merchant Navy, sailing in the Atlantic convoys. He didn't want them to know about his being here—the family I mean. He's a big tough—I rather liked the look of him, what I could see of him. I had an impulse to go over to Ingleborough and put up at the same Inn. He's going to stay the night at the Wheatsheaf, and then tramp on into Sleydale. I should rather like to get to know him—but I felt too lazy to tramp and I can't be bothered to hitch-hike."

Elizabeth had picked a scarlet apple and was crunching it thoughtfully. "Are you going to tell the others—Marion and Charles—about seeing him?"

"Not I! Why should I? I heard him ask John Staple not to say anything, so I'm not going to butt in. I had to tell you, though. I always want to tell you things."

She chewed her apple thoughtfully. "It *is* queer, Malcolm," she said. "I've heard about Richard, of course. I think Marion liked him—but your father won't have his name mentioned. It's rather funny. It was only the other day Charles was talking to Marion about Richard. Charles said he believed he was dead, because he hadn't been heard of for years and years."

"A sell for Charles, then, because Richard's very much alive. He's heir to this place, of course—only he doesn't seem to want it. He does hate the old man—just like I do."

"I've told you before not to say things like that to me," she replied. "I simply can't understand a family like yours, you're always at loggerheads. If I didn't like Marion so much, I don't think I could stand staying here."

"Lisa! What about *me*?"

"Oh, you..." her face softened. "I know, Malcolm, I'm not being horrid—not really—but I can't bear it when you start this hymn of hate business. It's horrible."

"All right. I won't talk about it, and Lisa—I wrote something for you up there in the heather. It's not much good, but it's for you, from me... I'm going to put it under your pillow, and you can read it when you go to bed. Will you?"

"Yes, you know I will. I always love your verse, Malcolm. Look, there's Charles calling us. We'd better go and get the cart and lorry out."

"Oh damn!" groaned Malcolm. "The land seems a sort of taskmaster, always demanding, always this urgency of toil and sweat... Why, oh why..."

"Because we live by the land," retorted Elizabeth. "Harvest time *is* urgent. We don't grow crops in order to let them rot in the fields. Come on—I love carting, it's fun."

IV

Green Holm was a great stretch of land just above the level of the flood plane. It was the first year it had grown grain and the crop was a heavy one, as though all the fertility begot of years of grazing had been turned to account when the old pasture was ploughed up. There had been fifteen acres of oats on Green Holm, most of which had been carted before the weather broke. Now only three acres remained to be brought into the great barn where Staple was housing his oat crop. Three acres and a falling barometer: when Staple saw the contingent of helpers from the home farm he knew the job would be finished that evening, for he had enough labour to create the endless chain which is the ambition of all farmers at harvest. With kindling eyes Staple deployed his forces: Elizabeth had brought the lorry. Staple himself mounted it while Elizabeth and Marion tossed the hattocks up to him. Young Briggs was in the barn to unload. Malcolm led the cart, into which old Mr. Garth and old Briggs tossed with the rhythmic unhurried skill of old hands, and finally there was Jem Moffat with a second cart and Charles to load. As one load was completed it was taken to the barn and an empty cart brought back to the field. As the sun went down and the long northern twilight spread greyly over the great stretch of level land there was never a pause or a break in the work: in order to keep the sequence going and to avoid breaks everybody had to work steadily, ignoring weariness or thirst: tossing rhythmically the harvesters worked on and as the clouds came up and the wind moaned louder from the west the great stretch of land was cleared of its last loads. The moon was waxing and shone high in the sky after sunset but at length the clouds blotted it out and as Elizabeth turned the lorry with its last load the rain storm burst over the valley—not a slight shower but a heavy steady fall which gave promise of a night's rain. John Staple chuckled to himself when he felt the first cold drops: he was just securing the last lorry load. "Aye, it can rain now and no harm done," he said to Marion, and she laughed back.

"It's a grand feeling to have got the whole lot in, John Staple. Towns folk never understand the feeling of urgency which makes us work and sweat to get the crops in. Even Charles, who was brought up on the land, can't see why we want to work all the evening to get the stuff carried. Well, it can rain as much as it likes now."

Staple clambered down from the lorry. "Aye. Thanks to you I needn't bother about the weather to-morrow," he said. "Happen I'd better get the beasts up from the dales. The river'll rise before morning."

Elizabeth had driven the lorry off to the barn, and Malcolm had already started home with the cart. As Staple made off to round up his beasts, whistling to his dog to follow, Marion trudged across the stubble making for home. She was tired, her arms aching from the effort of tossing the hattocks, her legs weary from a long day's work. Darkness was deepening swiftly now, as the moon was blotted out and indigo clouds piled up to the zenith. Her shirt was soon wet through and the driving rain blew in her eyes half-blinding her, but Marion was contented as she trudged uphill in the gloom, aware of a deep-seated satisfaction at a job well done.

CHAPTER THREE

I

ELIZABETH BACKED THE LAST LORRY LOAD INTO THE BARN and called up to young Briggs, who was on the top of the stack.

"We'll leave this lot here until to-morrow. It's too dark to unload now. It's all under cover and that's all that matters."

Young Briggs slithered down from the stack. "Aye, that's right," he said, and only his voice told of the satisfaction which his terse speech would not express.

"By gum, it's raining," he said, and Elizabeth laughed.

"Raining it is, and who cares. Good-night," she called.

Leaving young Briggs to close the door of the great barn she turned towards home through the downpour. Accustomed to bad weather the rain did not trouble her at all, and as she walked she pondered over the story Malcolm had told her before they started carting. Would Richard Garth come home after all, she wondered, and if so, how would his father receive him?

"It's a pity he's such a bad-tempered old devil," she said to herself. "I could admire him such a lot. He worked like a Trojan this evening, all to help John Staple. There's something fine in him, only he's so cussed. Of course Marion's just like him, though she doesn't realise it. I often wonder they don't have one blazing row and be done with it."

It was quite dark by the time Elizabeth reached the big house and she made her way, as usual, to the kitchen side, wondering where the others had got to. As she opened the kitchen door she heard the welcome crackle of burning sticks, and she found Marion working the bellows, with a fine blaze under the hanging kettle in the great open hearth.

"I'm going to have some tea, and some hot water to wash in after all that," she said.

Elizabeth reached out her hand to take the bellows. "Leave that to me—you're dog tired," she said.

"So are you—and drenched through into the bargain," retorted Marion. "Go and get into a dressing gown: by the time you come down the kettle will be boiling—and I've got a spot of rum to lace the tea with. We'd better take Malcolm a hot drink—save him from getting another of those foul colds."

"Is he in? I saw him taking Jessie back to the stable. Aren't you ever tired, Marion? To see you working those bellows anyone would think you were as fresh as paint. You've had an eighteen hour day—"

"And I'm not as young as I was. Thanks for the implication. No. I'm *not* tired. I just feel on top of the world. It was grand getting the oats in, just in time like that. Do go and get out of those sopping clothes, Lisa, and then come and have some tea."

"You beat me. You've got more energy than all the rest of us put together," yawned Elizabeth.

A few minutes later she came down into the kitchen again, clad in a vivid silk kimono, her fair hair brushed back, loose from its curls. Marion had closed the kitchen shutters, and lighted a big lamp which hung from a beam. In the golden light, with the wood fire roaring up the chimney, the great kitchen had a beauty all its own. Old copper and pewter gleamed against the dark oak of a huge mediæval dresser and the dark settles shone with the polish of age and centuries of wear. Marion had made a pot of tea and was measuring out rum into the cups when Malcolm strolled in, also in a dressing gown, an amused smile tilting his wide, mobile lips.

"Is this a sort of preliminary harvest home?" he enquired. "What a good thing the old malefactor's gone to bed—I heard him snoring as I came down. I bet he tumbled into bed just as he was—dung soaked breeches and boots and all. Where's Charles? It's not like him to be absent when there's a free toddy obtainable."

"He's probably asleep, too. He was dead beat, and his hands had blistered," said Elizabeth, lighting a cigarette.

Marion snorted. "Charles!" she exclaimed. "He's always getting blisters: he's frightened of hard work—that's what's the matter with Charles."

"He's a bit like a blister himself," said Malcolm, "in fact the description just fits him."

"Don't be so foul," expostulated Elizabeth, sipping her hot toddy contentedly. "I'm rather sorry for Charles. He's lived in the tropics, got a liver, never done a hand's turn of anything like work for twenty years, and then comes back home having lost every bean, to a life which is all hard work, plus abuse, with no trimmings and none of the luxury Charles dotes on. It's not to be wondered at he gets blisters."

"I never had much use for Charles," said Marion. "He always showed a genius for avoiding the dirty jobs, even as a child. Father may be a tyrant—unreasonable old devil that he is, I'm willing to admit—but he does know how to work and he never shirks, even now, when he's old enough to be justified in easing off. Well, well: he's got to face up to the idea of my Hereford bull. I'm going to have a straight talk with him to-morrow."

"Might as well save your breath," said Malcolm, and Elizabeth yawned again as she tossed her cigarette end into the fire.

"Go to bed, children," said Marion. "You're both half asleep already. I'm going to have a tub by the fire. There's nothing I enjoy more after a good day's work."

"Good Lord! You don't mean you're going to lug that ghastly great tub in here now," protested Elizabeth, but Marion only laughed.

"I'm going to have a hot bath and wallow in it in front of the fire," she replied. "Off you go to bed, both of you. It'll still be raining floods in the morning, as sure as my name's Garth. You can have a day off, Elizabeth, and get your hair washed in Lancaster for a treat."

"Sounds good to me."

Elizabeth yawned again as she lighted a candle and turned towards the door which led to the back stairs—her shortest route to her bedroom. Malcolm, candlestick in hand, made for the door on the opposite side of the room.

"I've left a book in the dining-room," he said. "Good-night, Lisa. 'Night, Marion. Don't go to sleep in that Heath Robinson bath."

Elizabeth went up the worn, shallow, oak stairs, shading her candle with her hand to prevent the draught blowing it out. The wind howled round the house—and through it, as the guttering candle testified. There was a door at the top of the awkward twisting stairway, and it banged to behind her as she reached the passage which led to her room. She stood still a moment, shielding the candle flame, which flattened out into a blue flicker in the wind which came along the passage. As she stood she heard a sound ahead of her and raised the candle to throw its light along the passage. Elizabeth had steady nerves and she was accustomed to the old house, but her heart gave an unaccustomed bump. In front of her, at the farther end of the passage, she glimpsed a tall figure in a long dark coat or dressing gown. It was old Robert Garth, walking along the passage with uncertain steps, touching the wall with his hand as he walked.

"He's walking in his sleep," said Elizabeth to herself. She found the door handle and slipped behind the door and stood on the landing, pushing the bolt home. Somehow, she knew not why, she was afraid of meeting the old man in the narrow passage and her heart thudded a little as she stood shading the candle with her hand. "I must buy a new battery for my torch in Lancaster to-morrow," she said to herself. "This candle business is enough to drive anyone bats. Why are we all so antediluvian in this house?"

She waited for what seemed an interminable time, hearing nothing but the wind howling outside and the rain beating against the windows. At last she drew back the bolt, opened the door and adventured along the now empty passage. She blew out her candle when she reached her own room: the windows were not blacked out and she was too tired to bother about closing the heavy shutters and pulling the awkward curtains over them. She went to the window and stared out into the gloom, listening again. For some reason she felt wide awake and unwilling to go to bed. There came a further sound of footsteps along the passage and she braced herself as the handle of the door was turned.

"Who's that?" she demanded.

It was Malcolm's voice which answered. "Lisa, the old devil's been in my room again, poking about. He's always spying on me."

"Oh, what does it matter, Malcolm? I saw him in the passage, he was walking in his sleep. Do go to bed, I'm dog-tired. If Marion hears you in here she'll fuss, you know that. I sometimes wonder why on earth I go on living here. You're enough to drive anyone mad, all of you. Go to bed, Malcolm."

She walked across to the door, and as though with a sudden sense of compunction, she kissed him, her lips just touching his ear in the darkness. Then, with unexpected strength she seized his arm and pushed him outside into the passage, saying again, "Go to bed and don't fuss. What we all want is a good night's rest."

She shot the bolt of her door, got out of her wrap and tumbled into bed, pulling the bed clothes up round her ears to shut out the wail of the wind which howled round the house like a witches' chorus.

Half an hour later Marion Garth went up to bed: every window and door in the old house rattled and strained in the tempest, as though the uncarpeted corridors were being patrolled by an eccentric's army. Marion did not care. She was asleep by the time she had pulled up the bed clothes, and it would have taken a bomb to awaken her.

Malcolm was the only person in the vast old house who bothered to black-out his window and light a lamp. He stood looking round his room with a frowning face. It was a pleasant room, despite the decrepitude of furniture and hangings. The panelling had been painted white many years ago and still retained something of lightness and elegance, and there were some fine old pieces, including a rosewood bureau, which Malcolm had contrived to collect in his own room. Generally the room gave him pleasure and a feeling of security, but to-night he scowled as he looked around and examined the papers on his bureau. As he had come upstairs to his room, Malcolm had seen his father walking along the passage, coming away from his (Malcolm's) room. The boy had an ever present horror of being spied upon, and it was a perpetual source of anger to him that he was unable to lock the door of his room when he left it. The key had been lost years since, and Malcolm had never found any means of getting another one cut. Even his beloved bureau had no key. It was because he dreaded his father's derision that Malcolm hated the old man to enter his room. Malcolm's main delight was in writing, and the writing of verse satisfied him and gave him moments of rare delight to counterbalance the depression which so often overcame him. To old Robert Garth the habit of writing poetry was a species of idiocy, all too characteristic of the weakling son whose nature baffled and exasperated him. The Squire had mocked aloud when he first happened to find some lines which Malcolm had written, and the boy had never forgiven him. Ever since he had had a dread of being spied upon, and above all Malcolm hated his father to go into his room and look at his books and papers. Standing there, intensely aware of the storm without which seemed to deprive the ancient house itself of stability or peace, Malcolm was overcome by a sense of frustration and wretchedness. In actual fact he was overtired by the evening's work. His physique was too frail to endure physical effort without exhaustion, and his bodily weariness resulted in a nervous reaction in which everything assumed abnormal shapes. The wind and rain, the rattling panes and shutters, the lamp which flared in the draught—all these seemed ominous, and the recollection of old Robert Garth stalking along the passage had a horrific quality to the overtired boy. He remembered Elizabeth's words—"He was walking in his sleep." Malcolm shivered. The thought of the old man walking about the dark house had a nightmare quality to him. "I hate him! Oh Lord, how I hate him," he said to himself.

Pulling a chest away from the wall, Malcolm shoved it against the door, because the thought of his father coming into his room

terrified him. He put out the lamp at last and got into bed. Because he was physically tired he fell asleep, but the storm entered into his dreams and he tossed and groaned like an uneasy spirit while the wind howled round the ancient house.

II

The storm which swept down Lunesdale beat with even greater fury over the limestone heights of Ingleborough. Richard Garth, after he left John Staple, had deliberately gone out of his way to tramp over the smooth turf of the great hill. He had climbed up the slippery slope until he could see the valley stretching away to the sea, and he had stayed up there until the rain had blotted out his surroundings.

He was wet through when he reached the Wheatsheaf, and had persuaded the landlord to let him have a wood fire in his room. Sitting beside the cheerful blaze, a hot toddy in his hand, Richard meditated into the small hours, recalling his walk, pondering over the familiar land he had seen, the river, the fells, the fertile valley and woodland. Now he had seen it again he was loth to leave it, but at the back of his mind the thought of his father still rankled.

"There's not room for him and me together," he told himself. "When I went away I swore I'd never come back—and I was right. Some scores can't be settled in a lifetime… but Lord, that fell side with the heather all abloom, it smelt good. There's something about the fells a man can't forget…"

CHAPTER FOUR

I

WHEN ELIZABETH MELDON CAME IN TO BREAKFAST THE next morning, she wondered why her nerves had been so unsteady the previous night. After milking the cows she felt as cheerful and hungry as usual: she liked milking and was as expert at it as Marion herself. The smell of fried tomatoes and eggs and bacon made her sniff appreciatively, and she forgot to comment on the weather when she saw that there was a letter waiting beside her plate. Malcolm studied her morosely as she opened it.

"'Morning. Foul day. Pouring all it knows how. The river's up already."

"Who cares?" demanded Marion, busy with a great bowl of porridge. "Elizabeth, Trant's taking his heifers in to market and he can take you on the van if you like. Charles seems to have cleared out already. I think he must have cadged a lift on the early lorry. Father's staying in bed for a while, too. I'm going to have a peaceful day."

Elizabeth looked up from her letter. "Thanks awfully. This is a line from Roger Wood. He's going to be in Lancaster to-day and asks if I can lunch with him. That'll give me time to do some shopping, and I can come back on the Carnton bus and walk from the cross-road. I'll be back in time to milk."

"Never mind about that. Jem and Bob and I can do it," replied Marion. "Come back late as you like—if you can find anyone to bring you back. Some of the farmers are sure to be in there for the cattle market, and they won't mind giving you a lift. You can say you were looking at some cattle for me if you're stopped by the traffic cops. I hope you'll enjoy yourself. You deserve to after the way you've been working. It'll be pretty beastly in Lancaster though, with this rain. It won't lift to-day."

There was silence for a moment, and then Malcolm asked, "Ever seen a fox hunt in these parts, Lisa?"

"A fox hunt? I've seen them hunting on Exmoor. Lord Varmoor still takes his hounds out."

Marion and Malcolm both laughed, and the latter went on: "No. Not that sort of thing—hunting pink and whippers-in and all the frills. When the farmers go a-hunting here, they do it to kill foxes, not for fun. They assemble all the guns in the neighbourhood, enrol the rest of the population as beaters, and shoot every fox they see."

Marion took up the tale. "Bob Moffat says there's a big dog fox in Lawson's Wood—he's seen it more than once, and he's lost some of his geese. He intends to get that fox. If you can shoot straight I'll lend you my gun. I can't be bothered to go myself—takes too much time. I expect father will go, though he always curses the whole show to blazes."

"It's against his ethical code to let a fox be killed without hunt-ing the poor brute and letting it be torn to pieces by hounds," said Malcolm. "That's sport, that is. Shooting a fox as vermin is unsporting. The only marvel to me is that something else besides foxes doesn't get plugged at the entertainments here. You've never seen anything so gloriously casual as the guns here—all popping off at anything. If a bunny or a hare gets put up by the beaters—well, it's all good for the pot and they just blaze away, every man intent on his own affairs."

"They generally auction the foxes afterwards," said Marion, "and give the money to the Red Cross. Some of the farmers' wives like a fox fur. No accounting for taste. You ought to go and see it, Elizabeth, it's quite an entertainment. When are they going to shoot, Malcolm?"

"Bob says the day after to-morrow—Trant's arranging it with John Staple." He turned again to Elizabeth. "They generally arrange a fox hunt before lambing-time—they shot four foxes last spring and were no end pleased with themselves. No one got plugged, but they're bound to have a casualty some time."

"Not they! Farmers have got more sense than you credit them with," replied Marion briskly. "I'm all in favour of getting rid of the foxes: they're a menace when you're raising poultry. Malcolm, what are you going to do to-day?"

"Why this interest in my doings? D'you want me to lend a hand with something. I do bar one thing—and that's pumping up liquid manure."

"My dear, I've more sense than to ask you to have anything to do with muck," replied Marion serenely. "It's much too valuable to be wasted. You go along up into your loft and play around with your bee-supers. You'll be nice and dry up there, and not in anybody's way."

"You seem too mighty keen on getting us all out of the way," grumbled Malcolm, and Elizabeth put in.

"Yes, what's the great idea, Marion? Don't say you're going to set-to house cleaning."

"Not I," replied Marion. "This house has got to wait a while before it's cleaned. If you really want to know what I'm going to do, I'm going to have a day at accounts. We've been so busy all the summer that nothing's got done in the booking line, and we shall be in a mess when the Income Tax assessment is due. Father thinks he does it all himself, but if I don't get things sorted out he'll never manage to get it right."

"Ha ha!" snorted Malcolm. "I see your little idea. You're going to work out the old man's profits and then tell him he'd better buy you a couple of good bulls to avoid paying any more income tax."

"It doesn't work out quite that way," said Marion placidly, "but it's quite true that I thought I'd have a talk with father to-day and see if we can't come to an agreement. It seems a good opportunity. It's too wet to do anything much outside—barring hedging, which father never does: Charles is out apparently—that's all to the good, because the sight of Charles lounging round the house is like a red rag to a bull to the old man—"

"And I'm out, and Malcolm's to keep out of the way," interpolated Elizabeth, and Marion nodded.

"That's the idea," she agreed. "Now all the harvest's in it's no use his saying to me he can't afford things, because he not only knows the value of his hay and grain and what he's made on milk and grazing stock this year, he knows that I know it, too. One thing about farming, it's no use trying to be too secretive over profits, because the profits declare themselves to anybody who's intelligent. I know how many loads of oats we've carted, and I've a good idea how they'll work out when they're threshed."

Elizabeth chuckled. "Yes. I quite see all that. I believe you could make out Mr. Garth's valuation from memory—crops, stock and all the rest—but do you really believe you can induce him to give you a free hand to buy the beasts you want?"

"No, not give me a free hand exactly, but I think he may be more reasonable than he was last time I broached the subject. He's got plenty of money lying idle—I know that because I know the prices he got for the last bunch of bullocks he took to market, and the in-calf heifers brought in an average £30 each. It's silly keeping money in the bank. Money ought to earn money. Besides, what's he saving it for? He doesn't want to leave it to me—or to anyone else so far as I know, and he can't live for ever."

"Don't tell him so. It'll only annoy him," said Elizabeth, and Malcolm put in abruptly—

"Talking of wills and all that, Marion, have you any idea where Richard is now, or even if he's dead or alive?"

Marion gave a start, and turned on Malcolm with surprise in her face and brows lifted.

"Richard! What on earth made you think of him? You've never even seen him. He left home before you were born."

"I know. It's a pretty story, isn't it—real old traditional melodrama. Do you know anything about him, Marion?"

Marion poured out another cup of tea before she answered, and Elizabeth waited for her answer with lively curiosity. How like Malcolm, she thought—both secretive and inquisitive. Remembering what he had told her the previous evening Elizabeth felt a sense of discomfort. Malcolm was hardly playing fair.

"Of course I don't know anything about him," Marion replied at length. "He went to Canada nearly twenty-five years ago, and nobody's heard of him since so far as I know. Charles was talking to father about him the other day. They were discussing the probability of his being dead—presumption of death, or something of the kind. Very stupid of them, because they've no reason at all to suppose he's dead. The Garths are a long-lived race." She paused, and then added: "I've always supposed he'd come back eventually."

"Eventually?" inquired Malcolm, his voice cynical. "Meaning when the old man's dead? How would you like it, Marion, if

he did come back, and interfered with all your private schemes here?"

"I don't know what you mean by private schemes," retorted Marion. "If Richard comes back, I suppose he'll farm his own land. He was a good farmer—Staple says so. I should go on just the same as I am now."

"And say if Richard didn't want you?" inquired Malcolm. "Say if he's got a wife, and wants the house for themselves?"

"Oh, don't be tiresome," said Marion. "This supposing game is just silly. If Richard didn't want me here, I should get him to let me one of the fell farms. I've thought several times lately I should like to start on my own. The trouble is I've no capital."

"Seems to me you can put up some very pretty arguments to induce the old malefactor to shell out some cash," said Malcolm. "Ask him if he's saving his money so that Richard can have a nice spot of cash to help him along when he inherits, and then add that you're thinking of taking a farm on your own account where you can put your ideas into practice."

"You are an ass, aren't you," said Marion. "He'd get into such a dithering rage that I should lose my last chance of talking him into a reasonable frame of mind. It's no use annoying father if you want to manage him. Once he's in a rage he's hopeless."

"Have you ever lost your temper with him?" inquired Elizabeth, and Marion nodded, a grimace on her usually calm face.

"Yes, I have, we've all got ghastly tempers, you know, though I generally manage to keep mine by hook or by crook. Look here, Elizabeth, if you're going to be ready for Trant's van, you'd better hurry up—he'll be round quite soon. Malcolm, I don't often ask you to keep out of the way, but if you can make yourself scarce till dinner time I shall be grateful."

Malcolm grinned. "Right oh. Suits me all right. I don't want to be found a job for."

II

Marion sat on over the breakfast table after the other two had gone. It was not often that her father came down late to breakfast, and she guessed that the wet day had given him a feeling that he could do with a rest. He never admitted to being tired, and Marion, in common with many other people, often wondered how long the old man's superb physique would stand the strain of his activity. She knew that he had been tired the previous evening—tired to the verge of exhaustion, but she had also seen the look of grim triumph on the worn old face. If Robert Garth had been tired, he had had the satisfaction of knowing that his son Charles had been even more tired.

Marion sat studying a local paper, reading lists of forthcoming sales of stock, until the door opened and her father came into the room, moving stiffly.

"Good-morning," she said. "I'll go and get you a fresh pot of tea. This one's cold. I've told Elizabeth to take a day off. There's nothing much we can do outside to-day, and we're well forward with hedging."

Mr. Garth merely grunted and lowered himself heavily into his chair. When Marion returned with the tea-pot and a bowl of hot porridge he did not bother to say thank you—and neither did she expect him to do so. She started collecting used plates and cups, saying:

"I thought I'd make some of the books up to-day. Will you have time to go over those Milk Board papers some time—about the new returns?"

Again old Garth merely grunted, but his grunt was a token of assent. He then inquired: "Where's Charles?"

"I don't know," replied Marion. "I haven't seen him this morning. He said something about going in to Lancaster to do some shopping, so I expect he got a lift on the early lorry. He's done that before."

"Shopping, eh? Where's he got the money to shop from? I always said that Charles had got a bit put away, for all that he pretends he hasn't a halfpenny. Charles was born cadging."

Marion paused in her task of clearing the table. "I don't think he's got any money at all," she said quietly. "He borrowed some from me."

"More fool you to lend it," retorted the old man. "You'll never see it back."

"Obviously I shan't, if Charles isn't able to earn any money," she replied; "but I'd rather lend him a few shillings myself than have him borrowing from John Staple or getting into debt anywhere they'll give him credit. A man's got to have some money—that's obvious. If you would only pay him a regular wage, it'd be much more satisfactory, father."

"Pay him a wage? Charles? My God, he doesn't do enough work to earn his keep."

"I think you're wrong there. Charles is quite useful here, and we're short-handed enough, goodness knows. If he goes off and gets a job somewhere else, it'll only make things harder. There's all the ploughing to be done, remember, and Elizabeth can't always be on the tractor. Charles is a good driver and quite a fair mechanic. It'd be worth while paying him a market wage—and you'd save the Income Tax on what you pay him."

Old Garth pushed his porridge plate away with a snort of

disgust. "So I'm to pay Charles, am I?—and to keep him as well, I
suppose. You'll be wanting me to pay Malcolm, next?"

"Not a bad idea—pay him piece-work, he's not strong enough
to work full time. It doesn't matter about Malcolm, though. He
makes a bit of money from his hives—he's clever with bees, you
know. But I don't like all the neighbours knowing that Charles
hasn't a penny. It's undignified. Better pay him a market wage—
and then I think he'll earn it. As it is, he's always taking Elizabeth's
cigarettes. It's not fair."

"Serve her right. Oughtn't to smoke. Filthy habit for women,"
grunted the old man.

Marion lifted her laden tray. "I'll come and find you in the office
about those returns," she replied placidly.

The old house was very quiet when Marion settled down to
her accounts. Outside the wind howled and the rain beat against
the windows, but indoors was no sound of voices or movement.
Old Mrs. Moffat was busy in the vast stone-floored kitchen, far
away from the untidy little room which Marion called the "office."
Somewhere upstairs Janey Simpson, a girl of fourteen, was "doing"
the bedrooms in her own half-witted way: otherwise no one
moved in the house. Marion pulled out her own private account
book from the corner where she kept it hidden and pondered over
the figures she had entered. She had made a very fair assessment
of the farm profits for the year and she studied the figures with
satisfaction: twenty-five milking cows at £38 per head, twelve
calving heifers at £30, seven yearling calves, ten small calves, one
hundred and sixty ewes with lambs at foot, six sows with litters,
two tegs, two boars, four horses and a foal, a hundred head of
poultry. Then followed crops—oats, wheat, potatoes, mangolds,
swedes, kale and seed grasses: Marion knew exactly the market

value of the crops she had toiled so hard to raise and harvest. Next came implements and gear of all kinds—tractor, plough, carts, and the food stocks and fertilisers. The stock could be valued at £2,000, the crops at nearly a thousand. The market value of all the gear had appreciated during the year, though Marion was careful to make a conservative estimate in all cases. Through the list she went, considering the prices she had set against the beasts, including pigs and poultry, gear and crops. The total totted up to nearly £5,000—several hundreds of pounds higher than the previous year's assessment. As Marion pored over her figures, her face showed set and obstinate. She had her figures, she had formulated her case, and she intended to pit her will against her father's for the first time in her life. For years she had worked for him without being allowed any say in the policy of the farm or any share in its profits, and at long last her slowly moving nature had revolted. She wanted to have some say in the working of the farm: to buy stock using her own judgment, to be allowed to use her accumulated store of knowledge and experience. Marion knew exactly the obstinacy she would meet in her taciturn father—but she had become aware of obstinacy in herself, and she knew the strength of her case. Shortage of labour was the lever by which she meant to move the old man. "There's me and Elizabeth and Charles and Malcolm," she said to herself. "Without us he has only got old Moffat and Jem and himself. He couldn't work the home farm with only them to help him—and if the land isn't farmed properly he'll be in trouble with the War Agricultural Committee. He knows what that means now. He's got to be reasonable for once in his life. It's the first time I've ever asked for anything—and I'm going to have it. I won't be put off any longer, as though I were a child."

She suddenly sat up, listening intently. She could hear old Garth's heavy footsteps coming along the bare wooden floor of the passage, and she pushed her private account book away under some papers, where it was ready to her hand.

"Come on," she said to herself. "I've been waiting for this for a long time. It had to happen—and now it's come."

III

Malcolm had done just what Marion had suggested: he had gone up to a loft over the kitchen which he used for storing his bee equipment. There wasn't any job he wanted to do so far as bee-keeping was concerned, but he was out of everybody's way and was likely to be left undisturbed. If his father saw him in the house, Malcolm knew that old Robert Garth was likely to order him to get busy on any of the odd jobs which accumulate about a farm and are attacked on wet days: anything from cleaning out shippons or pig houses, lime washing, shifting manure, hedging and ditching and cleaning implements. Whatever the job, it would certainly not be to Malcolm's taste. From under a pile of odd boards and fitments for his hives, Malcolm pulled out a heap of manuscript paper and began to read through his own untidy writing. He was at work on a novel, and he was endeavouring to revise his rather shapeless story and make it satisfy his own slowly-developing critical sense. He had written, as most beginners tend to do, about his own people, and the central figures in his narrative were his half-brother, Richard Garth, and their father. The happenings of the previous afternoon, when he had actually heard Richard talking to John Staple, and had seen him walking away across the fells, were still vivid in Malcolm's mind, and as a result he felt dissatisfied with the imaginary character study he had made while Richard was nothing more than a name to him. The real Richard had had a vitality and purposefulness about him which Malcolm felt that his own fictitious character lacked. Richard in the flesh was clear-cut, hard and determined, but there was nothing neurotic or melodramatic about him. Malcolm turned his pages discontentedly. Should he try again?—rewrite all those painfully written pages? His novel had become to Malcolm a symbol of escape. If he could get it published he could escape from an environment which he hated, from a father whom he loathed, and from whom he felt utterly alien.

He read on through the untidy pages, the already many times amended sentences, growing more and more depressed as he read. At last he put the sheets together and hid them again in the corner, and sat down listening to the dreary sound of wind and rain. He felt defeated and desolate, unable to make any effort adequate to help him to do the one thing he longed to do—to get away from this world of earth and dung and beasts into a world of thought and freedom and creative activity. He thought of Marion—arguing about the cost of a Hereford bull—and he clenched his thin nervous hands round his knees.

"Why am I so unlike them?" he asked himself. "Why, if I was born of this family and into this place, don't I fit here…?"

Exasperation begot loneliness: he jumped up at last and made his way down the rough ladder which eventually took him into the stone-flagged dairy and on his way to the front of the house. He drew near the door of the office without any thought of Marion and her discussion with her father, until he was reminded of them by the sound of voices. Marion's voice was clear and strong: "I've said all I've got to say, and I mean every word of it," she said. "If you persist in your present attitude you will have no one but yourself to thank for the consequences, father."

Malcolm paused outside the door, and as he waited he became aware that Charles was standing in the shadows farther along the passage. Old Garth's voice roared his reply: "Damn you! You're threatening me, are you? You think you can frighten me into submitting to blackmail, devil take you. Get out, I say, get out and be damned to you!"

"It's easy enough to say that, father. The consequences aren't going to be so easy, though. You turned Richard out, long ago..."

The sound of her voice was drowned in a crash, as of a heavy table overturned: almost simultaneously there was another crash, a reverberating report which echoed through the old house. Malcolm knew what it was—a gunshot inside the room. Sick and horrified he stood helpless, unable to move, but Charles sprang past him to the door of the office.

"Damn all!" he exclaimed, "someone's got to do something... can't stand and do nothing." He flung the office door open, and Malcolm peered over his shoulder, sick with apprehension. The sight which met their eyes was in the nature of a ludicrous anticlimax. A big heavy arm-chair had been pushed back and violently overturned, upsetting a table behind it. Old Garth was on the floor, swearing with a vindictive non-stop fury and with an energy which told Charles that he could not be seriously injured. Marion stood with her back to the wall, blank surprise on her face. A gun lay across the space between the overturned table and the wall, and the room was full of cordite fumes from the shot which had just been ejected from it.

"Here, what the devil's the matter?" asked Charles, his voice surprisingly normal. "It looks as though Marion had forgotten to unload that gun. Anyone hurt? Let me help you up, father."

He bent over the old man and managed to help him to his feet, and old Garth roared out: "Get out, all of you! Trying to murder me now! I'll have the law on you, you murdering graceless fools…"

Charles turned to Marion who was trying to make herself heard. "Here, clear out—he'll have an apoplexy. Go away and leave him to it. No use arguing now."

"I tell you it was an accident. He knocked the gun over and it went off," said Marion. "Do you think I'd be such a fool as to shoot him?"

"Oh, lord, get out. All that can keep," said Charles, under cover of old Garth's roaring imprecations.

Malcolm still stood as though transfixed. He saw that Janey Simpson had appeared, and stood gaping at the foot of the stairs, her face white and idiotic. Old Mrs. Moffat, with a saucepan in her hand, stared into the office as though to assure herself that murder had not been done.

"I can't stand any more of this here. 'Tisn't right," she quavered, and Marion came out into the passage.

"It's all right, nothing awful has happened," she said. "Father pushed his chair over, and the gun was leaning against the table and it went off as it fell. Nothing's the matter."

"Nothing… Deary me, I don't like it," said Mrs. Moffat. "Guns shouldn't go off, not with folks who know how to treat them. Here you, Janey, you get back to your work and don't stand gaping there."

"I'm goin' 'ome, I am. Don't like it," quavered Janey, and fled into the shadows. Mrs. Moffat turned on her heel and walked away, and Marion suddenly leaned back against the wall, shaken by spasms of uncontrollable laughter.

Malcolm, his nerves still aquiver, caught her by the arm. "Don't," he begged, "don't laugh… I can't stand it."

Marion pulled herself together with an effort and spoke normally, but a little breathlessly. "Oh, all right! Don't get all het-up. Come into the sitting-room. The whole thing was so ludicrous I had to laugh—it was relief, partly. When father fell back over the chair I thought he'd been shot."

She walked on into the wider passage and threw open the door of the living room, and Malcolm followed her. Marion found a cigarette and lighted it, and then turned to Malcolm.

"All the same it would have been pretty grim if… if he *had* been shot. Somebody must have borrowed my gun and brought it into the house again still loaded, with the safety catch off." She paused, and then faced Malcolm squarely.

"Do you know anything about it, Malcolm?" she asked. "If you *did* borrow that gun, you'd better say so. I know you say you hate guns, and that you won't touch one, but somebody has been meddling with mine."

He stood very still, looking white and stubborn. "I don't know anything about it," he replied. "I haven't touched your gun."

"Then who did?" she asked. "If I hadn't been so busy thinking about these accounts and what I was going to say to father, I should have noticed the way the gun was leaning against that table where he always sits. I always put my gun back in the rack—you know that."

Malcolm was obstinately silent, and at that moment Charles came into the room.

"Whew!" he said. "You seem to have had a proper old set-to. Father's perfectly certain you meant to shoot him."

"When he's thought it over he won't think anything so idiotic," retorted Marion. "It's true that the gun ought not to have been loaded. One of you borrowed it and put it back in the office, forgetting to unload it. When father jumped up in a rage he knocked his chair over and it fell against the table and jerked the gun to the ground. Of course it went off—but the whole thing was an accident. He'll realise that when he's recovered his temper."

"Recovered his temper, eh? D'you realise he's roaring all over the place that he's going to turn you out and put the police on to you and the Lord knows what else?"

"Quite probable," she replied calmly. "It's been known to happen before. When it comes to milking time this evening he won't be so anxious to have me out of the way, you'll find. As for the police—if he likes to get them here, he can. Perhaps they'll find out who last used my gun."

"My God!" said Charles. "This house defeats me! After all that, do we all sit down to dinner as though nothing had happened?"

"Quite possibly," said Marion. "I'm going to have some dinner anyway. When I'm ready to leave this house I shall do so. Not before. And the sooner somebody remembers who borrowed my gun, the better for all concerned." With that she walked out of the room.

Charles mopped his forehead. "I don't know," he said. "It beats me. The whole thing's like a lunatic asylum."

Malcolm stood and stared out at the rain.

CHAPTER FIVE

I

I T HAD SEEMED TO CHARLES, WHO KNEW LESS ABOUT THE violence of his father's temper than did Marion and Malcolm, that it would be impossible for family relations to return to normal: Charles was wrong. Despite the old man's imprecations and fulminations, by the end of the day he was behaving as though nothing unusual had happened. The reconciling force was a sick cow. Before dinner had appeared on the table Jem Moffat came into the house to seek the old man with a tale of woe about Bluebell—a heifer who was in process of calving. "Summat wrong," said Jem. Old Garth cared a lot about his cows: he hurried out to see if he could assist her.

"Better get Miss Marion. Her's champion with cows," said Jem.

The old man did not reply, so Jem hurried in again to find Marion. Together she and her father toiled in the shippon, and at length Bluebell's calf was assisted into the world and the cow dosed and wrapped in sacks to keep her from chill. Neither father nor daughter mentioned the scene which had occurred in the house: their only remarks related to the cow and her calf—it was a heifer calf, which gratified old Garth: bull calves were of very little value, but a heifer was a potential milking cow.

It was nearly tea time before Marion returned to the house and Charles saw her when she came into the kitchen, her clothes sodden with rain and dung, her face flushed and dirty but serene.

"How's things?" inquired Charles.

"Oh, she'll do. The calf's all right too," responded Marion, and Charles exclaimed:

"Well I'm damned—and what about the to-do this morning? Any police in the offing?"

"Don't talk rubbish," said Marion calmly. She was washing her hands at the kitchen sink.

"I see. All forgiven and forgotten," jibed Charles. "Well, you're a marvellous pair. Murder and shooting and denunciations one minute and all peace and goodwill the next."

"You exaggerate things," replied Marion. "Father lost his temper—nothing unusual about that—and when the gun went off under his nose he lost his head and said idiotic things. He's got over it by this time."

"And how was it that the gun *did* go off under his nose?" demanded Charles, lounging against the table.

"Because some idiot borrowed my gun and brought it into the house loaded," replied Marion.

"I see. That's that. Nothing more to be said, eh?"

"Talking about it won't help matters," replied Marion. "If I knew who used my gun without permission I might had have something to say—but I don't know, and nobody's likely to tell me."

"Perhaps it's as well," observed Charles. "Though it does occur to one that you aren't too anxious to have detailed inquiries made on the topic."

Marion flushed. "I don't know what you're talking about," she said brusquely.

Tea time was a silent meal. Only old Garth, Marion and Charles sat down to the loaded table, for Malcolm had not been in evidence since the morning's excitements. The old man had propped a copy of *The Farmer's Weekly* in front of him and sat studying it. Marion sat silent and Charles concentrated on putting down an ample tea, glancing from one to the other occasionally with twitching lips. At length the old man got up and stalked out of the room and almost immediately Elizabeth Meldon came in, flushed and pretty, her fair hair freshly curled, a rose pinned in the buttonhole of her neat suit.

"Mr. Thwaite gave me a lift back," she said. "I'll come and milk when I've had a cup of tea, Marion. How's everything?"

"All right. Bluebell's calved—a heifer. She nearly went west. I'm going out to see if she's all right."

Marion went out and Elizabeth turned to Charles who said: "Enjoy yourself? You looked pretty festive when I saw you in Lancaster."

"Did I? It was a pretty foul day—poured all the time. I didn't see you about. What's all this about Bluebell? Marion looked rather hot and bothered."

"It's been one of those days," said Charles. After a pause he told her of the excitements of the morning, and Elizabeth listened with a face which grew increasingly troubled.

"Oh dear!" she cried. "It's simply awful… I just dare not think about it."

"Well, don't think," said Charles. "It doesn't help. I've tried it and I'm stumped. Have a cigarette." He pulled out a packet of Players but Elizabeth shook her head.

"I must go and change and help with the milking. Where's Malcolm, by the way?"

"I don't know: he's cleared out since the fracas," replied Charles. "There's one bright point in the situation," he added gravely, just as Elizabeth reached the door. She paused and turned back to look at him.

"Bluebell's calf is all right," he said. Elizabeth slammed the door behind her.

II

On the following day—Thursday—John Staple was returning from the "fox hunt." Three foxes had been shot in Lawson's Wood and the victims had been auctioned outside the big barn in the dales, bringing in a profit of five pounds for the Red Cross. Staple had not gone to the auction: he had gone down to the river in order to see the amount of damage caused by the flood, which was now subsiding. He was also keeping his eyes open for some cattle which had strayed from the Home Farm. The river had flooded the pastures, bringing down much wreckage in its path. Staple noted that there was a quantity of timber—fallen trees, gates and posts, which would be worth carting for firewood. He had just turned upwards along a path which led up the steep sides of the valley when he saw a man's figure on the far side of some gnarled old thorn trees. Staple recognised Bob Ashthwaite—Richard Garth's father-in-law. Ashthwaite had been at the fox hunt, much to Staple's surprise, for the former seldom came near Garthmere these days. Staple called a cheery greeting: "Good-day, Bob! glad to see you again. Did you get a shot up yonder?"

"Nay. Might've saved myself a walk. Never caught sight of the darned foxes at all," returned Ashthwaite, and without pausing he continued his way towards the river. Staple looked after him, wondering a little. He doubted very much if it was the attraction of shooting foxes which had brought Ashthwaite on to the Garthmere land.

"That's odd, that is," said Staple to himself, recollecting his own meeting with Richard Garth two days ago. "Could it be that Richard's hereabouts still?" he pondered.

His way led up a steep old lane, sunk between banks on which fantastic ancient hawthorns bent their gnarled branches from the prevalent west wind. The ground beneath his feet was but a squelch of mud, for the lane was used for the cattle who grazed in the lower pastures, and after the recent rains a runnel of water flowed down the steep declivity. At its upper end the lane turned abruptly to meet the road, but the road was concealed from Staple by a barn and a small ancient building called a "hull," once used for housing a few cattle in the winter, now used as cover for any miscellaneous gear which could be conveniently packed into it. Staple noticed that the door had been left open and he went to close it with the instinct of the farmer, for if cows were driven up the old lane they would undoubtedly go into the hull if the door was left open, and thus cause trouble to the person who was bringing them in.

When Staple reached the hull and stretched out his hand to pull the rough door towards him he suddenly stiffened and stood stock still. In the shadows at his feet a figure lay prone on the trampled mud of the floor: the head was against the further wall, the feet in their heavy muddy boots were just against the door. The hull was dark inside, and the long figure clad in drab raincoat, whipcord breeches and leather leggings seemed of the earth, earthy. Staple rubbed his eyes, as though in very truth he could rub away a hallucination which had invaded his vision. Then he stood his gun against the outside of the rough stone hovel, and went in, squeezing past the door into the shadows of the hull. It was old Robert Garth who lay there, his gun beneath him, the stock sticking out from under his arm. Staple knelt down beside the man who had been his master for nearly half a century and touched the white head. There was blood on his hands when he withdrew them.

"He must have stumbled and the gun went off and shot him," was Staple's first reaction. Then he thought again. Old Garth carried his gun as a gun should be carried—barrel pointing down, stock under his arm. How then could he have been shot through the head with his own gun? There was sick horror and distress in Staple's mind, but his common sense never deserted him. He looked at the still figure: it was lying just where it had fallen—not so very long ago, either. The face was chilling, with the swift chill of death, but the body was limp, not rigid. Within the last hour Robert Garth had fallen prone in the dank mud of the hull, shot at close quarters by a gun whose charge of shot had nearly blown the old man's face away. He had not been moved since—where he had fallen, there he lay.

"I don't like it. I don't like it," said Staple to himself. He stood there, pondering, his slow countryman's mind at work on the ugly problem—how this had happened. He bent again to see if the button of the safety-catch on the gun was pressed home, and then he heard footsteps and a shrill cry. Looking up quickly, Staple saw Jock, the idiot boy who worked on Bob Ashthwaite's farm. Jock was standing close to the hull, his mouth wide open in his round pink face, blue eyes staring, tow-coloured hair on end all round his silly face.

"Killed 'im, shot 'im dead, hast tha?" said Jock. "Aye, shot him dead. Him's dead. Goody, goody. Him's dead. Dead as mutton."

"Stop that, Jock. Go along to the house at once and ask Miss Garth to come here. Tell her there's been an accident…"

"Him's dead," said the boy. He turned away, giving vent to his idiot's chuckle. "Shot 'im dead! Goody, goody."

A horrible misgiving arose in Staple's mind. Jock was devoted
to his master, Bob Ashthwaite, and it was more than probable that
Bob had cursed old Mr. Garth long and loud in the boy's hearing.
Jock was shrewd enough in some ways, for all that he was classed
as a mental defective and was in the habit of behaving like an idiot.
Had Jock done this thing? As Staple stood there he remembered
how Mr. Garth had threatened Jock with a thrashing if he caught
the boy on Garthmere land. For once Staple stood irresolute: he felt
that he could not go away and leave Robert Garth lying there, and
yet Jock of all messengers was the most unreliable. He stood wondering what he ought to do, and then, to his relief, he heard his own
name being called. It was Marion Garth's voice, and he called back:

"Yes, I'm here—" and then he broke off not knowing what to
say next.

Marion swung down the bank which divided the lane from
the road above.

"Is anything the matter? That boy Jock's madder than ever. He
says you've shot somebody."

Staple stood between Marion Garth and the door of the hull.
"Something bad has happened, Miss Marion, something very bad.
It's your father. He has been shot."

"Father? Good heavens! Is he badly hurt? Where is he?"

"He's in here. I'm sorry, my dear. It's no use my making a long
story about it—he's dead, Miss Marion. Shot through the head."

"Father... dead... Merciful heavens! Who shot him?"

The last words came out in a rush, and Staple saw fear in
Marion's eyes for the first time. He had known her all her life and
never before had he seen her look like that.

"I don't know," he said slowly. "I thought at first he had
tripped and his own gun had gone off, but I'm afraid it's not

that. Maybe it was that boy Jock. He came with Bob to the fox hunt."

Marion strode past him and stood by the door of the hull. Then, like Staple, she knelt down beside Robert Garth's body, her face pallid. "Poor father!" she said softly. "I can't bear to see him lying there like that. We must get a hurdle and carry him home."

"I'm afraid we can't do that," said Staple. "We shall have to report to the police. In a case like this one ought not to move anything. You see..." He broke off, and then added with an effort: "It will be the business of the police to find out who shot him. This wasn't an accident."

Marion stood very still, looking down at her father's body. Then she said: "Jock—what was he doing here?"

"I don't know," replied Staple. "In any case it's not for us to determine. The police must make inquiries."

"How awful!" she broke out. "How utterly and indescribably horrible..."

"I know, my dear. Don't think I don't understand. I've worked for him nigh on half a century, and I cared for him in spite of all his harsh ways. I hate to let him lie there... but it's got to be. Now I'll stay here, and you go in and phone through to the Sergeant of Police at Carnton. Tell him Mr. Garth has been shot and ask him to come at once."

Marion's face contracted, and she stood for a moment as though she was going to argue, then she thought better of it and turned quickly away, leaving Staple standing by the door.

A moment after Marion had gone, Staple heard voices again, and the sound of Jock's raucous chuckle. Then came the sound of Charles Garth's voice, raised angrily.

"What the devil do you mean, you imp of Satan? If I get my hands on you you'll be sorry for it. Be off with you!"

Staple heard the shuffle of Jock's running footsteps and his parting words, shouted out as he ran: "Shot him dead, goody, goody. In tha' ould 'ull. You go and see."

A moment later Charles Garth appeared from the roadway and jumped down the bank. He halted abruptly on seeing Staple.

"What the deuce is the matter—or is it all that idiot boy imagining things? He ought to be in an asylum."

"Maybe he ought. I suppose we ought to have kept him here." said Staple wearily. Suddenly he felt exhausted and incapable of further explanation. He stood aside from the door of the hull and motioned to Charles to come and stand beside him. Shoulder to shoulder the two men stood, gazing down at the prone body and at last Charles spoke, almost under his breath:

"My God! It's happened then. I was afraid of this. That gun didn't go off by accident yesterday... I never thought it did."

"What do you mean?"

Charles jumped and then stared at Staple. "Never mind," he said slowly. "How did this happen?"

"I don't know—any more than you know," replied Staple. "I found him here as I came up from the dales. Your sister has gone to ring up the police."

Charles pushed past him and went inside the hull. "Accident?" he queried. "He often left his gear in here when he was going round the farm. Could he have tripped?"

"Look at the way he's holding his gun," replied Staple.

Charles lit a match and peered into the dark recesses of the little building and went right into the further corner.

"There are some snares here," he said. "Father often set them himself. He was cunning at it—always spotted the rabbit runs. He must have come in here to fetch them and been shot just as he opened the door—point blank." He paused and added, "What about this for an idea? That boy, Jock—say if he came in here to pinch one of those snares and was caught by father. He might have shot if he'd got a gun with him. You were at the fox hunt, weren't you, Staple?"

"Aye. I was there. Jock was with the beaters. He hadn't got a gun."

"Ashthwaite had though. I wonder if he carried his own gun back with him—or gave it to the boy to carry."

"Bob Ashthwaite's odd in some ways, but he's not fool enough to give a loaded gun to Jock," replied Staple. "I saw Bob just now, down in the dales. He'd got his gun with him."

"What was he doing in the dales?"

"I didn't ask him."

The two men fell silent, and Charles asked: "You're sure he's dead?"

Staple felt suddenly exasperated.

"D'you think I've been standing here wondering if he's dead?" he demanded. "He was dead before I found him. It's not because I like it that he's lying there, like a beast that's been slaughtered. I'd move him if I had my way, but the police won't thank us for moving him. They've got to see him as he lies. This isn't an accident, Charles Garth. It's plain murder. Someone shot him as he opened the door—and it's the police have got to find out who did it." He paused a moment and then added slowly: "I tell you I wish it were me myself lying there in the mud. This is an awful thing—and I don't dare think of the consequences."

"You're right," said Charles soberly. "It's an ugly thought, Staple. The police will find plenty of mud about the place... My God! it's a grim prospect..."

III

Superintendent Layng was an able and energetic officer. He was not popular in his district, but that fact was due to a variety of circumstances, not all Layng's fault. First, he was not a local man, and he had never got on to terms of real understanding with the folk around Garthmere who had an innate distrust of those not natives of their own valley. Secondly, Layng had a slightly pompous manner and a tendency to regard the shrewd farming folk as being slow of understanding because they habitually spoke slowly and thought for a long time before they gave vent to speech. Layng had been born in a big midland city—he had never quite realised that the slowness of speech which often irritated him in these north countrymen was not a symptom of stupidity: far from it—their minds were as shrewd as Layng's own, while their knowledge of their neighbour's potentialities was far wider than anything that Layng could achieve by the exercise of an inquiring mind and an observant eye.

When Layng first questioned Staple by the door of the hull in the grey September evening, the superintendent shouted out his questions sharply, in a somewhat hectoring and military manner. The sharper and quicker the policeman, the slower and more terse became the bailiff. Staple, who had suffered a very real shock when he found his master's body, unconsciously put up a "defence mechanism" of obstinacy and slowness when he felt that he was being brow-beaten.

After a series of questions Layng dismissed Staple abruptly, saying: "Go up to the Hall and wait for me there. I shall come there immediately I have finished investigations here, and I shall want to see everyone in the house. Meantime, I caution you not to discuss this matter with anybody. I don't want to waste time over hearsay evidence. You can leave your gun here. I will see to it."

Staple thrust his hands into his pockets and turned away with his shoulders hunched up, walking slowly and heavily. Layng turned to one of the constables he brought with him.

"You can go up to the house and see to it that everyone is there when I want them." He turned to his younger assistant, who had acted as his chauffeur, saying: "We should be here all night before I got any facts out of that old fellow. Can't answer yes or no without five minutes time lag between question and answer."

Turning on a powerful electric torch, Layng examined the ground inside the hull. It was very damp, the mud heavy and squelchy, for the rain-water had drained through it in the recent storms, soaking through the unmortared walls and seeping in at the ground level. Obviously some sheep had been temporarily folded there not long since and there were plenty of fresh footprints. Marion had worn gum boots: Charles Garth and Staple had both moved about inside the little building, and Charles' footprints were plain in the far corner. Layng gave a snort of disgust. He had learned from Staple that three people had been inside the hull since the body was discovered—Staple himself, Charles, and Marion. "Galumphing around and confusing all the traces," said Layng. He soon arrived at the same conclusion which Charles had formed—that old Mr. Garth had been shot just after he stepped inside the door of the hull. Layng was a tall fellow—close on six feet, but the dead man had been taller still. Layng had to bend his head to get inside the door, and Mr. Garth would have had to stoop still further. It was probably that fact which accounted for his prone position: he had been bending right forward as he came in at the door and consequently had fallen forward on his face instead of going backwards as might have been expected when struck by a charge of shot at close quarters. If this argument were right, there seemed to be only one place where the murderer could have stood—in the corner of the hull diagonally farthest from the door. Examination showed that there was a pile of peat moss on the floor in that corner—probably put there long since as bedding for some sick beast. Its drawback from Layng's point of view was that it showed no footprints. Here the murderer could have knelt or sat—the sloping roof would have prevented him standing upright—and have left no trace on the resilient peat moss. Flashing his torch round in the dark corner, Layng pounced on something which reflected the light: he bent down with a pair of forceps and carefully raised his find without fingering it. He thought at first that it was a shilling, but closer examination showed it to be a twenty-five cent piece, the "quarter" of American currency. Layng put the coin away carefully in an envelope. How an American coin came to be lying in such a place Layng could not imagine, but he felt that he had found something of first rate importance. He noticed the rabbit snares, too, and tucked away into a corner was something which Charles had missed. It was an old haversack, containing odds and ends such as pieces of wire and twine, pliers and a jack-knife, as well as a heavy hammer. Staple had said: "Mr. Garth often left some of his odd gear here when he was going from place to place on the farm." Layng nodded to himself. He felt that he could guess what had happened. "Who?" was the next question. He came outside and spoke to the constable.

"You know a bit about the family at the Hall, Harding. Isn't there a son who has recently come back from abroad?"

"Yes, sir. Mr. Charles Garth. He was in Malaya, and got away to Australia just before the Japs took Singapore. No end of a time he had—got wrecked on one of those tropical islands and had a fearful time."

"He did, did he? Have you talked to him yourself?"

"No. I've only heard about it in the village yonder. Mr. Charles Garth isn't given to talking freely to anyone if you take me."

"Snob, eh? Did you hear if he came home via America?"

"I've never heard say so, sir. Maybe he did."

Layng stood and considered for a moment. "There's the surgeon coming out here, and the ambulance as well as a photographer. You are to stay here on guard until further instructions."

"Very good, sir. I've just remembered something you might like to know. Mr. Garth's eldest son, Richard, went to America years ago. Folks say he quarrelled with his father when he married Farmer Ashthwaite's daughter—him over at Greenbeck."

"Ashthwaite?" queried Layng, standing still and pondering for a moment. Then he inquired, "This eldest son, Richard, has he been back in these parts?"

"Not that I know of," replied Harding. "He left here before I was born, I believe. The only reason I know about him is that I heard two Gressthwaite farmers talking about Richard Garth only yesterday. I went past Howland's farm while his sale was on and I looked over the cars parked outside—just in case of any irregularity—and I heard two Gressthwaite chaps talking about the Garths. Funny how it should have cropped up just then."

"Very funny," agreed Layng thoughtfully. "You can tell me more about it later. I've got to go up to the Hall and get statements now. See to it that you don't let anyone near this place. What the devil's that?"

"That" was Jock's chuckle: a few seconds later his round red face appeared round the corner of the hull.

"Shot 'im dead, 'e did, goody, goody!" he exclaimed.

"Come here, boy! Who shot him?"

"Mr. Staple shot 'im, shot 'im dead!" cackled Jock. The next instant he had bolted down the old lane past Layng, who gave an exclamation of anger.

"Hi! Come back!" he shouted, but Jock, who had an unexpected turn of speed, had already disappeared down the steep winding lane.

"He's a natural, sir," said Harding. "Dotty as they make them. He works for Mr. Ashthwaite at Greenbeck. He can't even count, or make a mark beside his name, but I'm told he's clever with beasts and a wonderful milker.—That bit about Mr. Staple now, he'd just have made that up."

"Would he? Well, we'll have to see about that later on," said Layng, and turned away towards the road, intent on reaching Garthmere Hall.

CHAPTER SIX

I

WHEN LAYNG REACHED GARTHMERE HALL HE WENT UP to the great front door and pealed the heavy bell which hung beside the entrance. He had never been to the Hall before, and he had plenty of time to study the ancient door, set beneath a magnificent Tudor arch. The door was enriched with wrought iron spirals which sprung from the heavy hinges, and it was studded with square-headed bolts. The ancient weather-beaten oak had its own tale to tell to an antiquarian eye, for it still displayed the bullet scars of Cromwellian days, when the Hall had withstood the siege of the Parliamentarians. Layng was no antiquarian, and the door did not interest him: he only thought what an unconscionable time the inmates took over opening it. There was a rattle of chains and creaking of bolts before the oak swung ponderously back at last: truth to tell it had not been opened for years, for the Garths always used one of the side entrances or else the kitchen door. It was Marion who opened the door. The sound of the clanging bell had startled her—it had not been heard for so long and the deep note seemed to have an ominous significance.

When Layng introduced himself briefly, she looked at him with no friendly eye, saying: "I'm sorry to have kept you so long, but this door is never used now. Will you come in. I am Marion Garth."

Layng heard the rebuke in her tone and flushed awkwardly as he entered the dusty panelled hall. Marion pushed the creaking door and set her shoulder against it before it would close, and the two were left standing in the shadows.

"We use the other wing of the house. It's less inconvenient," she said abruptly, and walked ahead of Layng to a door beneath the great stairway at the back of the hall. She led him to the office and standing in front of him asked:

"Whom do you wish to see first? John Staple is waiting—he wants to get back to his own work. Farming has to go on, you know, whatever happens."

Her voice was abrupt, and Layng felt irritated. Marion had a dignity of her own, and she looked the Superintendent full in the face with an expression which Layng considered aggressive. Quite without justification he suspected her of trying to make him feel small.

"Other things have to go on as well as farming," he retorted, "and the law is one of them. I will take your statement first, but will you kindly ring and ask for the officer who preceded me here. It is customary to have a witness when a statement is taken."

She laughed. "The bells in this house are all out of order. If I rang one no one would take any notice. Bell ringing is no part of our routine these days. I will go and fetch your man. He's in the kitchen."

She turned swiftly and was through the door before Layng had time to reply. Truth to tell, he was nonplussed. The combination of the great house and Marion's forthright speech and working clothes struck Layng as an anomaly. He sat down at the desk and waited until Marion returned with the officer. He heard her voice as she came along the echoing passage:

"Yes. It's a huge house. Most of it's shut up these days. It would take an army of servants to keep it in order and we have no servants left save for an old lady in the kitchen and a child of fourteen who's a bit weak in the head."

She came into the room and motioned the officer to a seat with a nod of her head: then, standing with her back to the window she faced Layng.

"Yes? What do you want to know?"

"Please sit down," said the Superintendent, notebook before him. "You understand that I am a Superintendent of Police, and that I am conducting an inquiry into your father's death?"

"Yes." She uttered the word impatiently, but remained standing.

"I caution you to answer any questions accurately," continued Layng, "though you can refuse to answer if you wish. Your full name, please."

"Marion Elizabeth Anne de Lisle Garth. Age forty-five. Born on the tenth of July, 1898. Single. Occupation, farming. Only daughter of Robert John Stanton de Lisle Garth of Garthmere."

Her voice was steady and impersonal, very clear in diction, and deliberate. Layng wrote swiftly.

"When did you last see deceased?"

"At midday dinner. We eat at twelve."

"Did he tell you what he meant to do this afternoon?"

"No. My father did not ever say what he intended to do unless he needed help or wished to make arrangements about the farm work."

"Do you know what he meant to do?"

"No. I knew there was to be what we call a fox hunt, and he knew it. I assumed that he would go as the hunt was to be on his tenant's land, but I did not know for certain that he would go."

"You have not seen him since he left the house after his midday meal?"

"I have not."

"What were you doing yourself this afternoon?"

"From one o'clock until about half-past three I was helping to lift potatoes. Elizabeth Meldon—our land-worker—drove the tractor and I gathered the potatoes. About half-past three I came back and lifted onions in the garden here."

"By yourself?"

"By myself."

"And then?"

"I came in about five o'clock and had tea. Miss Meldon and my brother Charles had tea with me. After that I went out to milk in the shippon: the cows had not been brought in and I went to the fold yard gate to see if Jem was in sight. It was then that the boy Jock rushed up, calling out that someone had been shot in the old hull. At least that was what I think he meant, though he's difficult to understand. I went to the hull and saw John Staple, who told me that he had found my father's body. He also advised me not to have the body moved, which was what I wished to do, and he told me to come back home and telephone for the police."

The deep abrupt voice ceased and Marion stood in silence as Layng muttered: "Thank you," while he wrote down the gist of her statement. He then asked: "Can you account for your father's death in any way?"

"No. I can not."

Layng went on: "Do you know if Mr. Garth had any enemies, or any one who harboured a grudge against him?"

"I don't know," replied Marion.

Layng protested: "Come, come, Miss Garth: surely you can say yes or no. It is a plain question; had your father any enemies?"

"I don't know. If he had, he did not discuss them with me: neither did I discuss him with other people."

"I will put in your statement that you knew of no enemies nor of any persons holding a grudge against your father," said Layng. "Will you kindly tell me how many people reside in this house?"

"Seven—not counting my father: my two brothers, Charles and Malcolm, myself, Elizabeth Meldon, Mrs. Moffat and her husband, Bob, and the boy Jem who sleeps in a room over the stables."

"To your knowledge no enmity existed between any of these people and your father?"

"I don't know at all," replied Marion. "I lead a busy life on the farm, and I don't bother to be introspective over enmities and such like. It all sounds too much like melodrama. We are very plain folk here."

Layng paused. "Your father has just been shot, Miss Garth, and the circumstances indicate that he was deliberately murdered. I am asking for any assistance you can give in discovering who is the murderer." Layng paused, but Marion made no reply. She stood very straight and still, her face expressionless. Layng went on:

"I think you have another brother—Richard Garth?"

"Yes. He is my eldest brother. He went abroad twenty-five years ago, and I have not seen him since."

"He quarrelled with your father before he left home?"

"I believe so—twenty-five years ago."

"Have you heard from him since then?"

"No."

"Would you say that your father was a quick-tempered man?"

"It's probable that other people would say so. He was my father, and I was fond of him. You can ask for opinions on that subject elsewhere."

"Had any person in this house had any dispute with deceased recently?"

"We always argue to some extent. My father was old-fashioned, and I have tried to persuade him to try more modern farming methods. I don't know if you call that a dispute." Marion paused, and then went on: "There was one incident recently which will probably be exaggerated when it is told to you—so you might as well hear of it from me. Yesterday my father and I were in this room, going through some accounts. When he got up he knocked his chair over and it fell against my gun, which was standing in the corner. The gun fell to the floor, and as it fell it went off. That is all. No one was hurt and the whole thing was a stupid accident."

"I see. Your gun was loaded then?"

"Obviously, since it fired a shot into the wainscot."

"And the safety catch was off."

"Apparently—unless the shock of the fall jerked it back."

"Do you usually bring your gun into the house still loaded?"

"I do not—but everybody is liable to forgetfulness some time."

"Are you certain the gun was loaded when you left it in that corner?"

"Of course not—otherwise it would not have been left there."

"Could it have been borrowed by somebody else, and put back loaded?"

"Yes. Any one could have borrowed it, but as we all have our own guns I can't see the point."

Layng paused and looked at his watch. "I will go into this point again later, Miss Garth. For the moment all that I want to know about it is where are the guns generally kept?"

"In a small room called the gun-room close to the living-room. There are racks there. You can see them for yourself."

"Thank you. One last question. Did your father use the shed in which his body was found for any particular purpose?"

"I believe he dumped things there occasionally, when he had something which he didn't want to carry about with him, and there were some tools and posts in there as well."

"The fact was generally known?"

"I expect so. It was no secret."

"Thank you. Will you kindly ask Mr. Staple to come in here now—and I shall want to see the other members of the household later."

"Very well." Marion's voice was quiet and resolute, and she swung out of the room with vigorous but unhurried gait.

Layng sat meditating in silence, but the officer spoke: "She's a character is Miss Garth. They say she's a better man than either of her brothers, aye, and a better farmer than the old man was."

"She's a hard-looking woman," observed Layng.

II

John Staple gave his full name, his address at Lonsghyll Farm, his age as sixty-three, and his occupation as bailiff to Mr. Garth and farmer of ninety-three acres on the Garthmere estate. Then he waited to be questioned.

"When did you last see Mr. Garth alive?" asked Layng.

Staple considered this question and answered at length, "'Twould have been about three o'clock. The guns met at the High Barn, on the brow yonder. It is Mr. Trant's land—Lawson's Wood was where we shot. Mr. Trant, he arranged the guns. The wood was beaten from the valley upwards, and the better marksmen were placed where they were likely to get a good shot. Mr. Garth was midway, about fifty yards from me, and some way above me, in the gill."

"He was there all the time during the shoot?"

"Aye. He left when the third fox was shot—half-past four it would have been."

"Then you last saw him at half-past four?"

"Nay. 'Twas three o'clock as near as makes no difference. I heard Mr. Trant call to him at the end, 'That's about the lot, Mr. Garth,' he called—but I didn't see him, because he was above me in the wood and the undergrowth's thick there."

"Did he answer when Mr. Trant spoke to him?"

"I didn't hear him answer. Trant shouted that they'd auction the foxes at High Barn, and after that I went down into the dales. The beaters were around below me, and I saw Mr. Lamb and Mr. Hayman as I went."

"You'd better tell me exactly who was at the shoot," said Layng, and Staple, taking his time, gave the following information. The guns had been Mr. Garth himself, Staple, Trant, Martin Lamb of High Fell, Bob Ashthwaite of Greenbeck, James Hayman of Lower Stacks, and Tim Langhorn of Middle Field. The beaters had been the youngsters—Jem Moffat of Garthmere, Matt Briggs of Lonsghyll, Jack Lamb of High Fell, Giles and Peter Hayman of Lower Stacks and Will Langhorn of Middle Field. In addition, Jock had been among the number.

"Jock who?" asked Layng.

"Just Jock. Likely he's got a name, but I don't know it. He's simple, is Jock. He works for Bob Ashthwaite, and I'm told he's a tidy worker, though he can neither count nor write his name."

"Ashthwaite..." Layng pondered over the name and then turned quickly back to Staple. "This man Ashthwaite—Mr. Garth took him into court about some arrears of rent."

"Aye," agreed Staple stolidly. "Three years ago come Michaelmas that'd be."

"Does he often come to shoot on Mr. Garth's land?"

"Not so often—but this wasn't a pleasure shoot. Mr. Trant wanted these foxes shot, and Bob Ashthwaite's a good shot. Mr. Trant was free to ask whom he would."

Again Layng pondered. Then he asked: "Did you see Ashthwaite again after the shoot?"

Staple hesitated; then he replied: "Aye. I saw him in the dales, down by Lawson's close. After the hunt that was."

"In the dales, eh? What was he doing there? His place— Greenbeck, that's over beyond Middle Field, isn't it? A matter of five miles away."

"Three, if you take the bridle path over Brough's land."

"But the dales are in the opposite direction. What was he doing down there?"

"I didn't ask. Looking for some strayed cattle, likely. The heifers go mad for the fog grass in the dales the backend. Good feed that is."

"Perhaps it is, but have you ever known a heifer stray for five miles?"

"Ay. When they're bulling they'll go for miles."

Layng snorted impatiently—stock raising did not interest him. "Did Ashthwaite say he was looking for strayed cattle?" he demanded.

"Nay. I didn't ask him."

"Had he his gun with him?"

"He had. He'd been shooting at the fox hunt."

"Where was his place during the shoot? Above or below you?"

"Above. Ashthwaite was at the top of the gill above Mr. Garth. Trant said if one of the foxes diddled all of us, Bob would be safe to stop him."

"When you went down to the river, did you see Ashthwaite behind you?"

"No."

"Where was he when you first saw him?"

"By the old thorns, just above the ford."

"At the bottom of the lane leading down from that shed, eh?"

"Aye. How do you come to know that, Superintendent? That's Mr. Garth's land, that is."

"Never mind how I know. If Ashthwaite had followed Mr. Garth to the shed, he could have reckoned on getting away down along the river without being seen." Staple made no answer, and Layng went on, "About this boy, Jock. What was it he said when he first saw you standing over Mr. Garth's body?"

"He said, 'Tha's shot him.'"

"Are you sure he didn't say, 'He has shot him'?"

"That he did not," replied Staple, "though it would have been all the same if he had. The boy's a natural: what he says can no more be relied on than an idiot's babble."

Layng was silent for a minute or so, writing very swiftly. Then he said: "Were any other members of this household at the shoot, or fox hunt, or whatever you call it?"

"You'd better ask them. If I'd seen them I should have said so."

Layng leaned back in his chair. "Do you know anything about Mr. Garth's eldest son, Richard?"

Staple stared blankly in front of him. "I knew him as a boy and as a lad," he replied. "He left home close on twenty-five years ago, and I haven't heard any one name him since."

"He quarrelled with his father before he left home?"

"Maybe he did. 'Twasn't my business to inquire."

"Have you heard any one speak of him lately?"

"Nay. Not for years. Twenty-five years is long enough to forget—and to be forgotten."

"Now, Mr. Staple," and Layng faced the other squarely. "Mr. Garth has been shot—murdered so far as appearances can be relied on. Can you make any suggestion as to who had any motive for shooting him?"

"No, Superintendent. I've no suggestions to make. I found Mr. Garth, as I told you, lying in the mire in the hull. I don't know who shot him, though I can tell you straight that I'm not the one who did it. Neither do I believe Bob Ashthwaite did. It doesn't make sense to nurse a grudge for years and then go and shoot a man on his own land when every one knows you've a gun handy."

Layng paused again. "Did you know that Mr. Garth kept some gear in that shed?"

"In the hull? Aye. I knew that well enough."

"It was general knowledge? Every one knew?" asked Layng.

"You'd better ask them, Superintendent. It's not for me to answer for everybody. You're town-bred, and maybe you don't know country ways. That hull's on Mr. Garth's land, on the home farm. Farmers don't often go on each other's land, nor go meddling with gear in other folks' buildings, be it house or barn or hull."

"Thanks for the information." Layng's voice was sarcastic, though he should have known that it was a mistake to be sarcastic with a man like Staple. The Superintendent went on:

"Perhaps you can answer the question if I put it this way: would every one in this house have known that Mr. Garth kept his gear in the hull?"

"Nay, I can't tell you. Better ask them yourself," replied Staple.

Layng was beginning to lose patience. "You're the Garthmere bailiff, aren't you? What does that imply?"

"Not that I manage the home farm," replied Staple in his most stolid voice. "I see about letting the farms if they fall vacant: I collect the rents, I report on repairs and see they're done if need be—and I see that the tenants keep to their agreements: that they don't sell oats or hay to be consumed off their land, and that they keep the hedges and gates and ditches in order, and keep the land in good heart."

There was a pause, a deliberate silence on Layng's part, and then he asked: "Then it amounts to this: you can give no assistance or make any suggestion in the matter of discovering your master's murderer?"

Staple sat very still, his grey eyes bright, his face showing more colour than his wont, but his expression did not alter.

"There's no help I can give, for I know nought about it," he replied, "and as for suggestions, you'll get no suggestions from me that may put a halter round an innocent man's neck. You can suggest I shot Mr. Garth, or Bob Ashthwaite shot him, or Jock—and it'd be the devil and all to prove we had no hand in it. I know naught about it, and as God heard me, that's true."

III

Charles Garth was the next to be interviewed by the Superintendent. "Charles Laurence Philip de Lisle Garth, aged forty-seven, late of the Maramula Estate, Malaya, second son of the late Robert Garth. Landed in England in January last."

Layng made a small deviation from his precise manner of question and answer here.

"You were in Singapore, sir?"

"I was. I left in a Chinese tramp steamer with about a hundred others—one of the last boatloads to escape."

"It must have been a shocking experience," observed Layng.

Charles studied him coolly. "Undoubtedly—but it has no bearing on the matter in hand, Superintendent."

Layng took the implied snubbing quietly, and went on: "All the same, I should be very interested if you would tell me by what route you reached England."

"Via a nameless atoll in the Java group, where we lay exposed for seven bloody days, then via Java itself, Port Darwin, Sydney, Melbourne, Durban, Cape Town, St. Helena and Southampton." Charles studied the police officer with raised eyebrows. "Geography seems to me to be a little wide of the point, if I may say so," he added. "Correct me if I am wrong."

Layng mumbled something that sounded like an apology, then cleared his throat and said:

"I have been trying to find out what the members of this household were doing during the course of this afternoon, sir. Did you join the shooting party?"

"Meaning the fox hunt? I went to have a look at the arrangements, to see how the guns were posted, but I didn't stay. It looked a slow business to me—and in point of fact I haven't got a gun of my own here, and I can't get on to terms with the antiques I'm offered. I came back here before the shooting began."

"You were in the house for the rest of the afternoon, then?"

"No. I was not. I was out at the back, in the shippons. As you may have observed, there are farm buildings at the east end of this peculiar house. It's never made up its mind if it's a castle or a farm. Actually I was doing some lime-washing in a shippon close by the kitchens."

"Is there any independent confirmation of that, sir? It will simplify the inquiry if such points can be settled by additional witnesses."

"Thanks for explaining," said Charles. "You can ask the old Biddy in the kitchen if she noticed me in the shippons, or thereabouts. She'll probably complain that each time I came inside the door I spilt lime wash on her damned kitchen flags."

"Thank you. You were about the place until—?"

"Until tea time, when I came in and had tea with my sister. She went out to milk, and when I followed her, some minutes later, I heard that idiot boy shouting something about the old hull. I went along there and found Staple beside my father's body."

"Thank you. I think it will be accepted that Mr. Garth was shot within an hour of Staple's discovery of the body. The fox hunt broke up about half-past four, I gather, and most of the guns then went to the auction of the foxes at the High Barn. Mr. Staple went down to the river, he tells me. Can you remember hearing any shot between half-past four and half-past five?"

"I shouldn't have noticed it if I had," replied Charles. "There had been shooting all the afternoon, and one shot more or less wouldn't have been noticeable."

"This would have been one isolated shot."

"In any case, I didn't notice it. Actually, I believe Jem Moffat did some potting at rabbits after the hunt was over. He doesn't often get a chance of being out with a gun and he was enjoying life. Anyway, I didn't register any particular shot. I just didn't notice."

"Can you make any suggestion at all as to who might have held a grudge against Mr. Garth, or been at enmity with him?"

Charles shrugged his shoulders. "No. I can't," he said bluntly. "You've got to remember that I have only been back at home for a few months, after years spent abroad. I simply don't understand what might be called feudal politics. Anybody in this district will tell you that my father was a hard man; some call him mean, and every one knows he's obstinate, but I believe he was generally respected. He was over eighty, but he still took his share in the farm work, and believe me, he worked without sparing himself—and expected others to do the same. You can say if you like that he was a harsh old curmudgeon, always ready to abuse others, but to get him into focus you've got to remember his age and his position. He may have been a tyrant, both to his own family and to his tenants, but he's been the same for sixty years, I gather." Charles paused, and added at length: "No. I can't help you. It just doesn't make sense to me."

Layng turned back a page or two in his notebook, and then said: "Miss Garth tells me that there was some sort of accident with a gun yesterday—a gun was knocked over and went off unexpectedly."

"Yes," said Charles, looking the other full in the face. "You say my sister has told you about it—so you know as much as there is to know. I wasn't in the room when it happened—but even if I had been, it's not likely that my description of the matter would deviate from my sister's. It might help you in your researches if you get it firmly into your head that my sister is not only an accurate person, she's a strictly truthful one also."

Layng flushed a little and replied stiffly: "I had no suggestion to the contrary. As I explained before, we always try to get corroboration of evidence where possible. Were you in the house when this accident happened?"

"I was—and I came running to this room when I heard the shot. What had happened was plain enough. My father, who is—or was—an impatient man, had pushed his chair back in such a manner as to knock over the table against which the gun had rested. In falling, the gun had gone off. My father was furious over it—as any other man would be furious if a gun had gone off under his nose. He was swearing like a trooper. However, you will find out on inquiry that his rage soon evaporated. He and my sister spent the afternoon together assisting a heifer with its first calf. His rages were soon over—that was one of his outstanding characteristics."

"Thank you," said Layng. "In conclusion I ask you again—have you any suggestion to offer which may help the course of this inquiry?"

"I'm sorry, but I have no suggestion at all to make," replied Charles. "As I observed before—the thing doesn't make sense—that's as near a suggestion as I care to get."

Layng laid down his pen and studied the other deliberately. "I don't quite gather what you mean, sir," he said. "Are you implying that the murder was the work of an idiot—a mental defective, in fact?"

"Possibly," said Charles. "It's not for me to make assumptions. That's your province."

Layng glanced down at his papers. "You have an elder brother," he observed. Charles waited for the Superintendent to go on. "When did you last see him?"

Charles hitched an eyebrow—a habit of his.

"When did I last see Richard?" he seemed to ask the question of himself. "Sometime early in 1919. I can't tell you the exact date."

"When did you last hear news of him?"

"Later in the same year—1919. I heard that he and his wife went to Canada. In 1920 I went out to Malaya, and I heard from my sister a few years later that Richard had lost his wife. Since then I have heard nothing of him—and neither has any one else in these parts, so far as I know."

"He quarrelled with your father before he went away?"

"I believe he did—but your detection seems a bit hoary to me, Superintendent. Tell me, how much do you remember of your own quarrels of twenty-five years ago? Are you prepared to commit murder on motives a quarter of a century old? Once again, to use my previous expression, that doesn't make sense to me."

"And you have no sensible suggestion of your own to offer?"

Charles merely chuckled at the sarcastic tone. "None whatever, Superintendent. Don't think I'm frivolous. I'm not. I take things seriously. If I could help you, I would."

"Thank you, sir. Now might I see your younger brother, Mr. Malcolm Garth."

"My half-brother. He's not in the house at the moment and I don't know where he is. He often goes out on his own and we expect him when we see him."

"Then I will see Mrs. Moffat next."

"Right. I'll send her in to you."

CHAPTER SEVEN

I

I T WAS AFTER SUNSET BEFORE THE SUPERINTENDENT LEFT Garthmere Hall, but Malcolm Garth had not yet returned home. Marion had said that he had probably gone up to the fells to see his bee-hives which had been taken up for the bees to collect the heather honey. "He often comes back late because he's a poor walker and gets tired easily," she told Layng. "When he gets up there as likely as not he'll go to sleep in the heather. I've often known him do it."

"Does he take a gun with him?"

"Goodness, no! Malcolm loathes guns. He's like a gun-shy dog. He probably cleared out this afternoon because he dislikes the noise the guns make at the fox hunt. Malcolm's like that. He never shoots. I doubt if he knows how to load a gun even."

Layng pondered over this and other things he had heard at Garthmere as he got into his car and started on his way back to Carnton. He was conscious of a sense of irritation, a feeling that he had not done as well as he had hoped to do. When he had set out it had been with a feeling, "Here is my chance. I've been waiting for an important case and now I've got it." Had he but known it, the very urgency of his ambition to do well and get results quickly had been responsible for the resultant sense of frustration. He had tried to go quickly when he should have fitted in to the slower temper of those he questioned. He thought of Mrs. Moffat, and dismissed her with an irritable exclamation of "old fool." The fact was that

Mrs. Moffat had been frightened, and the result of Layng's sharp manner and abrupt speech had been to frighten her further into obstinate silence. When questioned in detail she got confused and had tended to contradict herself, parrying the Superintendent's question with "I couldn't be sure like." True, she admitted that she had gone running to the office yesterday, when she heard a gun shot in the house, but her description of the incident had been hopelessly confused. First she had said that Charles and Malcolm had been in the office with Marion, then she had said that only old Mr. Garth was in the office—"swearing like." Layng had next tried to question Janey, the fourteen-year-old maid, but the only result was a flood of tears. Mrs. Moffat had been called in again to assist, and had kept on reiterating "Her's a weeper. Comes over her if you're sharp-like." Layng had felt exasperated, and thinking back to the ignominious scene he swore to himself over the time he had wasted with a half-wit. He turned sharply to Harding who was driving him.

"Get a move on. There's no thirty mile limit here."

Harding accelerated, and a moment later checked the "Damn it" which was half-uttered as some cattle ran unexpectedly out of a gate on his left. He rammed on his brakes and the car slewed on the dungy surface of the road and hit one of the beasts so that it fell sprawling on the road.

"Blast the fools!" exclaimed Layng, and Harding said:

"Someone's left that gate open. Those are Mr. Garth's stirks, quite a bunch he's got. I'd better see if that poor beast's hurt."

He got out, and as he did so a tow-headed, red-faced boy appeared grinning at the gate.

"Tha's shot 'im! Goody, goody!" he exclaimed. Harding made a lunge at him.

"Here, you young limb! What did you open that gate for?"

Jock feinted and leapt clear of the threatening hand, uttering a burst of raucous laughter as he bolted along the field inside the hedge.

"Here, go after him and bring him to me," shouted Layng, and Harding went into the field in pursuit. While Layng sat waiting in the car a man came up from behind him and began to drive the scattered stirks into a bunch. The newcomer called to Layng with little respect:

"Hey, you! Happen you've let the beasts out on the road through leaving yon gate open, you'd better come and drive them in again."

"I didn't leave the gate open. Drive them in yourself," retorted Layng, sitting obstinately in his place, but feeling a fool nevertheless. The stirks were excited and unmanageable and started playing hide and seek round the car. When at last they were persuaded to turn into the open gate, proceedings were upset by the reappearance of Harding, who puffed red-faced up to the gate just as the cattle were poking their noses towards the field. Harding's appearance made them bolt again and the farmer who was trying to drive them into safety swore lustily. "Darn you—police or no police, haven't you got any sense?" he roared.

Harding promptly began to assist in collecting the scattered cattle, and eventually they were herded into the field and the gate was closed. Layng, his face more sardonic than ever, looked at his chauffeur.

"Who was that?" he inquired, nodding towards the roughly-clad figure of the man who had been herding the stirks. "Is he one of the Garthmere labourers?"

"Him? Gum, no!" exclaimed Harding, who was still startled out of his official stolidity. "That's Mr. Lamb of High Fell. Farms nigh on two hundred acres. He's well thought of hereabouts."

Harding's tone was a reminder to Layng—if he needed one—
that he had made another mistake. He had forgotten the fact that
the farmers hereabouts thought nothing of ancient clothes, dung-
laden boots and scarecrow hats. It would have been better to have
been friendly to Mr. Lamb of High Fell. Layng turned on Harding:

"And that half-wit you went after? You let him get away, I
suppose?"

Harding nodded, very red in the face. "Yes, sir. Yon lad's a
racer—and a twister, too. He just disappeared."

"Oh, all right. Go on—and don't hit anything else," snapped
Layng.

Harding drove in resentful silence, and Layng sat back and
pondered bitterly over his case. Mr. Garth had been shot—and to
Layng's resentful mind it seemed that the old man had chosen to
get himself shot on the very day of all others which made discovery of the culprit most difficult. Every farmer in the district had
been out with a gun: Layng enumerated them to himself as the car
went smoothly on: nothing like memorising all the contacts in the
case, he thought. Lamb of High Fell, Staple of Lonsghyll, Trant
of Blackthorn, Hayman of Lower Stacks, Langhorn of Middle
Field, Brough of Farrintake, Ashthwaite of Greenbeck; in addition to these had been the beaters, some of whom had guns, like
Jem Moffat of Garthmere. Any one of them might have done it,
thought Layng to himself, and how to prove which one might be
a proper teaser. His mind then reverted to the Garth family themselves. "A rum lot," was Layng's reaction. Somehow he didn't trust
them, and admittedly he found them hard to deal with. Marion and
Charles, for instance, both clad in working clothes, both bearing the
mud and muck and stink of a farmyard about them, and yet each
having a poise and arrogance which conveyed little respect for an

urban Police Superintendent. "Garths of Garthmere—it still means summat"—so old Moffat had coolly told Layng. "Garths—ay, they came to these parts with Roger of Poitu"—where had he heard that? "Norman blood—bunk," said Layng to himself. "I'll give them summat." What was Malcolm Garth doing?—and what about the Richard Garth who had quarrelled with his father twenty-five years ago and had gone to Canada? Layng thought again of the twenty-five cent piece he had picked up in the hull. He turned to Harding.

"What was that you were saying about some of the farmers discussing Richard Garth the other day?"

Harding looked blank: he had been nettled by the Superintendent's intransigence over the matter of the straying cattle and the pursuit of Jock, and, to put the matter in his own words, "he wasn't feeling chatty."

"Someone happened to mention him, just by way of talking about the family," said Harding. "'Twasn't nothing in particular. Just mentioned there was an older son who'd been abroad don't-know-how-many-years."

As it happened they had just reached a road junction, and an Army convoy was proceeding along it in the direction of Kirby. Harding concentrated almost obtrusively on his driving, observing due care and attention with great assiduity in solemn silence. Layng gave him one look and forbore to question him further. When they had reached their headquarters in Carnton the Superintendent said to Harding:

"You are to go back to Greenbeck—Ashthwaite's place, and find that idiot boy and bring him back to be questioned. That quite clear?"

"Yes, sir," replied Harding glumly.

II

Shortly after Layng had left Garthmere, old Bob Moffat repaired to the shippon where Bluebell was still tied up, convalescing after her recent difficult calving. Bob had once said to Elizabeth Meldon, "Aye, a cow's company like," and on the present occasion when feelings ran too deep for words and even Bob's own wife could not gauge the depth of his emotional disturbance, Bob made for the shippon to commune with the always understanding but unobtrusive Bluebell. He patted her vast flanks and the creature turned her head and curled out her long tongue to caress his dung-sodden coat. "Mm, mm, mm," she murmured comfortably, and "Cusha lass" growled Bob as he leant against her solid flanks and felt for his empty pipe. He was still standing thus, cow and man both ruminating in comfortable understanding, when Martin Lamb of High Fell appeared at the open door of the shippon and leaned leisurely against the door post.

"Well Bob," he said. "'Tis a sorry mess."

Bob Moffat grunted in melancholy agreement. "Aye," he said, "that be a sorry mess, that be."

Martin Lamb hitched himself more firmly against the angle stones of the old building. "Whiles we were shooting foxes, someone else had their own shoot like," he said, "but who 'twas, dang it if I know. I've thought, but 'tisn't likely…"

"Beats me to say," said Bob.

They fell silent in the manner of countrymen, an acquiescent sympathetic silence, comfortable to both. Lamb pulled out his baggy pouch and offered it to Bob, who was still leaning against Bluebell's flanks, his elbow on her neck. He filled his pipe with a gruff, "Thank y', Mr. Lamb," and at last got on to the epitaph which had been struggling to formulate itself in words.

"There been times when I've been main vexed with the old master," he said, "but he weren't so bad to get on with when you got to know him. Aye, he was a good master and I'm main sorry to see him go by sich a road."

"Aye, 'tis a sorry mess," reiterated Mr. Lamb, "and tell you what, Bob, no disrespect meant, 'tis a rum go, too. Happen it'll take more wits than that ower smart policeman in his swell motor-car to see to the bottom of this."

Bob spat—a firm, judicial yet comminatory spit, and Bluebell hiccoughed as though in sympathy.

"'Im?" he inquired. "Daft, I call 'im. Frightened our young girl till she was silly like and upset my misses so she mixed the beastings with the cream. Wants to make out we shot 'im 'ere—one of us in this house. What d'you make of that, Mr. Lamb?—one of us in this very house."

The unaccustomed effort of so long a speech made Bob sweat freely, but he stuck to it manfully, waving a gnarled wrinkled hand in emphasis. "Times was the master made me that mad I could've shot him myself," he declared, "but see here. Thirty years I've worked for Mr. Garth and not shot 'im. Stands to reason I wouldn't go and do it now all foolish like, with t'harvest in, and all fit for the ploughing again. Daft, I says."

"Aye. That's right that is," agreed Mr. Lamb, who was able to appreciate this rural reasoning. "Tell you what. I was up the road just now, and them stirks of yours was all over the road, the gate being open. The Superintendent, he sits in his car like any lord. 'You come and help drive 'em in,' I said, 'seeing you left the gate open.' 'Drive 'em in yourself,' he says. Can you beat that—and the beasts all over the road? 'Drive 'em in yourself,' he says."

"Aye. Reckon he would," said Bob. "Is them stirks all right, Mr. Lamb, thanking you kindly for looking to them. Fourteen there was in Cruft's intak."

"Aye, fourteen I made it. Happen you'd better go and look them over yourself, Bob. Now it so happened I saw young Jock up there, running like the devil and all, with a policeman after him. How'd that be, Bob?"

"Nay, Mr. Lamb. 'Twon't do. Jock, he can scythe proaper, and he can strip a cow, and the ewes trust 'im like he was one o' themselves, but Jock don't know t'other end from which when it comes to a gun or such like. He's good with beasts and he can mow a tidy swathe, but 'e'll muck up any gear 'e tries to 'andle. Silly like."

Mr. Lamb nodded. This was an expert opinion and he accepted it.

"Ashthwaite?" he murmured, and Bob looked at him in rather shocked silence. This was being almost too explicit for a cautious mind. At length Bob gave judgment, though he preserved a decent anonymity.

"If so be as shooting was in 'is mind, he had cause to shoot twenty-five years past. Aye, and he had cause, maybe, three years come Lady Day, for he had to shell out more'n was reasonable. Hot blood, that was, aye, and he'd reason. But to let that pass, and do't in cold blood. Nay. I wouldn't swallow it."

"But someone did it, Bob."

The old man shifted his ground a little, and Bluebell flicked her tail and tried to turn round.

"Steady, lass," grumbled Bob, ramming his weight against the cow. "Aye, someone did it, and 'twas a stranger, I reckon. Someone from furrin parts. No one in our house, nor in our village, neither. 'Tain't raisonable.'"

"Then 'twould have been some stranger who had a gey girt reason for coming here to do't," said Lamb, and Bob nodded.

"Aye. That's right," he affirmed, and then added, "And I'll tell y'what, Mr. Lamb. I was sorry to see the old master go, but I'll be mighty glad when that there Superintendent goes where he belongs, aye, and stays there, too."

III

As was to be expected, the Garth Arms was unusually full that evening. By nine o'clock the small bar was crowded to capacity, and the landlord—one Nathaniel Barrows, was anxious lest his limited supply of beer should prove inadequate to this important occasion. All the farmers on the Garthmere estate came in during the course of the evening with the exception of John Staple. His absence was much regretted by the company, who had hoped to get some first-hand information from him concerning the local tragedy.

A certain formality was observed during the course of the evening. Mr. Trant of Blackthorn was, by common consent, allowed to be leader of the conversation. For one thing, he was one of the oldest tenants in the sense that his family had farmed Garthmere land for generations, and the fact that he had organised the fox hunt which had been the prelude to the tragedy lent further reason to his unofficial "chairmanship." Mr. Trant was one of the first farmers to put in an appearance; shortly he was followed by James Hayman of Lower Stacks and Peter Brough of Farrintake.

Each of these uttered a sedate, "Good evening, Mr. Trant," while the farm labourers left the counter and stood respectfully against the walls. A couple more farmers from the higher fell district came next, and then Martin Lamb of High Fell came in and made proceedings more intimate by his "'evening, James; 'evening, Pete; 'evening William." There was a murmur of "'Tis bad news"; "Aye, a heavy day"; "'Tis hard to believe"; and "I can't think of him gone" as glasses were filled. Then, by common consent, William Trant was listened to in respectful silence. He spoke slowly, expressing the thoughts in the minds of all, achieving a simple dignity in his homely speech by very sincerity.

"Twenty-five years gone this midsummer; when my old dad died, I went to Mr. Garth and said to him, 'You'll be agreeable to me taking over the tenancy and farming Blackthorn, Mr. Garth?' and he answered, 'Aye, you take over, William. Your father was a tidy farmer and he served the land well, and I can trust you to do the same. You deal straight by me and I'll deal straight by you.' Reckon he did, too. Hard he might be, and gave me the rough side of his tongue often enow, but I knew where I was with him. Aye. He was straight, and he'd have no fancy dealing."

There was a gruff murmur of assent, and Trant took a good pull at his tankard of beer before continuing. "Mark you, I knew him years afore my old dad died. I was no but a nipper when Mr. Garth inherited at the Hall, and I remember my folks talking on't. 'A bad heritage, debts, mortgage and neglect,' they said. 'Twas said the Hall itself was mortgaged before Madman Garth as they called him, drank himself into his grave. He had a rough row to hoe had Mr. Robert Garth, and he didn't spare himself. These forty years he's toiled, good years and bad years—and some on you know that dun'a' many years have been mortal bad for farming—and I reckon he cleared debts and mortgage alike. No wonder he was hard—aye, he had to be hard to do what he did."

"Aye, that's right, Will." Mr. Lamb spoke heartily. "He was a wun'nerful old man, too. This very harvest I seen him tossing hattocks up as sweet and clean as may be, always just where they should ha' been, and it's not many men past eighty can hope to do that. Aye, he was a good judge of sheep, too, and he could clip a ewe as neat as any shepherd. But hard—aye, hard as flint he was. Once he'd made up his mind nought could move him."

Again there was a general murmur of assent, and at length Langhorn of Middle Field broke fresh ground.

"Nigh on half a century he's farmed at Garthmere; he took the home farm on when the pastures was nought but bull-toppings and thistles and scarce a decent bite o' grass in the lot—and as for the meadows, they wear sour right through. Now it's a different story. A very pretty crop of hay he lifted this summer. Now who'll be farming Garthmere from now on, Mr. Lamb? Who takes over?"

There was a general movement and a murmur of voices, and it was evident that the topic thus boldly mooted was in the minds of many. Martin Lamb tilted his old bowler forward and scratched the back of his head, and at last he said:

"That's hard to say. Richard Garth is heir—he's the eldest son, but who's to say where he is now? 'Tisn't even known if he's alive, I'm told. The lawyers, they'll have to advertise like, and I doubt if this here war will make it any easier. For the moment, I reckon Miss Marion will carry on. She's a good farmer, is Marion, and she knows the land. Garthmere won't lose nought if she manages it for a season. She knows her tenants, too, and she's reasonable. Meets your fair."

"Aye, and she'll lend a hand when she can," agreed Langhorn. "It was Miss Marion offered to help Staple cart his last bit of oats just before the river rose."

"And her father helped, too, tho' he'd done a man's day in his own fields already," said Martin Lamb. "That's neighbourliness, that is."

"Aye, she's a proper good sort—but she's not heir," objected Langhorn, and Mr. Brough of Farrintake said simply:

"More's the pity. Richard Garth's been away too long, and as for Charles…" Mr. Brough scratched his head to find a suitable expression, and then he said:

"Charles Garth now, he's what I'd call a watch and chain man, if you take me—he's no worker."

A rumbled subdued laughter greeted this effort, and a general murmur of agreement indicated that Brough had hit the nail on the head.

"Been out in furrin parts with gangs of lackeys to wait on him, I reckon," said Giles Hayman from his place by the wall. "I met him on the road one day when he was having trouble with Jessie, the ould mare, who's as quiet as any lamb. Got his load right athwart t'road, he had. 'Boy,' he shouts at me, 'shove behind this outfit,' he says. I just gave ould Jessie a chance and she righted t'cart in two twos. As for 'im—I didn't waste no words on him."

"Aye, that's right! 'Boy this' and 'boy that,' he says," agreed young Matt Briggs. Giles Hayman nudged him to indicate that silence on their parts was indicated again as Mr. Trant raised his voice.

"I'd like to say this," he began. "If Miss Marion carries on—as she's sure to do—until things is settled, reckon we'll help her where we can and stand by her—and play fair by her as we've played fair by her father."

"Aye, that's right," murmured several voices and Martin Lamb allowed himself a chuckle.

"Reckon if you don't play fair by Miss Marion you won't get no further than you would have done with her dad. She's got all her buttons on."

IV

At closing time the landlord, Nathaniel Barrows, murmured a word or two in the ear of Mr. Trant and Mr. Lamb, indicating that Mrs. Barrows would be happy to have a word with them in the parlour if they could spare her a moment. This was a formula, well understood between them, indicating that the talk could be continued between the principals, as it were, in the landlord's private quarters after the house was closed. In short, the meeting went into committee, the latter consisting of three old cronies, Nathaniel Barrows, Martin Lamb and William Trant. The two farmers were both big men, but they looked older than their years, respectively fifty-eight and sixty-one. Their shoulders were bent, their hair grey and their faces furrowed. Nathaniel was also tall, but he was stout and rubicund, his bald head having a spare fringe of reddish hair just above his collar.

There was a pleasant fire in the parlour, and Mrs. Barrows was officiating with a kettle and glasses.

"I'm sorry there's no lemon, Mr. Lamb," she said, uttering words familiar to all during this ritual, "but otherwise I think you'll find it to your liking—and you too, Mr. Trant." Having thus vindicated Nathaniel's truthfulness, Mrs. Barrows tactfully retired.

It was Martin Lamb who came to business first, glass in hand.

"I don't like it, Will," he said—and it was not to his hot toddy that he alluded.

Trant nodded. "Aye," he said lugubriously.

"What's this they're saying about Ashthwaite? Did you name the fox hunt to him, Martin?—because I didn't."

"That I did not," replied Lamb. "Seeing how things was I shouldn't have expected Ashthwaite to come shooting where he'd see Mr. Garth for certain. Let sleeping dogs lie, I say. Nay, 'twas a surprise to me when I saw him there."

"He'd never have come—for that..." said Trant unhappily. "'Tain't sense. If he'd wanted to do that, why he could have done it any day and never been noticed. Mr. Garth was always about on the farm."

"If he'd been so minded, he could have done it at the fox hunt. Dang it, by gum!" Lamb shouted, as though a great light had dawned on him, "that settles this nonsense about Bob Ashthwaite! If he'd wanted to shoot Mr. Garth he could have done it at the fox hunt, and no one any the wiser. Bob was above Mr. Garth and behind him, and there was others up there too, watching, some of them was. Brough was up at the top with his gun, and now I come to think of it old Joe Harrison potted a rabbit that bolted up the gill. Now if Ashthwaite had wanted to do that job, reckon he could've done it safely. He's a dead shot—and who was to know what gun the shot came from?"

"Aye. I see that," said Mr. Trant. "Come to think of it, I'm glad he didn't. 'Twould have been a gey bad job at the hunt and all."

"That 'twould—but Will, if so be as Ashthwaite didn't do it—and I can't see that he did, well then—who did?"

"Dang it if I know," said Mr. Trant, and then Nathaniel Barrows took his turn.

"If you'll pardon me, Mr. Trant, there was something I wanted to tell you." He lowered his voice and leant forward. "I don't like gossip," he said, "and you'll bear me out when I say I've never stood for any mischievous chatter in my bar. There's summat I've heard which it's right you two should hear, knowing I can trust you not to let it go any further if you don't think fit." He paused and leaned still closer towards the other two.

"You mind old Hodges at the Wheatsheaf over by Ingleton, Mr. Trant? He's an old friend of mine, and we meet and have a word now and then. I saw him in Kirby market the day before yesterday, and he told me he'd had a chap putting up for the night last Wednesday. You know how visitors has to register their names these days—that's a police regulation, that is. The chap I'm talking of registered his name as Richard Garth, Merchant Navy."

The effect of the landlord's words was electrical. Martin Lamb, who seldom took the name of the Lord in vain, exclaimed:

"God a'mighty!" as he slammed his glass down on the table, and William Trant groaned aloud.

"Deary me…" he said; "deary, deary me… I don't like it, Nat, I don't like it."

"That's just it," said the landlord. "I feel fair moithered, Mr. Trant. 'Twas the first thing jumped to my mind when I heard the news about old Mr. Garth. They quarrelled bitter, those two, and it's the first time I've heard of Richard Garth being home in all these years—and *that's* happened. Now what I want to know is this—what's my duty? Ought I to tell the police?"

There was a dead silence, and at length Trant said slowly: "I mind Richard Garth as a lad: I taught him to throw a cast and set a snare; aye, I taught him to shoot, too. Many's the time that lad came and tried his hand at potting rabbits in my roughs. I liked Richard, and I grieved when his dad treated him so hard over his marriage. Mary Ashthwaite was a right good lass. I'd find it hard to believe that Richard Garth did a thing like this. Shooting his own father? Why, 'tis against nature."

"Are you sure it's the *same* Richard Garth?" inquired Martin Lamb. "Maybe we're barking up the wrong tree."

"I taxed ould Hodges with that when he named it to me," replied the landlord. "He said the chap was getting on—nearing fifty may be, a hefty fellow and he'd the look of our old man here. Hodges tried to have a word with his visitor, but he was a close kind o' man and had nought much to say."

Martin Lamb, whose mind was more inquiring than Trant's, then asked:

"How long did he stay and how did he leave? Did he ask about buses and trains?"

"Nay. He left afoot, saying he was hiking a bit; left early, as soon as ever he'd put away some breakfast—and that was the last Hodges saw of him—or heard, either."

"Eh... but that looks as though he didn't come near these parts," said Lamb shrewdly. "If so be he'd walked this way he'd have come by way of Burton, and Melling likely, and many's the folks who might have noticed him, he being a stranger and yet favouring the Garths. 'Tis likely he went on into Yorkshire."

"Maybe he did, but that's nought to do with our problem," said Trant unhappily. "Is it our duty to tell the police about this?"

There was a lengthy silence. At last Martin Lamb spoke.

"I see it like this, Will. We've no proof the man was *our* Richard: we don't know he came this way, and we don't believe he'd have shot his dad. Let the police do their own job. I say—say nowt. Least said's soonest mended."

"Aye. Reckon you're right. We'll say nowt," agreed Trant, and the trio lifted their glasses with deep sighs of relief.

CHAPTER EIGHT

I

ELIZABETH MELDON HAD BEEN DEEPLY SHOCKED BY THE NEWS of old Garth's death. Horror and fear mingled in her mind because she was vividly aware that she had been afraid that this very thing would happen. Her main concern was about Malcolm: try as she would she could not rid her mind of the dread that this was just what Malcolm might have done in one of his fits of furious resentment. He had hated his father, and Elizabeth knew it.

Outwardly she went about her work as usual: she helped with the milking, drove the cows out to pasture again, strained the milk and set the cream, washed the dairy utensils, fed the calves and mucked out the shippon. She had just finished two hours of hard work when she was summoned to be questioned by the Superintendent.

Elizabeth had often laughed over the cautious manner of speech used by the north country folk of Garthmere, but she donned that caution herself while she was being questioned. Deliberately she set to work to "stone wall" while Layng, having satisfied himself that her time was accounted for, made his laborious queries about enmities, grudges and the like. Her blue eyes wide, Elizabeth disclaimed any knowledge.

"I'm employed here as a land worker, and I work hard," she said. "I'm well treated and quite satisfied—and no one has complained about my work. But farming is hard work, Superintendent. At the end of a long day's work in the fields, all one asks is to have supper and go to bed. One doesn't sit up discussing people's enemies. Also, as you may have noticed, the people round here aren't very forthcoming. They wouldn't have discussed Mr. Garth with me—a stranger."

"And you had observed nothing on your own account," inquired Layng.

"I'm afraid I'm not very observant," said Elizabeth sweetly, "unless it's about cows. I'm quite noticing-like about them."

Layng could make nothing of her. He thought she was probably rather stupid, in spite of her educated voice. In his heart of hearts Layng believed that all farmers were stupid—otherwise they wouldn't have been farmers. As a result, there was one thing which Layng had never learnt, and that was the best way of approach in getting information from country folk. No farmer who wanted information in the Garthmere district ever approached his subject directly. There was always a preamble, perhaps concerning the weather or the crops, in which the stage was set for discussion. Haste was but wasted time; it simply did not work.

Leaving Layng to do his irritated and impotent best with old Moffat—who was even less capable of speed than most—Elizabeth went and washed, changed her shirt, and set out by the fold-yard gate. She didn't want to talk to Marion—and she felt pretty certain that Marion didn't want to talk to anybody. As for Charles, Elizabeth shrugged her shoulders—still less did she want to talk to Charles. If Marion would be too silent, Charles would be too talkative.

Elizabeth wanted to find Malcolm. She set out through the lower meadows where the rich fog grass was heavy with dew, observing as she went that there was a second clover crop ripe for cutting. "They ought to make silage," she said to herself, "only the old man's too obstinate"—and she remembered with a shock that old Mr. Garth could obstruct no longer.

"I wonder what will happen... Farming's got to go on. Will Marion be given full control now?" she pondered. "Phoebe was to go to market when she calves, and Marion wanted..." Again discomfort overcame her. Perhaps Marion was free now to do what she wanted—but why had she left the potatoes so gladly to lift onions by herself that afternoon? "It's horrible," groaned Elizabeth as she crossed the higher pastures which led upwards to the fells. "One gets suspicious. One can't help it."

She left the fields and took a path through some woodland halfway up the slope. It was growing twilight now, and the wood was spooky, full of murmurous voices and scuttering leaves. She was glad when she struck the rough road which led through the sheep pastures to the open fell side, where Malcolm kept his bees. He always used this route and Elizabeth knew it. She loitered a little, picking some of the lush blackberries which weighted the brambles, and stopping to notice a squirrel throwing down hazel nuts. Here, high up above the valley, the evening light was still clear, the western sky still lucid gold above the blue distances of Morecambe Bay.

Elizabeth had nearly reached the open fell when she saw Malcolm. He was walking towards her, limping as he did when he was tired, his dark hair tousled. She called to him:

"Malcolm, you're late. What have you been doing?"

He quickened his pace when he heard her voice.

"Lisa! How decent of you! I was just hating the thought of walking back. I do hate walking back. It's grand up here."

He waved his hand to indicate the golden west and the mist shrouded valley far below. White swathes of mist now hovered waist high above the river meadows and the holmland.

Elizabeth fell into step beside him. "I'm not going to ask him any questions," she said to herself. "I won't give him a chance to lie to me... he might, if he's frightened, and I couldn't bear it."

"We've had a ghastly time, Malcolm," she said. "Old Mr. Garth was shot, and John Staple found his body in the old hull—"

Malcolm stopped dead, staring at her incredulously. In the dimness she saw his white face and wide dark eyes and the untidy lock of black hair over his forehead.

"His body? You mean he's dead... he's really dead?"

"Yes. He was killed instantly."

"Dead... I can't believe it. Lisa—I hated him. I was afraid of him. I can't pretend to you, I'm not sorry. I'm glad."

She shivered as though the evening air were chill. "Don't say that to any one else—don't say it to me, even," she cried. "There are police down there, waiting to question you, to trap you. They have to find out who shot him."

"Don't they know? Who moved him to the old hull?"

"Moved him? Nobody moved him. He was shot there."

"Shot *there*? I thought you meant he was shot at the fox hunt. Who did it?"

"I don't know, Malcolm. Staple found him, and told Marion to phone to the Superintendent of Police at Carnton. He came over here himself, and he's been asking every one questions—had Mr. Garth any enemies, had anybody a grudge against him—"

Malcolm laughed. "Well, he ought to get quite a nice lot of answers. Every one had a grudge against him."

"Malcolm, don't say things like that. The police suspect everybody, they have to. They suspected you just because you weren't in when they wanted to see you."

"Me? Oh, I see. Well, I've been up here all the afternoon. I just lay and baked in the sun and watched the curlews. There was a kestrel hovering just above me, and lots of lapwings, and larks, singing in the blue. Oh, I saw a lizard under one of the hives—have you ever seen a lizard?"

"No, not in England. Malcolm, did you meet any one up here—or see anybody?"

"Not a soul. That's one of the blessed parts of the fells. There's no one there."

"But you saw John Staple talking to Richard the other day."

"So I did—but that's only once in a lifetime. Richard. That's funny."

He broke off and Elizabeth said, "I don't think it's funny at all. If you tell the police you saw Richard, they're sure to believe he did it… killed your father."

"Perhaps he did. I don't blame him. He hated him—you should just have heard him. But don't be a juggins. Of course I shan't tell the police I saw Richard. Neither will John Staple. I bet he won't because he promised Richard he wouldn't tell any one he'd seen him. And that's that—and the others all lived happily ever after."

"Oh, Malcolm. Don't be flippant. The whole thing's horrible. He was murdered, and murder's beastly. It gave me the horrors—and I had to come and find you, so that you should know, and not have it jumped on you unexpectedly when you got home."

"Sorry, Lisa. All right, I'll be sensible. Look here, let's forget it all for just five minutes. Haven't you got a cigarette? Let's sit on the next gate and watch the gloaming. The owls will be coming out, and there are night jars in the wood down there."

Elizabeth laughed. "Oh, all right. I've got just one cigarette. I haven't had time to smoke it… I had an awful lot to do, I mucked the shippon out and did most of the milking."

She stopped and leant against a gate, with Malcolm beside her, and looked down into the mist-wreathed valley.

"Look!" said Malcolm softly, and a great white owl swept past them on silent wings.

II

Marion Garth drew a deep breath when the Superintendent had at last taken himself off. She listened while the sound of his car faded away; she was standing by the office window which she had just opened—it had been closed at Layng's wish. She had opened it instinctively "to blow the smell of the police away"—though Layng would have snorted could he have known her thought. He had been very much aware of the smell of dung hanging about the working clothes of these farming folk. Marion listened, and became conscious of the deep silence which had settled on the house. Every one had taken themselves off, it seemed. Probably Mrs. Moffat had gone to bed, as she often did at sunset. She had a long day, getting up at six o'clock, summer and winter alike. Old Moffat had gone outside somewhere and Jem was probably in the village. Elizabeth Meldon had disappeared, too.

Marion breathed a sigh of relief, closed the office window again, and went out into the orchard by way of the living-room window. There had been so much talking—she was tired of it all.

She strolled under the old apple trees, instinctively picking up the best windfalls—Mrs. Moffat's trug, half full of apples, still lay where she had left it when the news was brought in. Marion was glad to pick up apples, leisurely, peacefully, as the grey twilight deepened. She was not given very long, however, to commune with her own thoughts. Charles hailed her across the orchard.

"I say—what about some supper?"

Marion retorted: "Go and find something to eat yourself if you want it. There's plenty of food in the larder."

"That's all very well—but we've got to talk about things sometime," said Charles.

"I'm sick to death of talking. It doesn't get us anywhere," she replied.

"Perhaps not." Charles came towards her, lowering his voice a bit. "A few things have got to be settled, old girl," he said, his voice not ungentle. "First—who's going to run this outfit, *pro tem*? You'll have to advise the lawyers or you'll soon be in a mess. Wages must be paid, business must be settled. You can't carry on without the needful—and the bank won't honour your signature—or mine either."

"Oh, Lord! I don't want to bother now," said Marion. "We can't do anything to-night."

"No—but we ought to settle what's got to be done to-morrow," replied Charles. "I may be no farmer—I never pretended to be worth much in that direction, but I'm used to business. I can help you there if you'll let me."

Marion looked surprised. It was unlike Charles to volunteer help.

"I know you've thought I was an outsize in fools," went on Charles. "I'm no judge of cattle and I frankly loathe sweating and breaking my back hoeing turnips and lifting potatoes—but I've run a fair-sized business in Malaya without making a mess of it. It wasn't my fault the Japs messed it up for me," he added rather plaintively.

"I know it wasn't," said Marion, her voice more sympathetic. She turned towards the house. "All right. I'll come in. I expect it's quite true that you know more about legal business than I do. I know all the farm business—but, as you say, that's not going to help me to pay wages when I've got no money to pay them with. What happens? I don't know anything about wills and probate and all that."

"Let's go in and get a bite before we start talking," said Charles. "You never will admit you're tired, but you're tired now. I don't wonder. That Superintendent was enough to tire anybody. Typical policeman, official all through, and full of his own self-importance."

"I couldn't stand him," admitted Marion, as they walked towards the house. "I suppose he was competent—but he put people's backs up. John Staple's an even-tempered person, but even he was irritated."

When she reached the kitchen she said:

"Let's just slap everything on the table and pig it in peace. There's apple-pie and cheese—oh, and some cold bacon if you want it—"

"—and beer and pickled onions and a whacking big rice pudding," said Charles, looking in the larder. "O.K. by me. D'you want some tea? The fire's out but I'll pump up the primus. Here, you sit down. I'll get things ready."

Marion sat down. Tea? It was just what she did want. For once in her life she sat still, admitting a great weariness, while Charles "slapped everything on the table" and encouraged the primus stove. He made the tea, and Marion found herself laughing weakly as he lifted the lid of the teapot and stirred his potent brew, hitching up his right eyebrow in characteristic fashion.

"What's the matter?" he asked, as he heard her laugh.

"Nothing. It's just that it's funny to see you doing things," she answered, and he replied:

"I'm not nearly such an ass as you think. I'm quite a useful chap on safari—camping, y'know. The trouble is you've always told me not to interfere—and I was so fed up with everything I just took the line of least resistance. Here you are. Hot and strong. Do you good."

The tea did do her good, and she watched Charles tucking into a hearty meal of cold bacon and onions, regarding him with a fresh eye. It was true, she *had* thought him an ass—feckless and lazy. At last she said: "Well, what ought I to do about money and all that?"

Charles took a good draught of beer and then replied with surprising precision: "You see the old man's lawyer, find out who is named as executor or executors, and an interim account is opened at the bank by the executors on which they can draw until probate is obtained and the property distributed. He'd got a balance in his current account, I expect?"

"Oh lord, yes. He'd got a big balance. I know what he got from the sale of stock and the milk cheques. He's been doing very nicely these last three years."

"That's all right then. It'll be plain sailing if you go the right way about it. Who is his lawyer by the way?"

"Flemming and Barton."

"Have they got his will?"

"I suppose so. He never mentioned it to me, but he was always quite careful and businesslike about documents—policies and contracts and tenancies and all that."

"Right. Any idea who the executors are?"

"I believe Mr. Flemming's one—and I have an idea I'm the other one. I'm not certain, but I have a feeling he put me down—just from something he once said."

Charles sat back and lighted a cigarette. He had a new packet of Gold Flake in his pocket, and he offered Marion the packet. "Any idea how his property goes?" he inquired.

Marion shook her head. "No. He never told me. The land goes to Richard, of course."

"Yes. Eldest son. The point is—where *is* Richard?"

She shook her head. "I don't know. We haven't heard a word about him for years—but I've never believed he's dead. We should have heard if he'd died. Richard was a sensible creature. He'd have left some note of his origins so that news could be sent." She moved restlessly. "At the moment I'm more interested in where Malcolm is. I wish he'd come in."

Charles regarded her gravely. "Nervous, Moll?"

The use of her old nickname surprised her. "Oh, I don't know. I got fed up with the way that Superintendent kept on asking about Malcolm. He is—well, excitable, you know."

"Yes. I've often marvelled that the old man ever sired anything quite so imaginative as that boy. I suppose he gets his poetic qualities from his mother's line. She always seemed a bit Brontë-ish to me. Came from the Haworth district too, didn't she? Moll, is it true that Malcolm doesn't know how to load a gun?"

She flushed. "I told the Superintendent that, and I shall stick to it. I've never seen him touch a gun. As a small kid he howled at the sight of one. The sound of a shot always frightened him."

"Quite—but who left your loaded gun in the office the other day?"

"I don't know. I simply don't know, Charles. I can't bear to think about it. It only missed father by a fluke—his hair was singed."

"Pity it missed him at all," said Charles gloomily. "That'd have been brought in as accident. Not nearly so bad as this. Layng'll see to it someone's hanged for this. The trouble is he mayn't hang the right man. He looked damned stupid to me."

"Oh, heavens, isn't it all utterly loathsome?" Marion cried her words aloud. "Why couldn't they have waited... whoever did it? He was an old man... It's not fair to us that we should be plagued and pestered and bullied... I hate it all!"

Charles stared in surprise. This was unlike the Marion he was used to. "Bear up, old girl. Don't get jittered. The old man had to go the way of all flesh, and he died without knowing it. No lying in bed and dying by inches. Not a bad way to go. I hope I have as much luck when my number's called. As for you—if I have any say in the matter you'll be given a free hand to farm this place, and make your silage and plant your temporary leys and buy your Hereford bull—and buy a bulldozer for clearing the fells if you damn' well want it."

Marion laughed weakly. "Oh, Charles, I never knew you'd even heard of temporary leys... Look, there's Malcolm and Elizabeth. Thank goodness!"

Charles cocked an eyebrow. "Is that a case?" he inquired. "Looks O.K. to me. She might make a man of that kid."

III

The acting Chief Constable of the County, Major Havers, had been sent a report of the tragedy at Garthmere. All important cases were reported to him immediately, and the shooting of old Mr. Garth was a matter of outstanding importance. Major Havers originally assumed that the shooting was an accident—one of those accidents which do occur at intervals in the countryside where shotguns are habitually carried. When, during the course of the evening, he learnt that Mr. Garth's death could not be classed as an accident the deputy official felt perturbed. Murder... Hm. That was quite a different matter—and often a very lengthy and difficult matter: it meant a prolonged investigation which involved the employment of a considerable number of men—and Major Havers was fully aware that he was already short-staffed and that his men had more and more to do. Rural inspection, use of petrol, surveillance of aliens, registration of alien children arriving at the age of sixteen, black-out offences, licences for pig-killing, black-market offences—even bee-keepers added their quota to police work of to-day, for hives had to be officially inspected before the bee-keepers could get a certificate empowering them to get sugar for winter feed. All this entailed a lot of office work—particularly for Layng, who was very efficient in dealing with the multiplicity of government regulations and preparing Court cases. Major Havers regarded a prolonged murder investigation as a very difficult problem in the circumstances.

Shortly after Layng had returned to his headquarters, Major Havers came in to hear his report.

"A straightforward case, Layng?" he inquired hopefully.

Layng shook his head. "Hardly that, sir. Too many possibilities. It will take a lot of eliminating."

He gave the Major a terse, workmanlike account of his evening's investigation, and Havers listened with some consternation.

"It's going to be difficult," he said. "All these farmers out with guns, and some of the beaters, too. Probably one of these cases where there isn't anything but circumstantial evidence—and that's going to be a bit dangerous here, simply because there were so many guns out. I've heard of old Garth, and he had a name for being a proper Tartar. It's possible that any number of people had a grudge against him: not that any of them will admit it, or give one another away. They're difficult fellows to interrogate these farmers, especially when you haven't been brought up amongst them. Close as a clam, and suspicious too—altogether very chary of speech."

"Yes, sir, and slow! My country! I've had my work cut out to keep my patience with some of them."

"Ah, you've been doing mainly office work and duties in the town lately, Layng—gets you out of touch with these old farmers. I hear them talk when I go to the cattle market occasionally—they've got their own dialect when they're talking between themselves. I seldom get any of them to understand what I'm saying right away—I have to repeat everything at about half my normal speed. It'll take the deuce of a time to interrogate every one you've got on this list." He paused in his rapid speech and considered afresh. "You've got the one clue—that American coin—but I'm not sure it's so very valuable. With the number of Yanks we've got over here there's bound to be a lot of American coins about. The old man may have thrown it away himself, realising it was no good to him."

Layng felt depressed. All this was true, but it wasn't very heartening. "I haven't had very long to get at the facts, sir," he said, and Havers agreed immediately.

"Of course you haven't—and you've done very well in the time, Layng, very well indeed. You've given me an admirable report, clear and concise. Nobody could have done better. The difficulty is this—the amount of time this case will take up. We have got a lot of work on hand—there's all this Milk Retailing to be watched. The Ministry want the distribution to be supervised more closely, and it's a troublesome business."

"Yes, sir—but it's more important to arrest a murderer than to summons a milk retailer for selling an extra quart here and there."

"Quite so, Layng, quite so. Now I'll put it like this. If this Garthmere case promised to be straightforward, I should say go ahead with it. I've every trust in you, you're a competent and conscientious officer. The trouble is that I can't spare you. The Commissioner's office—the Yard, Layng—exists to assist the provincial police in criminal cases, especially when the local police are short-handed. Now in a case of this kind, the C.I.D. prefers to be called in at once—or not at all. I can quite see that it's exasperating for them to have a case handed over to them when every clue is stone cold and every witness jaded with repetition."

"Yes, sir," said Layng glumly. The effect of Major Havers' rapid utterance in contrast to the slowness to which he had been sub-jected earlier in the evening had made the Superintendent nearly giddy. Layng saw himself being relegated to supervision of Milk Retailing, and Court Cases in which offending farmer-retailers pleaded not guilty to serving Mrs. Gubbins with a pint in place of a half-pint. He cursed to himself over the complexities of this case—all those farmers out with guns—he couldn't pretend that it was going to be easy.

Major Havers went on: "I gather from your excellent sketch that this shed, or hull, as they call it, is on a by-road which is used almost exclusively by the Garth home farm people in the usual way. Did you get any report of any one seen on that road during the afternoon?"

"No, sir. The road isn't overlooked from the house. I couldn't get any reports in that line. Of course, the fact that Staple saw this man Ashthwaite down by the river indicates that Ashthwaite might have just come down the old lane which leads from the hull to the river."

"Just so. By the way, what does the word 'hull' mean, Layng? What's its derivation?"

"God knows," replied Layng gloomily. He was feeling so irritated that the exclamation escaped him against his better judgment. Derivations indeed! He made an effort and added hastily: "The farmers talk about a pig hull, or a calf hull, sir. I think it means a shelter—not a shippon or cattle shed in regular use. I should say this hull is centuries old—a very primitive building."

"Indeed? Very interesting—I must talk to old Bowles about the word. Such points interest me. Now to get to the matter in hand—you speak about this man Ashthwaite. Any connection between him and a twenty-five cent piece, Layng?"

"No, sir."

"You have also been making inquiries about deceased's eldest son, Richard, who left England twenty-five years ago. Is there any certainty that he's still alive? Have any of his family heard from him in the interim?"

"No, sir. According to their statements they have heard nothing of him since his wife died—over twenty years ago." (Layng recollected Charles's voice, "Your detection's a bit hoary, isn't it?")

Major Havers went on: "That will entail inquiries in Canada. Hm... A lengthy business... Then there's the mental defective, Jock. Has he ever been seen with a gun? Does he own a gun?"

"I doubt if he would own one, sir. Quite unlikely."

"And Ashthwaite was carrying his own gun when Staple saw him. Hm... How could Jock have laid hands on a gun, Layng? In the circumstances, any of the farmers who had missed their guns during the course of the afternoon would have reported it. Undoubtedly I think they could have been relied on to report it. There were several guns in the gun-room at the Hall, you say—but they had all been cleaned since they were last used?"

"Yes, sir."

"A mental defective might borrow a gun, but I doubt if he'd clean it and replace it in a rack."

"Yes, sir."

"Well, there we are. A very pretty case—complicated and full of possibilities…" Major Havers paused, and then went on in his rapid bird-like way: "By the way, Layng, to digress for a moment. That case you had on hand—the fellow at Arkwright who bought a hundred head of poultry last May and hasn't a hen left in his runs—have you investigated his records?"

"No, sir. I was going to see about it when I was called out to Garthmere."

"Just so—and there's that matter of suspected black-marketing of eggs at Nethergill—the official egg collector reported it. Needs looking into."

"Yes, sir."

"Well, it's like this, Layng: you've got as much work on hand as you can manage. In fact you've been doing the work of two men ever since I took over. I realise that—I'm a newcomer, a deputy, in fact, and I have to rely on your knowledge to a considerable extent. I can't spare you, Layng, and I don't want to put too much on your shoulders. In my judgment we should do better to apply to the C.O. for help immediately. They know the quandary we County men are in these days. We'll go straight ahead with the Inquest to-morrow, Layng—arrange it with the Coroner. It will be better to take only formal evidence and adjourn immediately for further investigations, so as to leave the Yard a free hand. I'll have a word with the Coroner myself and then I'll ring the Commissioner's Office. They'll probably send a man to-morrow. That, I'm convinced, is the wisest course."

As Major Havers spoke the telephone on Layng's desk rang, and he was informed that Harding had reported, bringing a witness with him.

Major Havers grasped what was being said over the line and said promptly: "Bring him in, bring him in at once."

Gloomily Layng passed the order on to Harding. He wanted to interrogate Jock, but he had no real hopes of the result.

The door opened and Harding appeared, holding Jock firmly by the arm. The boy's face was scarlet, his blue eyes bulging, his fair hair sticking up like straw. At sight of the other two men Jock gave vent to the roar of raucous laughter which, Layng was to learn, was his immediate reaction to surprise. It was an amazing sound, especially in a small room: his lungs had the power of a young bull's. Major Havers winced and Layng said sharply: "That'll do. We don't want any row of that kind. Behave yourself."

Jock roared again, pointing his finger at Havers. "Goody, goody, tha's shot him! I saw tha' shoot him!" he declared.

"Nonsense, nonsense," declared Havers, and Jock obliged again with his colossal mirth.

"He's been doing it all the way in the car, sir," said Harding, and there was satisfaction in his voice. "Hardly stopped once. You might as well have had a bull calf beside you."

Jock caught the familiar word, "bull calf," and responded heartily. "Moo-oo... Moo-oo," he bellowed. He was proud of his ability to simulate animal noises.

"Good God!" said Havers. "Make what you can of him, Layng. I've got to get on the phone…"

He hurried out and Layng looked at Jock sardonically. "I wonder what the experts from the Yard will make of *you*," he muttered.

CHAPTER NINE

I T HAD BEEN ON MONDAY, SEPTEMBER 20TH, THAT STAPLE SAW
Richard Garth on the fell side. On the following Thursday, the
23rd, the fox hunt had occurred and old Mr. Garth had been shot.
Major Havers had his way over arrangements for the Inquest,
which had been a brief, colourless affair, in which only the actual
evidence of identity, death, and discovery had been taken before a
prompt adjournment "pending further investigations." Meantime,
the Commissioner's Office had agreed to send a C.I.D. man to take
over the investigation.

Thus it came about that on a fine clear September afternoon
Chief Inspector Macdonald, C.I.D., arrived at Lancaster station—
choosing that route in preference to the more indirect and tiresome
journey to Carnton. A police car met him at the station, and Layng
greeted him somewhat gloomily.

"I'm sorry we had to bring you away from London to deal
with our hayseeds up here," said Layng, and Macdonald replied:

"Very kind of you, but I don't look at it that way. I've often
been through Lancaster, but I've never really seen the place. I like
your castle."

Layng grunted non-committally, and as they turned over the
bridge Macdonald leant forward to study the grand profile of castle
and parish church, clear cut against the sky high above the River
Lune, reflecting that it was the best thing in the way of a view
which he had seen since he was last up north. Edinburgh, Stirling,
Durham… Lancaster was not so tremendous as these but more

impressive than anything in the south to his mind. He glanced at Layng, tempted to ask him if he quoted "old John of Gaunt, time-honoured Lancaster" when he saw the castle—or if he carefully avoided those famous lines. Seeing Layng's expression, Macdonald said nothing. Layng broke the silence.

"The case in question doesn't concern Lancaster," he explained. "Garthmere is miles out in the country—the back of beyond."

"Good," said Macdonald. "I shall enjoy pitting my wits against the farmers. The folk in your valley resemble my own folk over the border, I expect. They're clannish, suspicious of southerners, and slow to answer questions."

"Slow," groaned Layng. "You've said it. I'm town bred, and these rustics try my patience. I've got a full report ready for you, of course, but if you'd like to have an outline of the case verbatim, I'll start straight away."

"Do," replied Macdonald cordially. "That will probably help me more than the official report. You can convey things in words which you could never put into a report. Hunches aren't evidence—but they're often quite as valuable."

"The trouble is I've got too many hunches," said Layng, with a glance at the long-jawed, dark-haired fellow beside him. "Decent sort of chap," the Superintendent thought. "Not condescending, anyway."

With a feeling of relief because he sensed fellow-feeling in the man beside him, Layng told his tale. He did it well, having a gift of orderly narrative which placed events in their right sequence and did not over-emphasise his own opinions.

At one point in his narrative, Macdonald nearly interrupted the Superintendent. This was when they had breasted the hills north-east of Lancaster and saw before them the whole stretch of the Pennine Chain, with Ingleborough like a titanic lion couchant clear-cut against a wind-swept sky, and the sun flecked shoulder of Pen-y-gwynt beyond. Macdonald loved hill country, and the wide prospect in front of him roused keen delight in his mind.

"Hoi—stop just a minute and let me take this in," he exclaimed.

Layng, quite uninterested in hills, assumed that the Chief Inspector had missed his last point: "the boy could hardly have owned a gun," he repeated, and continued talking. Harding, who was driving—and listening—slowed up and cast a quick glance over his shoulder. "Ingleborough," he said—and Macdonald chuckled silently.

When they arrived at Carnton, Macdonald found Major Havers awaiting him.

"Glad to see you, Chief Inspector, glad to see you! You probably wonder why it is that we country bumpkins say we've got too much to do. I expect you think life up here is pretty leisurely in comparison with town—it's all this extra inspection due to agricultural and marketing regulations. Small things, I know, but we can't let 'em slide. I thought if we were going to ask your department to take over we'd better call you in at once."

Macdonald replied courteously, but Layng observed the way in which the C.I.D. man checked Havers' garrulity and kept to his point. Macdonald pocketed Layng's report, produced an Ordnance Survey map of six inches to the mile which he had already studied, and asked Layng to underline all the strategic points for him. He then said:

"There's still a couple of hours of daylight. Can you lend me a push bike? If so, I should like to put it on the back of the car and Harding can drive me to the approaches of Garthmere—the pointer on the main road would do—and I can find my way about.

Is there any inn within a mile or so of Garthmere where I could get put up?"

Havers contested all these points: the Chief Inspector could have the car, he could put up at the Carnton hotel, he could... Very politely Macdonald kept to his point, and shortly he was in the car with Harding again, having booked a room by telephone at the Green Dragon, a good inn some two miles from Garthmere on the main road.

"I can leave my suitcase here and take the haversack," he said. "That will leave me quite mobile, as they say nowadays."

While Harding was driving him, Macdonald spent his time studying the big map, sitting in the back of the car asking questions at intervals.

Harding pulled up at the signpost which pointed to Garthmere, and helped Macdonald untie the bike from the back of the car.

"Lucky the signposts are back again, sir. It saves a lot of trouble. We've got them all back hereabouts."

"More than we have in the south," replied Macdonald. "Thanks very much and good evening to you."

The Chief Inspector mounted his bike with a keen sense of pleasure. This was one of detection's good hours. Free from streets and crowds, free from the smell of petrol, free from the sound of planes, so predominant in the southern counties, free to enjoy the keen sweet air and the silence of this sparsely populated hill country—Macdonald whistled as he spun down hill, and continued whistling as he pushed his bike up the opposite rise. On the breast of the hill he paused to survey his surroundings.

The low stone walls and occasional ancient thorn trees which edged the road did not interrupt the view. Macdonald's road ran parallel with the river valley, half-way up the scarp. A mile in front of him he could see Garthmere Hall, set on a level stretch some two hundred feet above the river. Above the great house and its outlying farm buildings the ground rose again to the crest of the fells, five hundred feet above sea-level. The pastures on either side of the road were known as "intaks"—Harding had provided this information; "intakes" from the fell, brought into cultivation throughout centuries of farming. Below and beyond the Hall, separated from it by a stretch of park land, the village stood just above the river. At intervals in the valley were patches of woodland, the trees lining the gills or watercourses, whose becks (Macdonald called them burns until he was corrected) ran down to join the Lune. The river was still high, and its shining curves wound in serpentine fashion westwards towards the sea.

The Chief Inspector remounted his bike and rode on towards Garthmere. Half a mile farther on the road forked, the higher right fork being the major section. The left fork, which dropped down to another gill, led to Garthmere Hall, and it was by this smaller road that the old hull stood, and the lane ran down to the river. Every barn and farm building was marked on the Ordnance Survey, and Macdonald picked out the High Barn where the foxes had been auctioned. This stood in a field on the higher road fork, and it was obvious that no one going from the High Barn would have needed to use the lower road fork unless they wanted to go to Garthmere Hall itself. Macdonald knew enough about farmers to realise their reluctance to trespass on other farmers' land, and though the old lane was marked as a public path on the survey map it ran exclusively through the Garthmere Home Farm.

Macdonald jumped down the small bank at the roadside and considered the hull, opening the door and observing its muddy interior. He agreed with Layng's observation: there was a probability amounting to a certainty that the murderer had crouched in the far corner of the dark little interior, and shot immediately the old man opened the door. The murderer would then have stepped over the body of his victim and have taken one of three routes: either by the road Macdonald had just traversed—at any rate as far as the fork—or by the old lane down to the valley, or by the road leading on to Garthmere Hall.

Macdonald decided to go down the old lane to the river. After one glance at its muddy depths—surface was a misnomer—he propped his bike against the hull and set off down hill on foot. This lane was obviously used for the passage of cattle up and down from the valley pastures, and it was sunk between banks in which gnarled old thorn trees leant from the prevailing west wind. The lane emerged into a pasture just above the river, where inquisitive bullocks followed at Macdonald's heels, as though intent on detecting a detective. From the time he had left Harding and the car, Macdonald had met no one and seen no one, but a dog gave a short bark as he reached the river bank, and he saw a stocky, square-shouldered man approaching him. Seeing the man's age, and remembering Layng's comments on the Garthmere folk, Macdonald made a guess at the identity of the man on the Home Farm pastures. This was probably Staple, the bailiff. Macdonald bade him good evening, adding that as the old lane was marked on the Ordnance Survey map, he hoped he had not been trespassing. The other regarded him with shrewd eyes.

"Aye, it's a public road, if you like to call it a road, but few people use it. The fields are cleaner going."

"Aye," Macdonald fell easily into the familiar affirmative, "but I don't like making free with farm land."

"'Tis little matter on those pastures," replied Staple, "though
it's true we don't like folk being over free, and leaving gates open
as likely as not. Many's the hour I've wasted after cattle who've
strayed by reason of an open gate."

"Aye. That's the hardest thing to teach the real townsman,"
agreed Macdonald. He fell into step beside Staple quite naturally,
and they walked downstream slowly.

"It's a grand evening," said Macdonald, following a gambit
familiar enough to him in his own highland country. "The glass is
going up. It looks like settled weather. I see you've had the river
up of late," he added.

They had reached a gate in the hedge which enclosed the
pasture and as though by common consent they leaned upon it
and continued talking, while Staple looked ruefully at the flood-
flattened grass in the dales beyond.

"Aye, more's the pity. It's spoiled the fog grass, as you see—all
mucked up with sand and river mud. It's rare good feed in the dales."

"Dales?" queried Macdonald. "You call these river meadows
dales? This fog grass, it's the aftermath of the hay, I suppose?"

"Aye, that's it. It's wonderful meadow land. We got six cartloads
to the acre when we cut the hay."

"What are the stones in the grass there?—like mile stones?"
queried Macdonald.

"They're the dale stones," replied Staple. "In old times the best
land was divided out between the village folk, a strip to each man,
share and share alike. The stones mark the strips and the dales
continue across the river. Those stones are centuries old, and they
go deep—four to five feet into the ground, I believe."

John Staple had been talking easily, his slow deep voice very
pleasant to listen to as he talked about familiar things. He turned

an inquiring eye on Macdonald. "You're just taking a walk along the river? It's a fine valley is Lunesdale."

"Aye, it is that," agreed Macdonald, making a quick decision. Frankness would pay best with John Staple, he decided.

"I wish I were just taking a walk along the river," he went on. "I could do with a holiday in Lunesdale—but I'm not on holiday. I'm on a job. My name is Macdonald and I belong to the Criminal Investigation Department of Scotland Yard."

"A detective. I shouldn't have known that," said Staple, and his voice sounded dejected, all the pleasure gone out of it. "It's a sorry business," he added.

"Aye, it is that," replied Macdonald. "I'm sorry it should have happened here. It seems foreign to the place."

"Aye, that's just it!" burst out Staple. "It's not like the folks round here. Take me—I'm one of them. I've lived all my life on Garthmere land. I've worked for Mr. Garth over thirty years—and now I'm suspected, along with men I've known since I was a lad, of shooting him. 'Tis perishing nonsense!" he declared.

"Yet somebody shot him," said Macdonald. "You'll be Mr. Staple, I take it? Are you willing to help me? I've come here to find a murderer, and to clear innocent folk of suspicion."

"It's a heavy business," said Staple slowly, his voice troubled. "If I'd known who did it, I'd have named him, no matter who it was—but I don't know. I'll answer any questions you like to ask about the folk round here—but I'll not go casting suspicion around haphazard like. It's easy to say 'maybe So-and-so did it.' It's not so easy for the man named to prove he had no hand in it."

Macdonald guessed that this was a long speech for Staple to make—but he guessed a good deal more. He knew, as clearly as if he had been told outright, that Staple was uneasy in his mind, and that uneasiness was not based on total ignorance, but on some disquieting knowledge. Macdonald had not worked in the C.I.D. for twenty years without gaining an insight into men's minds.

He leant on the gate and did not hurry to answer. At last he said: "Aye. I know exactly what you mean. Think of it this way. It's as much my job to vindicate the innocent as to outwit the guilty. Folks talk—you know it, and I know it. I'm a Highlander by descent. I know the Highland folk. They don't talk much to strangers, but they talk amongst themselves. If Mr. Garth's murderer is not found, the folk around here will talk, and suspicion will fall on this man and that—aye, and suspicion will rest. The only way of disproving it is to find the guilty man."

Staple looked straight ahead of him, his face furrowed and sad. "True enough," he replied, "but what can I do? What do you want to know?"

"I can't tell you yet, Mr. Staple. I've only just come here. I set out this evening to learn something about the district, to study the roads and paths, and to get the hang of it, the feel of the land. It's no use rushing to ask questions when you're ignorant of a place, especially a place like this. As I see it, coming here as a stranger, this crime is conditioned by the place. To understand the one you've got to study the other."

"Aye, there's something in that," said Staple, and Macdonald went on:

"I'm not going to ask you any questions now. I don't know enough to ask the questions that matter. Only one thing has occurred to me so far. The murderer went to the hull; he also left it—and the routes by which he left were limited."

"Aye, that's sense, that is," agreed Staple. "I've thought the same: there's the road to the house, there's the Carnton road, there's the old lane—and then there's the fields."

"Do you think it's likely he'd have taken to the fields?" asked Macdonald. "Wouldn't a stranger seen in the fields look more noticeable and suspicious than a stranger on the roads?"

"Aye—but how do you know it's a stranger you're after?"

"I don't," replied Macdonald simply—he now knew that Staple was sure in his own mind it was not a stranger. "I really meant someone who does not belong to the Home Farm. Other farmers wouldn't walk over Mr. Garth's fields, I take it?"

Staple scratched his head and considered: "I couldn't say that, not as a hard and fast rule," he said at length. "'Tis true we don't go over other folks' land without reason—but if I saw Mr. Lamb or Mr. Trant on the Home Farm land, I'd know they'd have had a reason for coming—seeking strayed cattle, may be, or getting to help a beast quickly—but they'd generally say something about it later." He turned and faced Macdonald. "Anyway—no one was seen on the Home Farm, barring Bob Ashthwaite in the dales after the fox hunt."

Macdonald did not follow this up by a question as to what Ashthwaite was doing in the dales. He considered that he had probably said as much as was advisable for the moment. At any rate, he had made contact with Staple on more friendly terms than might have been hoped. To question him rapidly would be a mistake, Macdonald judged. He went on:

"There's another way you could help me, Mr. Staple. I've been studying the Ordnance Survey map to learn the geography so to speak, but I haven't got things clear yet. If you've got time, could you come up the bank with me and point out the different farms? There's a bonny view up yonder."

"Aye, I'll do that gladly," replied Staple. "My own place is on the higher land, above the Home Farm. I've ninety acres, most of it fell pasture, though I've got one bit of land down by the gill and some arable holm land—ploughed for the first time this year. If we cross the dales and go up by the brow you'll be able to see what's what. We shall skirt the village that way."

"Good. That sounds just what I want," agreed Macdonald, and Staple opened the gate and they went through, keeping to the path by the river until they turned at right angles by a clearly defined track, and later left the rich valley grass and climbed by a steep hill which followed the line of a gill, overhung with beech and alder and thorn.

Macdonald said: "Then your land will be rather scattered, Mr. Staple?"

"Aye, it spreads a bit. You'll soon see. My land lies like a big T, with rough pasture across the top and a long slip-down the gill ending in that piece of holm land by the river. That piece used to belong to the Home Farm, but my father wanted a better bit of pasture, and Mr. Garth let him the holm land. He'd only seventy acres before that."

"You'll have had a lot of work with all this ploughing," said Macdonald, and Staple talked on happily enough, giving it as his opinion that it wasn't going to be too easy to return the wartime arable to the permanent pasture which was valued in the district.

The hill was steep, but Staple kept going steadily, his short sturdy legs managing the stiff gradient as easily as Macdonald's longer ones. They did not pause until they had reached a road above the Hall, and at length Staple halted and stood by a gate.

"My place, Lonsghyll, is above us, to the north," he said. "Higher Fell—that's Mr. Lamb's, lies to the east. You'd have passed his land and Mr. Trant's—Blackthorn, that is—as you came from the Carnton road. Farther west, downstream, the land's farmed by Mr. Langhorn, Middle Field, his place is named. His land goes with mine—you see, down yonder?"

"Aye, I see. I've got all that clear," replied Macdonald. "Garthmere Hall and the Home Farm in the centre of the picture, Blackthorn to the east bordering the river, Higher Fell north of Blackthorn, Middle Field in the valley to the west of your holm land and gill, Lonsghyll just behind us to the north."

"Aye, you've got it. That's fine," said Staple. "Now you can just see a clump of pine trees to the north-east—that's Mr. Brough's land—Farrintake."

"Farrintake? That'll be the far intak?" asked Macdonald.

"That's right, that's right." Staple was pleased with his pupil. "And Greenbeck—Bob Ashthwaite's land—lies to the west of mine, a mile or so farther north. You can't see it from here. It's not Garthmere land."

"I'm very grateful, Mr. Staple," replied Macdonald. "You've taught me more in a few minutes than I should have learnt in hours studying the map."

"You're welcome," replied Staple.

Macdonald looked down at Garthmere Hall, a grey mass in the greying light.

"That's a fine house," he said. "It'll be ancient—centuries old."

"Aye, it's an old house. 'Twas old before Flodden Field," said Staple—and Macdonald did not say how stirred he was by the mention of that ancient and bloody battle. Did they date their houses here before and after Flodden Field?

"The Garths were great folk then, aye and right up to the time of the enclosures they prospered," went on Staple. "You can see from the size of the house—but these last hundred years they've gone down hill. I respected old Mr. Garth, mind you," he added. "Folks called him hard, but he dealt fair by me, and by my father before me, and he cleared his lands of debt by honest hard work."

"You could have many a worse epitaph," said Macdonald gently and Staple nodded. They stood in silence for a moment or so more, and then Macdonald said:

"Thank you again, Mr. Staple, and good-evening to you."

"Good-evening," replied Staple, and Macdonald left him leaning against the gate, looking down at Garthmere Hall.

CHAPTER TEN

I

MACDONALD RECOVERED HIS BIKE AND RODE TO HIS INN without meeting a soul. The daylight was nearly gone and there was nothing to bring hard-working farmers afield these September evenings. Over his supper—and never had ham and eggs tasted better—Macdonald congratulated himself that he had kept to his own scheme, and that he was not supping in company with either the gloomy Superintendent Layng or the ebullient Major Havers. There was a good fire and an abundance of logs, and the Chief Inspector settled down to Layng's report feeling that he had now a very good chance of understanding it.

When Macdonald laid the typed sheets down he said to himself "Good for Layng." It was an admirable report, concise and yet detailed, and Macdonald knew well enough that he was in for no easy task. He remembered Layng's exasperated voice—"all those damned farmers out with guns"—and who was going to talk confidentially to Macdonald about those same farmers? He had established good terms with John Staple—but Macdonald was far too shrewd to cherish an optimistic belief that Staple would be willing to discuss his fellow farmers freely. It was quite plain that Staple would be very averse from anything of the kind. Macdonald racked his brains. A parson? There was no resident parson at Garthmere, the tiny church was served by the clergy of the parent parish of Claughby—and the farmers seldom went to church save at harvest festival. The village innkeeper might be willing to talk, but he again was of the district, one of the clan. There was no schoolmaster, no post office. At length Macdonald had an idea. All the farmers must deal with a corn miller—a firm which supplies cattle food, poultry meals and fertilisers. These firms have travelling representatives whose job it is to call at the farms at regular intervals and take orders, and in these wartime days to collect coupons for rationed feed. The traveller would need to be on good terms with the farmers, and he would probably discuss the news of the district with each. This seemed a possible source from which news might be evoked.

Macdonald sat back, his pipe between his teeth, and stared at the fire. He thought of old Garth at the fox hunt: this had taken place in Lawson's Wood, a spinney edging a gill to the west of the Home Farm. Old Garth had not gone to the auction at the High Barn, so presumably he had returned home and had gone into the hull on his way to the house. The fox hunt had finished at half-past four—rather too early for the old man's tea. Macdonald studied a list of the oddments found in the hull; these were a scythe, a mall (a wooden block like a large mallet), some chains and posts and wire, some rabbit snares, some sacks, and an old haversack containing some big nails, twine, a hammer and a jack knife. In addition had been found the quarter-dollar piece among the peat moss. Macdonald reviewed these. Granted that the old man had best part of an hour to put in before tea, what would he have been likely to do? It seemed plain that he kept some of his own working gear in the hull—a convenient storage place. The old scythe was probably kept there for scything thistles—Macdonald had noticed that the pastures had been well cleaned of these. The mall, the posts and the barbed wire were for mending fences or hedges; cattle have a habit of breaking through any weak place in the hedge, being obstinately convinced that the pasture in the adjoining field is always better than that in their own. The nails and wire would be handy for mending a gate. Macdonald made mental notes of points he must determine. Had any cattle strayed that day on the Home Farm? Had any gate been broken? Did any gate show signs of recent mending? It seemed to him that a task like this would have been likely to have filled in an odd hour of old Garth's time. Labour was short, and every one emphasised the fact that the old man had been a worker. A broken gate would have annoyed him— and gates had had but little attention during the war.

Stubbornly Macdonald worked backwards, bringing to the task a genuine interest and imagination which Layng lacked. Marion Garth had said in her statement, "I do not know what he intended to do. My father never told me what he meant to do unless it were some work on the farm for which he needed help." That was a definite statement, but if asked in a more detailed way, "had any gate been out of order, any hedge or fence broken, any wire been down—or had any such defects been reported or observed?" it was possible that someone on the Home Farm would be able to provide an answer.

Macdonald next turned his mind to the matter of Ashthwaite. Layng had not interviewed him, but he had told Macdonald that Ashthwaite had the name of a dour, difficult man—and he had certainly had reason to hate old Robert Garth. Macdonald was not in a position to judge whether the landlord's action in claiming arrears of rent from Ashthwaite had been something other than fair dealing, but he guessed that the hard-working farmer would have grudged paying out money for arrears of rent. The chief point to establish about Ashthwaite was his route from Lawson's Wood to the dales, and his reason for being there. Macdonald had recourse to the Ordnance Survey again, and he studied it, not very hopefully. During the fox hunt Ashthwaite had been posted at the top of the gill, nearest the road that was. He could have come up to the Carnton road when the shooting party dispersed and went to the High Barn. In that case somebody would almost certainly have noticed him. Old Garth had not intended to go to the auction, and it was probable that he returned to Garthmere across the fields. John Staple had gone down to the dales, but he had turned upstream towards a pasture where some bullocks were grazing; when he returned downstream he had seen Ashthwaite. Macdonald pondered over the itineraries of these two men, but considered that it was unlikely that these could lead him to anything important. Farmers traversed land at their own pace; they might stop to examine gates or hedges, to study the condition of their cattle, or merely ponder over the future cropping of a ploughed field. In short, either Staple or Ashthwaite might have taken half an hour to cover a distance which would have taken Macdonald five minutes.

Knocking out his pipe and standing by the now dying fire, Macdonald considered his itinerary next day. He would see Staple again before he tackled Ashthwaite; then the Garthmere Hall people. Remembering his notion of finding the corn miller's representative, Macdonald wondered how he could find out unobtrusively about such a firm. His eye fell on a calendar pinned to the wall. Sure enough he found that it was an advertisement of Bowden, Corn Millers of Carnton. Macdonald noted the telephone number and decided to ring up the firm next morning.

He stretched himself and yawned, sleepy after the keen air and the warm fire. He remembered saying to John Staple: "I wish I *were* on holiday." "That's a likely salmon river," he said to himself, as he made for bed.

II

Mrs. Sandford, of the Green Dragon, took a fancy to her guest.

"He's a schoolmaster on holiday, I reckon," she said to her husband. "More considerate than most, and a tidy fellow."

Edward Sandford meditated. "If he's a schoolmaster, I reckon his holidays ought to be over. He's a Scot, all right. His first word told me that—but 'twas a London address he registered. I thought he might be from one o' them ministries evacuated hereabouts, or may be one of those big firms from London, who've taken a place in Kendal."

"Whoever he is, he's a pleasant fellow," said Mrs. Sandford.

"Maybe he's looking for some land. I've heard there's a retired schoolmaster over at Thaugon who's raising calves as though he were born t'ot."

The object of their conversation was pedalling towards a public call-box he had noted the previous day. He put a call through to Bowdens, the corn millers, asking quite straight-forwardly in what district their travelling representative for Lunesdale would be working that day. The reply came without any argument. Their Mr. Toller would be calling at Gressthwaite in the morning, and would work his way back to Wrafton Bridge and the Wrafton farms after midday. Was there anything the firm could do?

"No, thanks; I just wanted to make sure I shouldn't miss him," replied Macdonald and rang off.

Continuing his ride, he considered his best way of dealing with John Staple, and once more concluded that frankness would be the best policy. He found Staple engaged in thatching a rick in a field at the road side, and Macdonald apologised for interrupting him at his work.

"I know you've got plenty to do without spending time talking," he said, and Staple replied:

"Well, I'm not so pressed now. I've got my oats in, and the potatoes and turnips won't hurt for a bit."

He leant against the gate and waited and Macdonald went on: "I'm going to see Mr. Ashthwaite to-day, and I wondered if you'd care to give me any advice before I see him."

Staple's shrewd eyes smiled a little. "Eh, but you're cut to a different pattern from yon Superintendent," he observed. "He didn't want advice—no, and he wouldn't have taken kindly to it, neither. It's hard to say about Ashthwaite. He's queer these days. He's a dour chap. You'll find it hard to get an answer out of him. I reckon your best way would be to tell him your name and business right away. Don't be ower sharp. If he thinks you're threatening him, he won't answer at all. He might order you off his land—or try to chuck you off it, if so be he lost his temper—and that's not going to help," he concluded. "He's got a dog, too. Don't you let that dog get behind you, it's an ill-tempered beast." He rubbed his head thoughtfully. "Mind you, I've nothing against Bob Ashthwaite. He thought Mr. Garth treated him hard—but that was because they didn't have things down on paper. 'Tis no use having spoken agreements. Likely one or t'other doesn't understand what's meant."

"You're right there," agreed Macdonald, and ventured on his next inquiry. "After the fox hunt, you went down to the river, Mr. Staple. Which way did you go?"

"The shortest way—by the gill. It's rough going, but I'm used to it."

"I see; so you reached the river at a point some hundred yards upstream from where you saw Mr. Ashthwaite?"

"Aye, that's it. Mr. Trant's got some bullocks down there, and I was keeping my eyes open for two stirks which had strayed from the Home Farm."

"Do you know how they broke out? They'd be out at pasture all day and night this month, I take it?"

Staple again studied Macdonald, and the latter suspected that the reason for his question had been understood.

"Aye, they stay out," replied the bailiff. "I've been looking at the fences. I'd say those stirks broke through into the old lane and got down to the river. I found them in the Pardon's Field—that's downstream from the dales."

"Did you see Mr. Ashthwaite at the close of the hunt?"

"Nay. I went straight down to the river. I saw Mr. Lamb and Mr. Hayman as they went up the fields beside the gill and I saw one or two of the lads. Bob was above me at the shoot. Even if he came straight down to the river, I should have got down first."

Macdonald was alert to every word, listening for an opening. He replied: "You say even if he came straight down! Do you think he had business up above?"

Staple was slow in replying. He chewed a straw meditatively before he answered, staring out towards the fells.

"It's like this," he said at length. "I don't believe Bob Ashthwaite shot Mr. Garth. I tell you that plain—but you can see as far before your nose as most, aye, and a sight farther than that Superintendent. What was Bob doing on Garthmere land after the hunt was over, you're asking yourself—and by gum, I've asked myself the same question. I'm willing to say that Bob had a down on Mr. Garth—it's true, and it'd be silly to deny it. Maybe he's been brooding over it. Living as he does, alone with Jock and no kith nor kin of his own, nor woman in the house, 'tis likely he would brood."

Staple broke off here and paused, as though so much conversation were an effort. Macdonald put in easily:

"I can well believe it. It must be a sad sort of life for a man. No one really likes being lonely."

"Better be lonely than aye bothered with someone cracking," said Staple, "howsomever, it's likely Bob did brood ower much—and what then? He's no murderer, take it from me, neither would he play any dirty trick that'd go against the grain with a farmer." He turned and faced Macdonald. "Bob's a proper farmer. Remember that," he said. "He wouldn't drive off another man's beasts, nor see his ewes worried, aye, and he'd send word if any beasts were in trouble. That's second nature to a farmer. But maybe he brooded till he felt he must have his say. He maybe wanted to tell Mr. Garth just what he thought of him and get it off his chest. I reckon that'd be about the size of it."

Macdonald had listened with the liveliest interest to all this. It rang true, and it was helpful. Here was the judgment of a man by one of his peers.

"I'm very grateful to you, Mr. Staple," he said. "You're helping me more than you know. To understand this problem it's necessary to understand the nature of those concerned. You know them—and I don't. I should be all at sea without the sort of advice you're giving me. Now tell me—do you think Ashthwaite *did* have his say?"

"Nay. I don't. So far as I can tell he never got a chance," said Staple. "Bob was at the top of the gill, and Mr. Garth, he was lower down. When Trant called, 'That'll be the lot,' Mr. Garth took himself off over the fields, and Bob didn't see him go, the trees were between them. I reckon Bob came down the gill and saw he'd missed him, so he came on down to the dales. For why? Because he was so vexed he'd missed his chance, he couldn't just take himself off. He wandered down there in the dales, brooding like."

Macdonald pondered: "But surely Ashthwaite wouldn't have wanted to abuse Mr. Garth when his fellow farmers were at hand and could hear?" he asked.

Staple chuckled—the first sound of amusement Macdonald had heard from him.

"You're wrong there," he replied. "'Tis just that that Bob would've wanted—to shame him in front of t'others—and 'twould have vexed Mr. Garth too. A man don't like to be called a flint-skinning bastard in front of all his tenants."

Macdonald laughed outright at that, and Staple concluded: "'To've said his say in front of t'others—that would've been sweet to Bob—aye, and it'd have caused a good laugh behind Mr. Garth's back. That story would've gone all up and down the valley. I'd say Bob was properly sorry he missed his chance—but shoot him, he didn't. I'll lay my life on that."

"Well, thank you very much, Mr. Staple. I've learnt a lot," said Macdonald. Staple replied:

"Some can learn and some can't. We've a saying hereabouts—a man's got all his buttons on. Good-day to you."

"That's a new one on me," said Macdonald to himself, as he mounted his bike again. "If Staple's right, then I'm wasting my time going to see Ashthwaite—but seeing I'm half-way there, I might as well go on and try my luck."

Greenbeck was two miles farther on, and the road was uphill, but it was exhilarating country and Macdonald enjoyed it. He found the approach to Greenbeck Farm was a stony track edged with a stone wall. Above the wall was rough sheep pasture, mainly consisting of agrostis and rushes, too poor for dairy cattle to thrive on.

The house was the usual long, low stone building, house and barn under the same roof; it was a small building and looked in poor condition. As Macdonald reached the fold yard gate, a dog rushed at him, barking. It was a vicious-looking beast and Macdonald swore at it, his Scots speech surprisingly harsh and vigorous. The dog hesitated, as though recognising something to be reckoned with, and a voice came from the barn calling the dog to heel. Then a tall thin man appeared at the shippon door and stared at Macdonald.

"Mr. Ashthwaite?" inquired Macdonald.

"Aye." The curt rejoinder was not encouraging—nor was the farmer's expression. He had a thin, lined face, a harsh mouth, drawn down at the corners, and light expressionless eyes which seemed to be looking a great distance away.

"My name is Macdonald. I am an officer of the Criminal Investigation Department, and I am in charge of the inquiry into the death of Mr. Robert Garth."

Ashthwaite's expression did not change. He turned and swore at the dog again, and then turned back to Macdonald and waited. He did not invite him to come in, and the Chief Inspector leaned on the fold yard gate, reflecting that he was getting used to carrying out interrogations thus.

"I am making inquiries of all those present at the fox hunt," he went on. "I understand that your position was at the top of the gill."

"Aye."

"Could you see Mr. Garth during the shoot?"

"No."

"Did you see him leave the gill at the end of the hunt?"

"No."

Macdonald wondered if he could get more than a monosyllable in reply. "What did you do when the hunt was over?"

"Went down to the river."

"Why did you go down to the river?"

"Because I chose."

"Hell's bells, this is thirsty work," said Macdonald to himself, and changed his tactics a little. "You know that Mr. Garth was murdered in the hull at the top of the old lane, Mr. Ashthwaite?"

"Aye."

"How do you know that?"

At last Ashthwaite's expression changed; there was wariness in his eyes. "Heard it from Mr. Lamb at Higher Fell," he replied.

"Very good. I have told you who I am. It is my duty to caution you and to tell you that anything you say may be taken down and used in evidence. That is not a threat, Mr. Ashthwaite, but it is fact. You can refuse to answer my questions. In that case I report your refusal, and you will probably be summoned to the Coroner's Court to be questioned there. On the whole, it'll be much less trouble for you to answer my questions here—unless for any reason you prefer to have a solicitor present."

Again Ashthwaite said nothing. Macdonald went on: "It seems to me it would be much more comfortable if we both went and sat on the bench yonder. I don't expect you to show any respect to me, personally, but as representative of the law of the land I demand attention."

Without waiting for a reply, Macdonald unlatched the gate and opened it, being interested to know if Ashthwaite would "order him out or try to chuck him out," as Staple had suggested. Ashthwaite did neither. He made no comment as Macdonald went to the bench and sat on it, but he followed him a few steps and stood leaning against the door post of the barn. Macdonald took his notebook out:

"You were seen in your place at the top of the gill at the end of the fox hunt. Nearly half an hour later you were seen at the bottom of the old lane by the river. That lane leads directly down from the hull where Mr. Garth was shot. He was killed by a charge from a shotgun, fired at short range. I think you would be well advised to tell exactly what you were doing in the half-hour I have mentioned. It is stated by the doctor that Mr. Garth was probably shot during that half-hour."

"Are you charging *me* with shooting the ould varmint?"

"No. I am not. I am giving you a chance to prove that you could not have done so."

There was a moment's tense silence, and then Macdonald went on, slowly and conversationally: "Think it over, Mr. Ashthwaite. I've no doubt Mr. Lamb told you as much as is known of the murder. He may have told you that only three of those known to have been present at the fox hunt did not go to the auction at the High Barn—Mr. Garth himself, Mr. Staple, and yourself. He may have told you that your lad, Jock, was seen at the hull when Mr. Staple found the body. Considering all these points, I think you would be well advised to give a clear account of how you spent your time, from the moment you left your place at the top of the gill until the moment you met Mr. Staple down by the river."

Ashthwaite was in no hurry to answer. He leant back against the door post in silence, and Macdonald pulled his pipe out and began to fill it. He wanted Ashthwaite to regard him as a human being, so that they could get on to better terms. He also wanted to manœuvre into a position where he could see the other's face and hands. Macdonald always found that he learnt something by using his eyes. Feeling in his pockets as though to find a match, he stood up and rummaged in his trousers pockets, at last producing a match. Setting a foot on the bench, he bent down to obtain shelter to light his pipe, his back to the wind. This accomplished he stood straight again this time facing the other man.

"Well, Mr. Ashthwaite—what do you think? If you'd rather not answer, I won't waste any more time."

Ashthwaite put out a hand as though to check Macdonald were he about to take his departure.

"I've no need to think," he replied. "I didn't shoot him and I tell you so plain."

"But that's not an answer to my question," said Macdonald.

Ashthwaite paused again. Macdonald was pretty certain that his delay in answering was second nature to this man who lived alone, save for an idiot boy, on this lonely fell farm. At last he said:

"The river'd been in flood. I wanted to see if the dales was mucked up. Time's, when Mr. Trant's got more feed'n he needs, I put some of my grazing cattle on his land. 'Tis poor pasture for cattle up here."

"Well, that's plain enough," said Macdonald. He knew at once that if Staple stuck to this story—and if no one else had seen him in the interval—the story could not be disproved. It was a perfectly reasonable thing for a farmer like Ashthwaite to have done. Macdonald decided to try another angle.

"How was it you went to the fox hunt?" he inquired. "Did Mr. Trant ask you to go?"

Again suspicion showed in the man's curiously light eyes. Macdonald knew at once that Trant had not asked him, and awaited his reply with some interest.

"The corn miller's man towd me on't," was the reply. "I didn't need ask any leave to go and join a fox shoot on Mr. Trant's land."

"Aye, I see that," said Macdonald. He felt he was getting on a little bit. This last statement could be proved or disproved.

"I've got a difficult job, Mr. Ashthwaite," he went on. "I'm a stranger to these parts and it's not going to be easy to get at the truth. Now you have known the Garth family for a long time."

Once again, studying the thin lined face of the farmer, Macdonald sensed a reaction, an uneasy change of mood. Ashthwaite shifted his stance too, and replied:

"Maybe—but I've got some work to do, and talking don't get me any further."

"But my job can't be done without talking," replied Macdonald, still good-humouredly. He was racking his brains for the best way to exploit that unease which had made Ashthwaite try to terminate the interview. This man's daughter had married Richard Garth, twenty-five years ago. With this in mind, Macdonald asked suddenly:

"When did you last see Richard Garth, Mr. Ashthwaite?"

This question succeeded in so far as it startled the other altogether out of his immobility. Ashthwaite started, his gnarled hands clenched, and his thin lips disappeared into a hard line as the jaws contracted like a spring.

"Richard Garth?" he queried.

"Aye. Your son-in-law. Mr. Robert Garth's heir."

Ashthwaite spat, deliberately. "I last saw 'im the night afore he and Mary went to Canada," he replied. "1919, that were."

"And when did you last hear him talked about, Mr. Ashthwaite? Villages all over the country are alike in one way—they're rare places for talking."

"Aye, then you go and ha' a crack wi' 'em," replied Ashthwaite.

"Right," replied Macdonald, straightening his broad shoulders. "I'll take your advice. The problem is this—to know what to believe.

If honest men keep their mouths shut, liars are most likely to be believed."

Ashthwaite peered at the lean, well-tanned face of the detective with an almost painful intentness.

At last he said:

"I'll tell you this, mister. If any says Richard Garth shot his own father, they're dirty liars. He deserved shooting, maybe, but Richard never did it, and no more did I."

He turned abruptly into the side door of the barn, and Macdonald went his way, not entirely dissatisfied with his interview. As he got on his bike again, he said, "Well, if that's the way of it, Garthmere Hall seems indicated right enough."

CHAPTER ELEVEN

I

MACDONALD WAS BEGINNING TO KNOW SOMETHING ABOUT the Lunesdale farmers. The term "gentleman farmer" belonged to the south: these independent north country men were workers. A farmer might own stock and crops and gear worth some thousands of pounds, but he would still cart his own muck, milk his own cows, and wear garments which would have classed him as a tramp in the south while he went about his business. Farm houses had front doors, but these were seldom used. Farm labourers might be employed, but the term which described them was "hired man." They generally lived under the farmer's roof and ate at the farmer's table.

Macdonald hesitated before he approached Garthmere. Did he uphold the dignity of the law by ringing at the front door, or did he study the convenience of the inmates by going to the back door, by way of the fold yard gate? Common sense prompted him to do the latter. Layng had said there were no domestic servants at the Hall, and it seemed futile to bring busy people to the front of that vast house to open a front door. The Garths were farmers; they were likely to be found, if about the place, in barns, shippons or kitchen.

So it came about that the Chief Inspector leaned his bike against the fold yard gate just as Marion Garth was persuading a new-born calf to drink out of a pail. Macdonald watched, conscious of a feeling that he wished he were holding the pail, gripping a tiny calf between his knees and holding his fingers in its mouth while it learnt how to drink milk from a pail. Marion, aware of someone standing at the shippon door, called: "I won't be a minute, Mr. Toller. Go and sit down."

Macdonald obeyed, pondering over her voice. A north country voice, but with a clearness and decision in its diction which differentiated it from the other voices Macdonald had listened to in Lunesdale.

He walked up a cobbled slope and turned into a flagged yard. Here he found a big stone slab, supported on stone uprights which must have once formed part of a very different structure, for they were moulded and foliated. Sitting in the mellow sunshine, Macdonald was not impatient: words came into his mind:

"No time to stand beneath the boughs
And stare as long as sheep or cows."

Leaning against the sun-warmed stone of the barn he wondered if he could make a success of farming. Calves, he meditated, were more attractive than criminals—and this house had "been old before Flodden Field."

Marion caught him unawares; she was wearing Wellingtons and came quietly over the flags.

"So you're not Mr. Toller," she observed.

Macdonald jumped up. "No, but it didn't seem worth while explaining while you were busy. Are you Miss Garth?"

"Yes."

"My name is Macdonald," he began, and saw enlightenment in her eyes.

"Oh yes. John Staple spoke of you last night," she said, and then added abruptly: "Would you like to come indoors—or shall we talk out here?"

"Out here," said Macdonald, and added, he knew not why:

"I was just wishing that calf was mine."

She laughed. "You can have it for a pound. It's a bull."

She sat down on the bench and waited for him to speak.

"Staple will have told you why I'm here, Miss Garth. I realise I've got a lot to learn before I can tackle this problem." He paused a second and added: "I'm not forgetting that it was your father who was killed. I should like to offer you my sympathy."

"Thank you." Her voice sounded surprised and she went on without any prompting: "I wish I could help you, Mr. Macdonald—but I don't know anything about it. I simply can't imagine who shot him. I can only be quite sure that certain people did not."

"That may help," he replied, glad of the gambit. "I have just been talking to Mr. Ashthwaite."

He saw her face frown a little, and she replied:

"Of course I can't be certain about *him*. Admittedly he bore my father a grudge—but if he had wanted to shoot him, why wait all this time? So far as I know, they hadn't spoken for years."

"When you talked to Superintendent Layng, Miss Garth, he asked you if you could make any suggestion of any kind about the case, and you replied that you could not. You have had time to think the matter over, since then. Can you add anything now?"

"Oh, I've thought all right," she said. "In fact, I've hardly thought about anything else, but I can't make any sense out of it. The most probable suggestion is that daft Jock did it. He'd got into trouble with my father once or twice, and he'd been warned off—told not to come on our land again or he'd get a thrashing."

"Why did your father object to Jock coming on his land? Because Ashthwaite employed him?"

"Partly, but more because he didn't trust Jock. He's like all idiots—cunning in some ways. Father believed he would try to steal—hens or ducks or geese—and if the cattle strayed or a gate was left open, Jock was always suspected. After all, he'd no business here. It's natural to suspect him."

"Yes. I see that. Have you had trouble recently with cattle straying?"

"Not on a large scale, but some of the young beasts have broken out, and father said that someone had meddled with the fences. We say 'fences' here when we mean hedges. The hedges are often too thin to keep the cattle in, and they are reinforced with posts and wire in weak places. If the wire is cut or a post pulled out the cattle always find the gap."

"And you think that has happened recently—deliberate meddling with your fences?"

"My father did—but I doubt it. Five hundredweight of bullock can do a lot of damage, and the beasts get wild with the flies."

"Yes, but what you are saying interests me a lot. You say Jock had no business on your land; then why did he come here?"

"I don't expect he knew himself. He's inquisitive, and he's a big powerful lad. He's nothing to occupy his spare time, he can't go courting like most of the lads because no one would look at him, and he can't go to dances or the pictures—he just wanders when he's not working."

"Has he wits enough to realise that Ashthwaite was at enmity with your father?"

"Oh, yes. I've no doubt he understood that. Ashthwaite would have to talk to somebody. It's only human nature to talk sometimes."

"Of course. Now do you think that Jock could aim a gun and fire it?"

"Our men say no—the Moffats and Staple, for instance. They say he just wouldn't know how, but it seems to me that there's a likelihood, if he got hold of a loaded gun, he'd be able to fire it. He must have seen it done so often. It's very easy to cock an old-fashioned shotgun and then pull the trigger. I can imagine Jock, if he managed to get hold of a gun, hiding in the hull, and shooting when he was found—when father opened the door."

"The chief problem is—where did he get the gun?"

"The only gun he *could* have got was Ashthwaite's."

"In that case Ashthwaite is a guilty party. He must know if he parted from his gun."

"Yes. I suppose he must, and I must admit that I can't see him doing it. A man like Ashthwaite, when he's out with a gun, doesn't lay it down or give it to someone else to carry. Also, Ashthwaite was carrying his gun when John Staple met him in the dales." Marion Garth turned to Macdonald, puzzlement in her eyes: "So you see," she went on, "all my thinking hasn't got me anywhere. I'm just as much at sea as I was at first."

"You've told me a number of interesting things all the same," replied Macdonald.

"Have I?" She turned and looked at him, noting his long limbs, his leanness, and appearance of physical fitness. Marion Garth assessed men in terms of the work they could do, and Macdonald looked as though he would be capable of much more physical endurance than Layng, whose figure was getting bulky. Somehow she liked this deep-voiced stranger.

"All I have said is a commonplace to ourselves," she went on, "what I call common sense." A smile lightened her weather-beaten face. "Your Superintendent thinks all farmers are fools, doesn't he?"

"I don't own him, and if that's his opinion, I don't share it," replied Macdonald. "On the contrary, I believe if you all held out on me, I'd get nowhere. It's only with your help that I can understand this business."

She laughed. "John Staple said he thought you were a good learner. I expect you're a Londoner, aren't you—but you do seem to understand what we say, which is more than most Londoners do."

"Your speech up here is nearer my own than London English," replied Macdonald. "I'd probably have fought against you at Flodden Field, but I understand your speech all right. Now there's another point, Miss Garth. Layng's point—I'm working on his report, of course. Incidentally he made out a very able report. He mentioned your eldest brother, Richard."

"Yes; he asked a lot of questions about him. All I can tell you about him is that he quarrelled with my father when he married Mary Ashthwaite, and went to Canada in 1919. I haven't heard from him for nearly twenty years. The lawyers are going to advertise for him. He inherits the land, you know. It's entailed."

"That seems rather hard on you," said Macdonald, but she answered:

"Oh, no. I don't want to be a landowner. I'd be quite content to be a tenant farmer. I shall farm anyway, and provided the government doesn't let us down, farming's quite a good proposition these days." She faced him again with her square face resolute. "Some people would be quite capable of saying that I shot my father to gain independence. I do inherit some capital under his will, and it means that I *am* independent for the first time in my life—but I didn't shoot him. I know it's no use saying that, because I've no means of proving it, and it could be argued out that I had plenty of time to do it. I was by myself from half-past three until I came into tea about five."

"Provided you didn't do it, you've nothing to worry about," returned Macdonald. "I wish you would tell me this. Is there any means by which Ashthwaite might have known that your father would go to the hull when the hunt was over?"

"None that I can think of. I didn't know myself."

"Look at it this way, Miss Garth. Supposing your father was out and you needed him for some purpose or another—needed him very badly. Wouldn't you try and put two and two together to argue where he might be?"

"Well, I'd know or not know."

"Doesn't it depend on the season of the year? At haymaking or harvest you'd know which field he was in."

"Yes—because I should be there, too."

"If the river rose suddenly and no one had gone down to the river pastures to drive the beasts up, wouldn't you have expected him to do it?"

"Oh, yes. He had an extra sense about the river, he always knew when it would rise."

"Very well. Now you said you didn't know that he'd gone to the fox hunt—but didn't you think there was a very strong probability that he had?"

"Yes—but I didn't *know*."

"Quite. If you'd wanted to make sure, you could have gone to see if he'd taken a gun with him?"

"Yes—but I didn't."

"All right. Now isn't it true that you—or someone else on the Home Farm—told John Staple that two stirks were missing from their pasture?"

"Yes. I told him. I asked him to look out for them. Didn't he tell you so?"

"No. He only said he was looking for them. Now if they'd broken out, didn't it mean a fence was probably defective or needed mending?"

"Yes—unless a gate had been left open."

"There were materials for mending a small break in a fence in the hull itself. Do you know if your father heard you ask Staple to look for those stirks?"

"I don't know. He might have done."

"And isn't it possible that if he did hear you say so, he might have gone to look at the pasture and the fence on his way to the fox hunt? He could have gone to Lawson's Wood that way, couldn't he?"

"Yes." She turned and looked at Macdonald with a frown of concentration. "You're being clever over this—much cleverer than the Superintendent. You've thought it out much more clearly than I could have myself. The upshot is that if I'd used my brains that way, I *could* have argued out that father might go to the hull for a post and a mall after the fox hunt was over—but I didn't."

"Was there any way you could have known when the fox hunt was over and the guns dispersed?"

"No. I might have noticed that there were no more shots—but that might have indicated that they were beating for another fox. As it happened I didn't notice the shots at all. Until about half-past three I was helping lift potatoes, and the noise of the tractor prevented me hearing anything else. Then I came back here and started on the onions, and I certainly didn't notice any shots."

"Why was it you decided to leave the potatoes and start on the onions?"

She chuckled. "You're thorough, aren't you? I like that question. It's one I should have asked myself. The tractor went wrong. Do you know the contraption we use for potato lifting? It's a bit like a small propeller, and its blades turn over the soil and throw up the potatoes. We've only had it this year. Unfortunately nobody has ever invented anything for picking up the potatoes, and you have to do it by hand. It's a poor job. When Elizabeth Meldon said she'd have to spend some time on the tractor engine to get it to rights I wasn't sorry. Frankly, I prefer onions."

"Had you no one to help you gather the potatoes?"

"Not that afternoon. I had told Jem he could go as beater, and Bob has taken his gun out. He doesn't often get a chance of any sport."

"Your brother Charles didn't help?"

"Lifting potatoes? You haven't met Charles. He has a back which aches—though he's quite useful at some jobs. Not that one, though. As for Malcolm, the mere mention of potatoes made him find it necessary to go and look at his hives up on the fells. Actually he's lame, and a bending job nearly kills him."

She paused and said: "That's Charles just coming in if you want to see him. I don't think he'll be very helpful. He's been in Malaya for years, and he doesn't notice things here very much."

Macdonald heard the footsteps as a man strolled up the cobbles and turned into the flagged yard. Charles Garth looked disillusioned, Macdonald thought, as well as rather weary. Remembering Marion's statement "He has a back which aches," Macdonald had to control a chuckle as he got up to face the newcomer.

II

"This is Chief Inspector Macdonald, Charles. He has been trying to make me use my wits, but his own are much more efficient. He'd better try his conundrums on you." She turned to Macdonald. "I'm going in to wash. Newborn calves are messy creatures to handle. If you want me again, I shall be indoors."

"Thank you very much for being so patient," replied Macdonald.

"You remind me of my dentist a bit," she answered unexpectedly. "He's always very polite, but he pulls my tooth out just the same."

Macdonald laughed outright at that, as he turned and exchanged nods with Charles Garth. "I've never been likened to a dentist before," he said.

"Rather apt. My sister's a bit of a wag at times," replied Charles, seating himself rather heavily on the stone bench. "God preserve me from you if you *were* a dentist," he added. "You'd look a formidable fellow with a pair of forceps. Well? Come to any conclusion yet? We're finding this business a bit wearing."

"I'm sure you are, very wearing indeed," replied Macdonald. He had sized up Charles pretty quickly: the ex-rubber planter was finding English farming heavy going, but he retained something of his erstwhile manner—bonhomous but a touch condescending. His voice had none of the north of England quality so noticeable in Marion's: Macdonald diagnosed it as "only one vowel and hardly any consonants." He went on: "I only arrived in these parts last night, so I haven't had much time to look around. I have found your sister and Mr. Staple very helpful, because they have enlightened me on conditions round about here. I admit I find the problem a complex one. There are so many possibilities. What is your view, Mr. Garth?"

Charles shrugged his shoulders. "It's difficult for me to have any views. These farmers are an unknown quantity to me after twenty years out east. My sister says that none of the farmers did it—she should know, she's lived amongst them; I say that no one in this household did it. I can't imagine that a homicidal maniac hid in a calf hull on the off-chance of shooting someone. That brings me to my last point. There's that idiot boy. He seems the strongest probability."

"But where did he get his gun from?"

"Ashthwaite—to a certainty. Ashthwaite would have known that Jock had been promised a thrashing by my father, and that Jock would have hated him. An English half-wit isn't so different from a Malayan or Goanese half-wit when all's said and done. They're the same mixture of idiocy and cunning. Give one of my half-witted boys in Maramula a gun and he'd have shot the overseer who'd bullied him. I think that's the likeliest explanation."

"You may be right—but Ashthwaite took a risk. If he'd been seen without his gun, people might have remembered it."

"Certainly—but Ashthwaite knows the lie of the land and the habits of the farmers. He would have thought all that out. However, I'm only offering you a theory. Obviously I've no proof. It's a matter of elimination."

"Quite. I only regret that no one can produce any evidence, as, for instance, if anybody had seen your father coming back over the fields—or seen Jock in the interval between the end of the hunt and the time the shot was fired."

"But the time isn't fixed, is it?"

"No. There's a margin of half an hour at least—probably more. There's one piece of evidence I should like your opinion on, Mr. Garth. First, will you answer a question. Have you, since your arrival in England, had any American coins in your possession?"

"American coins?" Charles stared. "What are you getting at? The answer is 'no.' When I arrived in England I had no money. That's a literal fact. I reached Java in shorts and a ragged singlet. I was lent a coat and a sun hat. When I reached Australia I contacted a firm I'd done business with, and they booked my passage to England for me, and also, very generously, gave me a small guarantee at an English bank. One of them—a personal friend, lent me a fiver so that I should have a spot of money on board. A fiver—I ask you. I played bridge in the hope of doubling it: I did win a bit—but by the time we reached Liverpool I hadn't a shilling left on me. As for American coins—where the deuce do you think I got them—and why on earth do you want to know?"

"The reason's very simple. A twenty-five cent piece—U.S.A.—was found among the peat moss in the hull."

"Good God!" Charles Garth stared, his face frowning. At last he said: "I begin to see daylight on one point—the Superintendent's interest in geography. He wanted to know by what route I reached England. Why the deuce couldn't he have asked me about the coin straight out, as you have done? I suppose he thought he'd got a likely suspect. Well, well… Anyway, I've never had any American coins on me. I know that."

"Can you help me by making any suggestion as to how such a coin got into the hull?"

"God help us—what a question. I haven't the faintest notion. One thing's pretty certain—Jock didn't drop it. Of course…"

He broke off, and sat forward, leaning his chin on his hands, his elbows on his knees, staring at the flags. Macdonald waited for a while and then echoed Charles's last words.

"Of course?..."

Charles raised his head. "Nothing. I was just thinking. It's damned odd."

"What connection can there be between Garthmere and an American coin?" went on Macdonald. "There haven't been any Yankee troops about here, have there?"

"No, not to my knowledge at least. I haven't seen a Yank since I came here. In any case, troops never come to this back of beyond—not even English ones."

"Your elder brother went to Canada, I'm told."

Charles groaned. "Oh lord, you're trotting that out again. I told the other police wallah his detection was a bit hoary when he got on to Richard. Damn it, man, he left here twenty-five years ago, and no one's seen him since. If Richard had put in an appearance in these parts the whole place would be buzzing with the news. There's mighty little to talk about in Garthmere. Weather, crops and beasts—and then beasts, crops and weather for a change. If any of the farmers' sons come home on leave, or a stranger is seen at a farm sale, the fact is chewed over *ad infinitum*. No. If Richard had been seen, we should have heard about it."

"Is this possible—that he has been seen, and that folks are careful not to mention the fact to you?"

"Why on earth?—of course they'd tell us."

"I wonder... It might look rather like making a suggestion that he was responsible for the shooting."

"Tact, eh?" asked Charles. "D'you think our farming neighbours are that tactful? Well, anyway, I can't go round the valley asking, 'Have you seen Richard lately?'—you must do that yourself."

"I'm doing it—of necessity. Not that I expect any result that way, but it's got to be inquired into. The other point which strikes me is this. I don't believe your brother Richard—even if he did it—went and secreted himself in the old hull on the off-chance that Mr. Garth might visit it some time."

Charles began to laugh. "Sorry. I'm not being flippant, but the picture you conjure up is rather priceless. Returned prodigal goes to eat husks in a hull, and waits patiently for days, or weeks, as the case may be, until hated parent puts in an appearance. Not too good, what? Incidentally, it's my brother you're talking about."

"Yes. I hadn't forgotten—neither had I forgotten that it was your father who was shot."

"All right. Don't let's lose our wool. I'm willing to discuss the Richard possibility, but don't talk to Marion about it. She's had enough to put up with lately, for all that she looks so tough. If you're going to put it on to Richard—though the idea's mad to my mind—kindly explain two things. One is: how did he know the old man would go into the hull? two is: how did he get a shotgun? Did he bring it from Canada with him?"

"Both very cogent questions, Mr. Garth. Let us consider the second one first. We don't know that your brother has been in Canada all these years—or do we?"

"Search me!" said Charles. "We've just taken it for granted."

"In detection we can't take anything for granted. He may have been living within a few miles of this place—unknown and unrecognised. He may have been in Wensleydale, or up in the Lakes, or up by Kirby Stephen. Folks here don't go far afield."

"Damn it, you're right there! So what?"

"If he intended to do what we are suggesting, he wouldn't have wanted to be seen carrying a gun, even though he had changed out of all recognition. He would have known there was one place he could find a gun—and ammunition as well. Here, in your gun-room. He could have counted on the fact that nothing would have changed here while your father was alive."

"My God!" groaned Charles. "You're suggesting he came *here*, to this house?"

"Why not? How many people were in this vast house that afternoon?"

"Here? Nobody—except the old Biddy—Mrs. Moffat. She was in the kitchens, because I saw her half a dozen times."

"Exactly. Jem and Bob Moffat were at the hunt. Your brother Malcolm went up to the fells. Miss Garth and Miss Meldon were lifting potatoes. You were about the shippons. I haven't been over this house, but I should imagine that there are a good many ways of approaching and entering it, unseen from the kitchen quarters."

"Lord, of course there are—dozens of them." Charles mopped his forehead. "I can't get used to this idea," he said. "It gives me the hump. Richard and I played in this house as kids… it's a beastly idea."

"Murder *is* beastly—with apologies to the beasts," said Macdonald. "Now here is a theory. I put it up like a skittle for you to knock down. Richard Garth may have been in the neighbourhood unseen. He may even have made contact with someone who told him about the fox hunt."

"Ashthwaite?" burst out Charles. "If so, he'll never admit it. Never—no matter how you third-degreed him."

"Anyway—assume for the moment that your brother knew about the fox hunt. It was an opportunity—there's no disguising it. Every one in the place was out with a gun. He could have guessed that no one would be left in the house on a fine September afternoon. Could he not have got into the house and borrowed a weapon?"

"Of course he could," replied Charles. "Equally, of course, he didn't. It's fantastic. Anyway, you haven't answered the other part of the question. How did he know that father would go to the hull?"

"He couldn't have known, but if he were in touch with Ashthwaite, he could have guessed at a probability. Isn't it true that two of your stirks broke out and were missing from their pasture on the morning of the hunt?"

"Were they? God knows—I don't, and neither do I see what that has to do with it."

"It means that a fence or gate was broken, or the beasts wouldn't have got through. Who generally did odd jobs like mending fences? Did Mr. Garth ever do it?"

"We all do it—it's one of those never ending jobs. The hedges on this farm aren't thick enough, and they're always having to be reinforced. The old man would bung a post in, or cut some thorns to fill a gap if he noticed one."

"It's a poor sort of job I should imagine. Cutting thorns isn't every one's notion of fun."

"Fun? If you think farming's fun you come and try it," growled Charles. "It's just one damned grind from morning to night."

"One needs to have done it all one's life to enjoy it, I expect," said Macdonald. "To get back to my theory: if a fence had been broken and your father knew of it, wasn't it likely that he would have gone and mended it after the hunt was over?"

"Possibly—but how could any one have known in advance that the cattle *would* break out?"

"By the simple expedient of tampering with the fences."

"My God!" Charles sat up and took a deep breath. "I'll hand it to you for brains," he said. "I shouldn't have thought of that in a hundred years. Where are we now? Richard moves a post out of one of the fences and makes a psychic bid that the old man will go and mend it after the fox hunt, first fetching a post and a mall from the hull. It's a bit far-fetched, y'know. I might have gone to the hull, or Jem or Bob."

"Certainly. Therefore I think it's probable that your father was watched, and that brings me to my next point. Is there anywhere on these premises where a man could have hidden and watched the fields between Lawson's Wood and the hull?"

"No. You can't see the hull from here. Come and look—the trees get in the way."

Charles got up and led the way to the highest point of the paddock which adjoined the fold yard, and Macdonald followed him.

"There you are: that's the best vantage point looking east-wards—but you can see neither hull nor field path."

"No, you can't," agreed Macdonald, "but I wasn't thinking of a place in the open, like this. It would have been too risky. I mean somewhere in the buildings."

"Up on the roofs, for instance? You could see right over the fields from there, but it would be the devil of a business getting up and down. You can come in and see the house if you like. I'll show it to you with pleasure."

"Thanks very much. I'll take advantage of that offer some other time. Now I've got to get on and see to another job. Meantime, think over what I've been saying, and let me know if you think it hangs together."

"Right—I'll think it over. I admit you've made out the deuce of a clever case—but I don't believe it. There are too many assumptions and loose ends. There's also this to it: Richard's my brother—I never was very devoted to him and I'm not sentimental over blood ties, but I'll tell you this. I don't believe he did it. It's all out of character. We may be a rum lot—every man jack in the valley will agree that we are—but we've never been in the habit of murdering one another. Got that?"

"Yes—and I respect you for your statement, Mr. Garth."

"O.K. Well—you want to be getting on. When you want another crack, as they say hereabouts, you know where to find us."

"I do. Many thanks, and good day to you."

CHAPTER TWELVE

I

"NOTHING LIKE TRYING IT OUT ON THE DOG," WAS Macdonald's remark to himself when he left Charles Garth. "Taking the two of them, Marion and Charles, I'd say Marion was the better man. Moreover, if she'd made up her mind to a certain course, she'd follow it out. Now where was I going to pick up the corn miller's man?"

Macdonald was lucky in this matter. After only one inquiry, made of a farmer who gave the stranger a prolonged stare, the Chief Inspector found a blue Austin car waiting outside a farm at Wrafton, and shortly saw a grizzled, rather worried looking little man coming out to the car.

"Are you Bowden's representative, Mr. Toller?" inquired Macdonald.

"Yes, sir, that's right," was the reply.

Macdonald was amused to note that this was the first "sir" which had come his way in Lunesdale. "He must be a Southron," he said to himself.

"I should be glad if you would spare me a few minutes' conversation, Mr. Toller," went on Macdonald. "Could we talk in your car? My name is Macdonald." He produced his official card, and Mr. Toller looked at it with a mixture of lugubriousness and excitement.

"If you wouldn't mind, Chief Inspector, I would suggest we get in the car and drive on a short way. The fact is, if the farmers saw me talking to a detective—well, it might go against me. I have to be careful in my job. No talking about one farmer's business to another is my rule."

"Quite right too," agreed Macdonald. He got into the car and Mr. Toller drove on until he was clear of the farm premises.

"You see," he explained, "if the farmers thought I gossiped they wouldn't trust me, and confidence is everything to a traveller."

"Of course it is," replied Macdonald. "The reason I have come to you is this: it seemed probable to me that you, going from farm to farm, would hear a good deal of the gossip of the neighbour-hood—and you'd hear all the more because you're careful not to pass it on. Now you can guess the job I'm here for. I'm investigating the circumstances of Mr. Garth's death."

Macdonald sat and talked to Mr. Toller for some time, and at the conclusion of his talk he knew that he was working along the right lines. There *was* a rumour abroad that Richard Garth had been staying in the neighbourhood, and that rumour had its origin in a village near Ingleton.

"To tell you the truth, I've been very worried," said Mr. Toller. "You know what these farmers are. They don't tell you anything directly. It's more in the way of question: 'Have you heard anything about so-and-so?' they'll ask, and then change the subject—but something's being said. It may be all rumour, but I don't know. I don't know."

Before he parted from Mr. Toller, Macdonald gave assurances that he would do his best not to disclose the source of his infor-mation. Mr. Toller obligingly drove Macdonald to a spot where he could get a Carnton bus, assuring him that his bicycle would be perfectly safe where he'd left it.

"The folks about here are very honest," he said. "They'll prob-ably report that bicycle to the police some time next week."

Macdonald reached Carnton just when Layng was returning from his midday meal.

"Hallo—any luck?" inquired Layng.

"More than I deserve—though it may turn out to be rumour," replied Macdonald. "I've heard a vague report that Richard Garth has been seen in Panstone, near Ingleton. Can you let me have a car? I want to go over there and see about it."

II

It was by sheer good fortune and nothing else that Macdonald went into the Wheatsheaf Inn, near Ingleton, about two o'clock that day. He had not had any lunch, and while he did not expect that the Wheatsheaf could provide him with a meal, he thought a glass of beer and a sandwich might help him on. The landlord, a grey-haired, toothless fellow, tall and gaunt, was not encouraging when Macdonald first inquired for "a bite," but after a moment or two he said there was a bit of rabbit left in the pot, and eventually produced a plateful of steaming stew rich with vegetables. Macdonald sat down to his meal in a dark little parlour, furnished with the solid oak and elm of the neighbourhood, with some fine spindle-backed chairs. There was a small table on which were piled old copies of the *Farmers' Weekly*, the local paper, and old editions of *Bibby's Annual*. When he had finished his meal, Macdonald rummaged under the papers and found an ancient exercise book which had seen many years of service as visitors' book. The later pages were ruled out in conformity with regulations to show the name of visitor, home address, date of arrival and departure and nationality.

The last entry ran September 20th–21st. Richard Garth. British. Merchant Navy.

Macdonald sat with the page in front of him, hardly able to believe his eyes at first. He then went to the door and shouted for the landlord.

"Aye. Will half a crown suit you?" demanded Matthew Hodges.

Macdonald put some coins down on the table.

"As good a dinner as any man could want, landlord," he said, "and now for a word on a different subject. My name is Macdonald. I'm a police officer, and here is my warrant. Can you read?"

"Not without my glasses, but I'll take your word for it."

"Right. Have you looked at this last name written in your visitors' book?"

"That? 'Twas a seaman—a right good chap, he was. Name of Clark, or summat like that."

"No, landlord. Not Clark. Garth—G-A-R-T-H. Have you ever heard the name in these parts?"

Matt Hodges scratched his stubbly chin.

"Garth?" he muttered doubtfully. "There's none of that name in our village. There's Garths down the valley."

"Aye—there've been Garths down the valley since before Flodden Field," said Macdonald. "Have you heard any news from Garthmere lately, landlord?" Matt Hodges sat in silence, and Macdonald went on: "Aye, you're in a cleft stick. News travels. It's being said by a good many that Richard Garth was seen hereabouts lately. Now we'll not argue over that. There's no law which forces a man to report on the doings of his neighbours when he's no proof that his neighbours have broken the law."

"Ah… Eh… So you're looking at it that way," said Matt Hodges, and there was relief in his low growl.

"Yes, I'm looking at it that way—unless I find reason to look at it any other. I'd say you're not the only man in these parts who has reason to believe Richard Garth was in this district. You haven't refused any information to the police, so far as I know, and you've told no lies—so I've nought against you. Now say if you tell me all you know about Richard Garth, remembering that I am a police officer, and I ask in the name of the law."

"There's little enow to tell on. Last Monday evening 'twas—and a gey girt dirty evening too. About half-past eight, when the rain was coming down in floods, a chap came in here and asked for a bed—and a bite of supper. He was wet through, and I wasn't that anxious to take him in, but my wife said yes. He looked like a seaman, and our Mitsy's married a chap in the Navy. Anyhow, there 'twas. We gave him a room and lit a fire for him. Next morning he had some breakfast and took himself off—and that's all there was to't. He put his siller down and went his way."

"Didn't you have a crack with him, or your missis—for Mitsy's sake?"

"Nay. He weren't no talker. I said to him, 'You're come from afar?' but he wouldn't say nowt. 'Twasn't till he'd left I looked in yon book—and then I knew who he'd minded me of. But I'd no proof, mind you."

"We won't quarrel over that," replied Macdonald. "Do you know where he went? Did he wait for a bus?"

"Nay, he just walked out. Hiking like."

"And that's all you can tell me, landlord? You know the oath you'll be asked to take—the truth, the whole truth, and nothing but the truth."

"So 'elp me, God," concluded the landlord. "Aye, I know it— but there's nowt more I can say. He came in here and asks for a bed and a bite. I had a word with t'missis, who saw him come in. 'Give him a bed,' she says, 'and there's some eggs he can have for supper. Looks like a seaman, he does, and he's wet through anyway.' He had his supper in this room, and we took his coat to dry it. 'If you've any logs to spare, let me have a fire in my room,' he says, and the missis, she saw to't. He went upstairs when he'd finished his supper—never came in the bar even. Aye, he was a close one—but none the worse for that. The morning 'twas the same. Paid his reckoning and went."

Macdonald sat silent for a moment. "How many people did you tell this to, landlord?"

Again Hodges scratched his chin. "Can't call it to mind," he said. "I may've named it. Why not?"

Macdonald did not press him—he knew the loyalty of these folk and guessed that Hodges would not admit to whom he had passed on his news.

"I want a description of him—what he looked like and what he wore," was Macdonald's next demand.

Mrs. Hodges was called in to assist here, and the description arrived at was summarised by Macdonald thus: Richard Garth. Age about fifty. Grey hair, short greyish beard, weather-beaten face, blue eyes, prominent nose. Wearing navy blue trousers, a blue seaman's jersey with roll collar and short navy blue coat. No hat.

"He must have been a noticeable figure, quite different from anybody hereabouts?" queried Macdonald.

"Aye. Outlandish he looked to me. I wondered what he was until he spoke," replied Hodges. "His voice was all right—bit o' twang, maybe, but he said 'Aye' same's you and me, and he said 'twas a gey dirty night. I reckoned he came from these parts."

Having collected all the information he could, Macdonald drove to the nearest constabulary and set out an all-stations call with a description of the wanted man, as well as an inquiry via Trinity House to all ports and harbour-masters. He then turned his car back to the inn, and set out on foot by the route which Hodges informed him his visitor took. A by-road, which later became a footpath, took him to the base of Ingleborough, and Macdonald started climbing the great limestone hill. Underfoot the turf was short and slippery, and larks sang overhead as he made his way up the vast shoulder of the hill, the wind whistling ever more keenly as he climbed.

Truth to tell, Macdonald wanted to think—and walking helped the process. He visualised Richard Garth—arriving from the unknown, gone into the unknown. He would have been a noticeable figure in this remote countryside: he had carried no suitcase, and could therefore have had no change of clothes. Had he walked down the valley towards Garthmere it seemed inevitable that he must have been noticed, not by a few people but by every one who met him. Surely someone would have reported seeing this unusual stranger. Yet it seemed to Macdonald that a man like Richard Garth, reared in Lunesdale, must surely have wanted to see his own home land again. Had he climbed this great limestone mass, which stretched for miles north and south across the head of Lunesdale? Ingleborough must have been the most familiar sight in the world to Richard Garth when he was a boy—it seemed to close in the world to the east of Lunesdale, a barrier across the sky. So Macdonald thought, as he climbed up the slippery turf until he could see the Lune and its valley, the heights of Clougha above Lancaster, the sands of Morecambe Bay and the Lakeland hills. Had Richard come up here to see all this? And if so, where had he gone? He could have reached Yorkshire or Westmorland or Lancashire, chosen any of a hundred routes. Sitting on the limestone turf—midway between earth and sky it seemed, Macdonald smoked one pipe while he wrestled with his problem and weighed alternate theories in his mind. It seemed to him that he could put forward a case against six different people which, if argued by an able counsel, could persuade any jury to convict any one of them.

III

It was nearly half-past five when Macdonald drew his borrowed car up outside Lonsghyll. He went in through the yard and drummed on the back door with his knuckles. John Staple appeared immediately and Macdonald said: "Here I am, back again for another consultation, Mr. Staple."

"Step in and have a cup of tea," replied Staple. "I'm just having my own and you'll be welcome."

"Thanks very much. That's very good of you," replied Macdonald. He followed Staple into the kitchen and sat down at the table. "Losh keeps! We don't get teas like this in London," he said.

"Eh, but happen you don't work in haytime from three o'clock in the morning to midnight," replied Staple. "'Twas three o'clock I was out cutting on Midsummer Day. That's young Malcolm's honey if you'd care for it, and the butter's our own churning. How did you find Bob Ashthwaite, Mr. Macdonald?"

"Well—he didn't try to chuck me out," replied Macdonald, "but I've got other news I want your opinion on. It's this. Richard Garth stayed on Monday night at the Wheatsheaf Inn, outside Ingleton." He watched the older man's face as he spoke, and added: "You knew that?"

"Aye. I knew," replied Staple, looking Macdonald full in the face. "I met him and talked with him upon the fells yonder. I still say what I said before: Richard didn't do this job." He paused, settling himself more comfortably in his chair. "Mark you—I've told no lies," he went on. "No one asked me 'When did you see Richard Garth last?' The Superintendent asked me 'Did I know anything about him?' I answered I'd known him as a boy and that I hadn't heard any one name him for years—and I hadn't, neither. Why didn't I tell you, you might ask—seeing you trusted me. Aye. I know that. I'll tell you for why. Because I promised Richard I wouldn't say I'd seen him."

"He asked you to promise that?"

"Aye—and I say again—he didn't do it."

"How do you know that, Mr. Staple?"

"Because I knew Richard. He's been on the Atlantic convoys these past three years, bringing tankers over so that our boys can beat Hitler. D'you reckon a chap like that would come and shoot his own father—aye, and run away, leaving an honest man to hang for him, maybe? D'you believe that?"

Staple's voice was fierce and his grey eyes shone with indignant fire.

"I know. It's hard to believe, Mr. Staple," replied Macdonald, "but I'll answer you straight. You can tell me later if I'm wrong. Richard Garth's appearance wasn't entirely unconnected with his father's death. Don't take me amiss. You could have saved me a lot of trouble—if I'd only asked you that one direct question which I did ask Bob Ashthwaite—when did you last see Richard Garth?"

"Aye. I'll admit all that. I've been troubled in my mind over it. You see I knew Richard as a boy: many's the time he's sat in that chair you're sitting on, swining into the apple cake. He asked me to say nought, and I promised. Was I to break my promise? I tell you I lay awake and sweated after I talked to you last night. You'd met me fair, and you'd trusted me. Still, I knew you'd find out pretty soon: you're no sort of fool."

Macdonald laughed, he couldn't help it: the conclusion of the sentence struck him as comic. "All right. We'll let that pass. Now, will you tell me what Richard Garth had to say?"

"Aye. I'll tell you that."

John Staple gave a very fair report of his conversation with Richard on the fell side, though he did not stress Richard's admitted hatred for his father. "Now see here," he concluded. "Richard told me he'd four days ashore between voyages. I saw him on Monday. His father wasn't shot until Thursday. What was he doing in between whiles? And tell me this: if that was what he planned, would he have come and had that crack wi' me? Wouldn't he have kept out of my way? I didn't see him until he came up to me and spoke to me."

"So he told you that he was tramping over into the Yorkshire dales," said Macdonald. "I climbed half up Ingleborough this afternoon, racking my brains as to where he went and what he did. That's a long stretch of hill, is Ingleborough."

"Did y' think he might have dropped something handy for you to pick up whiles you did your detecting?" asked Staple, and Macdonald laughed.

"To look for a clue on Ingleborough has got the proverbial needle in a haystack beaten hollow," he said, "but maybe I did hope I'd find summat as you say. Aren't there any Ramblers' Associations I could persuade to go over the ground for me, and save my own legs?"

"You'd better try the chaps who go exploring the potholes," said Staple. "There's a fair company of them—make a hobby of going down those great holes."

"No accounting for tastes," said Macdonald. "Now I've got a job I want you to do for me, and some more questions for you to answer. The job is this: come up the fell with me and show me exactly where you saw Richard Garth and talked to him."

"Aye, I'll do that right now—but you won't find him there now."

"No. I don't expect I shall, but I want to see the place. Now for the questions. Where were you when you were told those stirks were missing from the Home Farm, and who told you about them?"

"Miss Marion told me. 'Twas the morning of the fox hunt. I looked in to see young Malcolm, to get some of that heather honey if so be he'd got any to sell. I was talking to him in the fold yard and Miss Marion called to me from the barn."

"Was old Mr. Garth anywhere about at the time?"

"Aye. He was nearby—at the grindstone if I remember rightly."

"Any one else within earshot?"

"I can't rightly say—but any one could have heard. Miss Marion called to me from the barn—sung her question out, so's I could hear." Staple pondered, and said at last, "You're thinking it was that took the old man to the hull, to get a post to mend the fence where the cattle had broken through?"

"I think it's probable, Mr. Staple—don't you?"

"Aye. It's a good plain bit o' reasoning. Shows sense—and you're no farmer, neither."

"No—I wish I were. Tell you what, I'll try to come up here next hay time and lend a hand with the carting, and you can tell me how I shape. Now come along—I'll drive you up the fell as

far as the car will take us, and you can show me where you saw
Richard Garth."

Five minutes in the car and then ten minutes rough walking
brought them to the wall where Staple had stood and talked to
Richard. With the keen wind in his ears, Macdonald stood and
faced north, looking over the valley to the opposite fell side. He
had to turn his head away from the wind to hear Staple's words
when he spoke.

"If you've reasoned right about the old man making up his
mind to mend that fence when Marion spoke o' they stirks, then
you can't say Richard was there to hear."

"I can't be certain, Mr. Staple. I've played in my uncle's barn
in the Highlands, and I've hidden in the hay in the loft when I'd
earned a leathering... I tell you it's not impossible."

"Meaning he lay hid in that loft for days and listened, biding
his time? Nay, lad, you're wrong. You've got a good head on you,
but you're wrong there."

Macdonald turned away and looked over the wall. Malcolm's
bee-hives were in a wired-off enclosure just beyond the wall. In
one spot, where the heather grew high and the wall broke the
wind there were signs that someone had been there not many days
ago. The heather was bent and broken where a tall man might
have rested at full length. Into Macdonald's mind came Marion's
statement to Layng, "Malcolm was probably up by his hives... He
often goes to sleep up there."

Before Staple realised what he was doing, Macdonald had got
over the wall without disturbing a stone. He looked down at the
bent heather and saw a small book lying half hidden by the wall.
It had been drenched with rain, and was still limp and damp—a
little copy of Coleridge's *Ancient Mariner*.

Putting it in his pocket, Macdonald called to Staple, "What direction did the wind blow from last Monday when you were up here?"

"Nor'west. 'Twas a keen wind, caught my rheumatism. It veered to full west later, and the rain came on as we finished carting. Nine o'clock that was. We worked by moonlight to get the oats in—aye, and we got a proper drenching."

As Macdonald got back over the wall again, Staple was still talking half to himself. "Ould Mr. Garth, he came to help me cart my oats, and he worked three hours that evening, tossing them hattocks. How many landlords 'd do that for their tenants, and him an old man over eighty?"

"Aye—that's a good memory," said Macdonald. "You won't forget that, Mr. Staple."

"I shan't forget... and I tell you this, though you're a London detective and you've got a head on your shoulders, 'twas as likely I shot the old man myself as that Richard did. You can think and think again, but all your thinking won't make sense o' that."

CHAPTER THIRTEEN

I

MACDONALD DROVE STAPLE BACK TO HIS FARM, AND THEN went on to the nearest telephone call-box and put a call through to Layng, asking him to arrange certain matters for the next day—Sunday. This particular course of action had been suggested to Macdonald by a remark of Staple's. He then drove back to Garthmere, left his car close to the old hull, and went in by the fold yard gate.

There was nobody about. Macdonald paused to consider. It was Saturday, and probably Jem and Bob Moffat had both knocked off at middle day, since both haymaking and harvest were over, and there was no urgency over lifting potatoes or turnips. The milking would be done, the cattle turned out to pasture again, and probably the Garths were having a belated tea.

Macdonald went into the barn by the side door and waited until his eyes grew accustomed to the half-light. It was a fine structure, the great roof beams more impressive than those of many an ancient church: regarding them thoughtfully, Macdonald decided he liked the beams all the better because they were not shaped to a smooth finish, but showed the original irregularities of the wood. The open space of the barn where he stood held bins and chests and gear; at the farther end, beyond the double doors which admitted the hay carts, was an open loft, loaded with hay to the pent roof above, save at one side where a ladder ran up to give access to the store. Below the loft the floor of the barn was some feet lower than the main parts: here were the cow stalls or shippon, where a dozen cows could be tied up at milking time or housed in the winter months. They were empty now, and the shippon door stood wide open.

Macdonald walked across the rough floor of the barn and mounted the ladder leading up to the loft. There was no window here, but high above, just under the angle of the pent roof, a small space had been left open to admit daylight. It was twelve feet above Macdonald's head, but he found another ladder lying by the wall, presumably used when the hay had been piled up to the roof. Not without difficulty Macdonald upended the ladder against the hay, tested its stability and mounted it. As he had expected, the gap up in the gable was a fine view point: he could see over tree tops and hedges and irregularities in the ground, right to Lawson's Wood in the distance, and to the door of the old hull nearer at hand.

"Here a little and there a little," he said to himself as he descended to the loft floor.

He had just set foot on the rungs of the lower ladder when a change in the light told him that someone was standing at the side door of the barn, impeding the daylight. A cool voice said:

"And what the dickens do you think *you're* doing?"

Macdonald reached the ground and turned before he answered the unfamiliar voice. A tall lanky lad stood by the door, regarding Macdonald with amused dark eyes. The latter answered:

"Are you Malcolm Garth? My name's Macdonald."

"Scotland Yard in the Shippon, or The Corpse in the Hay Loft," responded the other. "Have you found anything?"

"Only what I expected to find—a good view," replied Macdonald. He pulled from his pocket the damp little copy of *The Ancient Mariner* he had found by the wall on the fell side.

"I think this is probably yours. I found it in the heather," he said.

"Oh damn... I mean, thank you very much," replied Malcolm. "I *am* a fool! I like that book—and look at it now."

"Yes. Distinctly damaged," replied Macdonald. "Considering the way it rained on the Monday night and all day Tuesday, it's only surprising that the book's recognisable as a book at all." He paused and then went on, evenly and deliberately, "How much of the conversation did you hear when John Staple talked to Richard Garth up on the fell side near your hives last Monday?"

Malcolm stood quite still, his pale face curiously white in the half-light of the barn. "I heard most of it—but I wasn't much the wiser," he replied, and his voice was quite steady. "You won't be much wiser either," he continued, "because although I listened-in, I'm not going to repeat what I heard."

"I haven't asked you to, laddie," replied Macdonald. "I've heard the gist of it from a pretty reliable witness named Staple."

"Hell! He never told you he'd seen Richard! I don't believe it!"

"If it interests you, I knew that Richard Garth had been in the neighbourhood before I asked John Staple about their conversation," replied Macdonald. "Now I may have a lot of questions to ask you later on. For the moment, one question outweighs the others in importance. That is—how many people did you tell about having seen Richard Garth on Monday?"

"I didn't tell anybody."

"Quite a good effort, but it's not true," replied Macdonald. "If you're interested in detection, you might like to know that the motives which make people give untrue answers are among the chief points to elucidate. It's quite often done from the best intentions, such as shielding someone else."

"I'm not shielding anybody."

"No? Then you're lying from a baser motive—the desire to shield yourself."

"Damn you, I'm not!" burst out Malcolm furiously.

"Don't be silly," replied Macdonald, not condescendingly and quite good-humouredly. "You've got plenty of wits," he went on. "Consider this. I'm more than double your age, and for more than twenty-five years I've been interrogating people like yourself—people who have no idea of the amount of patient donkey work which is described as detection. If I hadn't learnt the elements of my job in that time I should have been kicked out years ago. I have come here to find a murderer, and you know it, and yet you give silly answers which are obviously untrue because you won't face the issue clearly."

Malcolm was stubbornly silent, and Macdonald went on: "You can answer my question truthfully now, or you can come into the house with me, wait until I have collected every member of the household, and listen while I interrogate each one of them concerning the question I have asked you. It will probably be a long-drawn-out and rather painful business, because it will involve a detailed account of exactly how every one spent his or her time on Monday evening and on Thursday between dawn and five o'clock." Still Malcolm was silent, and Macdonald continued: "The word 'alibi' has a romantic flavour, but the proving or breaking of an alibi is often a tedious—and generally unromantic—business. But it can generally be done. Now for Thursday afternoon, you have no alibi at all. I don't know what is your estimate of human nature, but I tell you this. If you stick to your statement that you told nobody about having seen Richard Garth, I shall have no alternative but to arrest you. You may be willing to face that yourself, but do you think every one else is going to be willing to see you charged with murder and make no effort to help you by telling the truth?"

In the silence which followed, the sound of footsteps on the stone flags outside rang out clearly, and next moment another figure was silhouetted against the light at the side door of the barn. Elizabeth Meldon, in a gay cotton frock, called "Malcolm! Do buck up! Whatever are you doing?"

"Oh, go away, Lisa! Go away!"

"Will you come in, Miss Meldon? I am trying to get an accurate answer out of young Garth here, and I'm not making much headway. You know who I am?"

"I suppose you're the Scotland Yard man," she said, and Malcolm cried again:

"Go away, Lisa—it's not your business!"

"I think it may be Miss Meldon's business," replied Macdonald. "The question I want answered is this." He turned to her and asked: "Did Malcolm Garth tell you that he had seen his half-brother Richard on the fell side on Monday? I know that he did see him, and he hasn't denied it. All I want to know for the moment is—did he tell you that he had seen him?"

Elizabeth soon made up her mind about answering, and her answer was plain: "Yes, he did tell me."

"Have you repeated that fact to anybody at all?"

"No. Not to a soul. If the Superintendent had asked me, I should have told him, because I don't believe it's any good telling lies—but I didn't see that I'd got to tell unless I was asked."

"We won't argue over that," said Macdonald, and turned again to Malcolm. "Now we've got that point clear, will you tell me if you passed the same information on to anybody else?"

Malcolm did not answer, and Macdonald became suddenly aware that the lad was swaying as he stood. It did not need Elizabeth's cry of "Catch him!" to make Macdonald spring forward and save him from falling. He lowered the boy neatly on to the floor of the barn and lifted his inert wrist.

"Is he liable to fainting fits?" he asked Elizabeth, and she nodded.

"Yes. His heart is funny. He faints if he gets upset or over excited. I'll go in and get some water and sal volatile. He'll be all right in a minute."

"Tell them he's fainted—I'll bring him into the house in a little while," said Macdonald.

He stayed beside the lad in the shadowy barn, and presently saw his eyes open.

"All right. Keep quiet for a moment, you'll soon be better," he said.

Malcolm frowned in a concentrated effort of recollection. "She didn't have anything to do with it," he said, and closed his eyes again.

Elizabeth came back with a glass in her hand, and Marion Garth followed her. Marion expressed no surprise at seeing Macdonald there; she only said, "We must get him to bed. Can you carry him, or shall I help?"

"I can do it. He doesn't look very heavy," replied Macdonald.

He lifted the lad skilfully and took him into the house. There was a settee in the kitchen, and Macdonald obeyed Marion's injunction and laid Malcolm thereon.

"He'll be all right after a bit, and then he'll be able to get upstairs on his own feet," she said. She walked to the door, beckoning to Macdonald to follow her, and she led him outside into the yard.

"It's no use talking in there where he can hear us," she said. "What happened—or can't I ask that?"

"I think you've every right to ask," replied Macdonald. He told her, very simply and clearly. Marion sat down on the low stone wall as though all the strength had gone out of her.

"Richard..." she said, her voice very low and sombre. "How unbelievable... I still don't believe it. Charles told me what you said this morning, but we neither of us believed it. Do you know where he came from?"

"He's in the Mercantile Marine, or so he told Staple."

She looked up at Macdonald, her heavy eyes lightening a bit.

"Then he will have gone back to his ship?"

"I don't know," he answered. "I've got to find out."

She looked down, her face heavy and brooding: "I suppose that's what Malcolm has been worrying over. He's looked like a ghost all this time. I was afraid..."

She broke off, and Macdonald said: "Will you go in and ask Miss Meldon to come and speak to me?—and I'm afraid I shall have to wander round the house a bit. Perhaps you had better understand this: I think it's probable that the gun used for shooting your father was a gun in this house. I shall have to look at them, and study exits and entrances."

"Do as you like. The whole thing is so horrible I'm incapable of thinking clearly about it. I'll send Elizabeth Meldon out, and if you want me again, she will fetch me."

II

Elizabeth came out and joined Macdonald in the shadowy evening. "What is it you want to know?" she asked.

"I want to know exactly when, where, and in what circumstances, Malcolm Garth told you that he had seen Richard talking to John Staple."

"It was on Monday, after tea—about six o'clock. If you'll come

round to the other side of the house, I'll show you exactly where
we talked."

She led him to a gate at the farther side of the flagged yard, and
they then turned the corner of the house.

"This used to be a formal garden in the long ago," said Elizabeth,
"but it's a very long time since any gardeners worked here."

"You've got a grand crop of onions over yonder," said
Macdonald, and Elizabeth replied:

"Yes. They ought all to be up by now. Miss Garth has been
working at them every minute she can spare, but it's always the
same trouble in the country—there isn't enough time."

They had passed a stretch of level grass, which had once been
a lawn, where some geese were preening themselves happily. On
their right was the house, on their left a low wall of dressed stone
with smooth slabs on top.

"That's the window of the 'parlour' where we have meals,"
said Elizabeth, indicating the long french window. "We had had
tea on Monday, and Marion had said that she was going to offer to
help John Staple cart his last load of oats. She went to telephone
to him, and I was waiting by the window when I heard Malcolm
calling to me. He was by the orchard gate—over there. I went
over to him, and we walked in the orchard, and he told me how
he'd been asleep up in the heather, and had woken up and heard
two men talking just on the other side of the wall where his hives
are. He listened to them, and realised that it was his half-brother,
Richard, talking to John Staple. Soon after they had left he came
home here to tea. That was all."

"Thank you for telling me about it so clearly," replied Macdonald.
"Now I'm afraid there will be a lot of other questions I want to
ask you, but if I'm going to look round inside the house, I think

I'd better take advantage of what daylight is left. There isn't any electric light, is there?"

"Gracious no! The only modern thing in this house is the telephone, and Marion had an awful tussle to get that. It was such a nuisance not being able to get at the vet, and the cattle-van people and the corn millers. You'll find most of the farmers round here are on the phone."

"I wonder if you'd show me my way about inside a little? This house looks a formidable proposition."

"Oh, no—you see we only use a small part of it. Hardly anybody except old Mr. Garth used the big staircase. We all use the kitchen one. Of course I'll show you the house. Shall we go in by the parlour—it's the usual way—when we don't use the kitchen door."

She led Macdonald through the parlour and as she opened the farther door she said:

"This passage leads to the kitchen—through that baize door; if you turn the other way you get to the office—where Mr. Garth and Marion kept their bills and forms and accounts—and to the big dining-room which is never used and then the main staircase."

"And the gun-room?"

"That's just here—it's really under the kitchen stairs."

She opened another door and Macdonald switched on his torch. The small room was used as a cloak room; there were Wellington boots and mackintoshes and ancient tweed coats and cloaks hanging on the walls. The guns—six of them—hung on racks, and Elizabeth explained:

"The two top ones are—were—old Mr. Garth's, and the rifle is his, too. The double-barrelled shotgun below that is Marion's, and the lowest two belonged to Charles and Richard. I believe they're very old. Charles has tried both of them, but he says they're hopelessly antiquated. Marion says he only complains because he's a rotten shot."

"Is he?"

"Oh, yes, hopeless. He tried potting rabbits at harvest until I told him I wouldn't go on driving the tractor unless he put his gun down. He's a menace with a gun."

"Do you shoot?"

Macdonald was looking round as he spoke, observing the boxes of ammunition on the shelves above the gun racks.

"Well—I can, but I'm a pretty poor shot, and it doesn't give me any pleasure. Mr. Garth was a wonderful shot once, and Marion's very good. She gets wild duck sometimes—and that's not easy."

As he listened to the girl's quiet, unembarrassed voice, Macdonald thought what a queer place the world was now. Elizabeth Meldon could have taken her place anywhere, in university or drawing-room—and she worked as a farm labourer worked, at any job on the farm. While she talked, Macdonald lifted down the guns, broke and examined them: each one was unloaded, cleaned and in good condition. Anybody, on that afternoon when old Garth was shot, could have come into the empty house, borrowed gun and ammunition, used it, cleaned and returned it to its rack.

He switched off his torch and turned to Elizabeth. "Shall we go on exploring? I only want to see the kitchen, and any other entrances on the ground floor which are generally used."

"There's a side door which leads to the kitchen stairs—close beside the kitchen itself, then there's the kitchen door, the scullery door and the dairy door. Most people come to the kitchen door. It saves time."

Macdonald paused just before passing through the baize door:

"If anybody had wanted to enter the house without going through the kitchen on the afternoon of Mr. Garth's death, how many entrances were there for them to choose from?"

"At least three: the parlour window, the side door by the back stairs, and the office window. It's nearly always left unlatched, and it's a long window so it's easy to get in by. Then there's the dairy: you can go through the dairy and come out into this passage—look, through there and down the stone steps."

She led the way down the steps into the stone-flagged dairy, which had another door leading out into the fold yard as well as the door into the kitchen. A flickering light was showing in the kitchen, and Macdonald went in there to find Marion lighting a lamp and Charles sitting on the kitchen table.

Marion looked up from her task. "Malcolm's gone upstairs, Elizabeth. I think he's all right now. Do you mind going and blacking out for him and seeing his lamp is all right? Don't let him talk too much."

"All right. I'll go up."

Elizabeth went quickly out of the room and Marion began to close the heavy shutters.

"Can I help you with that?" inquired Macdonald, and she replied:

"No, I'm used to it. These shutters are devils to move."

Charles heaved a ponderous sigh. "Where are we now, Chief Inspector? It all looks pretty grim to me."

"So far as the evidence goes, you know as much as I do," replied Macdonald. "It seems perfectly plain that it would have been quite easy for anybody to have come into this house on Thursday afternoon and borrowed a gun—and returned it later."

"I told you you oughtn't to have touched those guns," growled Charles. He turned to Macdonald. "When Marion came back in here, after she'd phoned to the police, she went and checked up on each of the guns in the gun-room," he explained.

Marion cut in in her usual decisive way: "I wanted to know if any of the guns were missing—or if they'd been used or left loaded. I'd been worried about leaving my own gun about... It went off in the office one day."

"Yes. I heard about that," said Macdonald. "When you examined the guns after your father was shot, what did you find?"

"Nothing. They were all in order—unloaded and cleaned."

"Perfectly correct," said Charles. "I looked at them, too. I suppose we ought not to have touched them—but there it is."

"But I *still* don't see how anybody could have known father would go to the hull," protested Marion. "It's all so stupid and inconclusive... Richard *might* have done this, *might* have done that..."

"Your brother knew this place well," said Macdonald. "He would have known that it was possible to see as far as Lawson's Wood from at least one point easily accessible here—that is, from a ladder on the loft of the barn. You can see right out over the fields from the gap up in the gable."

Marion sat very still, staring at Macdonald. "Even so, even if he'd seen father coming over the fields towards the hull, he wouldn't have *known* he was going in there."

"No—but if your father had seen the door of the hull was open, isn't it almost certain he would have gone to shut it—as John Staple did?"

"Oh Lord, yes, I suppose so." It was Charles who answered, his voice depressed and irritated, as though he found it an effort to control himself. He drummed with his fingers on the table and went on: "Admittedly you've made out a case, and a damned clever case, but you haven't any proof at all. It *might* have happened as you say—or it might not. Personally, I don't believe it."

"What are you going to do?… or is that an idiotic thing to ask?" Marion spoke wearily, and Macdonald replied:

"The obvious thing to do is to find your brother, Richard. That may take time—but it's got to be done. Meanwhile I'll be getting on my way. I hope that lad won't be any the worse. Good-night."

Macdonald walked to the kitchen door and Charles followed him. "Good-night. I can only say again—I don't believe you're right."

It was dusk as Macdonald made his way outside to his car, and just as he was getting in a voice called to him softly, "Mr. Macdonald, just a minute."

It was Elizabeth Meldon, and he stood up and waited for her.

"I've been talking to Malcolm," she said. "He didn't tell any one else except me that he'd seen Richard. I'm quite sure he's telling the truth about that. He's been worrying about it all—that's what made him so queer." Her voice was hurried and a little breathless, and she went on: "I expect you think I'm silly, trying to explain things, but I'm so sorry for Malcolm. I *know* he didn't do it, but it's so hopeless to try to prove it."

"There's one thing you could do, if you would, Miss Meldon," replied Macdonald. "It's this. Will you try to write down a description of everything that was said and what happened at tea time on Monday afternoon, from the time Malcolm came in until you went into the oatfield—where you all sat and what every one did so far as you can remember?"

"Yes. I'll try—but nothing much was said or done… However, I'll do my best, though I'm not much good at writing things down. Wouldn't it be easier if I tried to tell you?"

"If you'd rather. Will you come with me in the car a little way and we can talk?"

"Of course." Elizabeth got in the car and Macdonald drove on for a few hundred yards in silence. As he pulled up Elizabeth spoke again.

"I've been thinking: perhaps I'm all wrong and just being horribly suspicious, but I have remembered something a bit queer about Monday evening..."

And Macdonald listened to the girl's low breathless voice talking in the gloom.

CHAPTER FOURTEEN

I

MACDONALD STAYED AND TALKED TO ELIZABETH MELDON for well over half an hour, and it was almost dark before he drove on. About a mile from Garthmere he made out a man's figure walking ahead of him in the gloom and he slowed up as he overtook and called, "Would you like a lift?"

"Thanks! Would I not! Footslogging isn't my idea of bliss."

Charles Garth scrambled into the car beside Macdonald saying, "I've come out for a drink. The fact that I'm willing to walk two and a half miles to a pub and then two and a half miles back may give you an idea of how much I want a drink."

"You don't care for your village local?"

"My God!" groaned Charles. "Think it out—and have a heart. If I go into the bar there's a sudden deathly hush—and then they start talking about the weather in hearty tones. I know what they've been talking about—and I don't blame them, but I'd rather not butt into an argument concerning the probability of my sister having shot my father, and variations on that theme."

"But surely the farmers round here wouldn't discuss your sister in such a way?"

"Oh, wouldn't they! You don't know them; they'd be careful enough over what they said in front of you, or any other stranger, but amongst themselves I'd lay a bet they've hanged one and all of us. Human nature's the same the world over. The devil of it is they all know everything that's gone on at Garthmere."

"Such as...?" inquired Macdonald.

"Oh, use your wits. You're not lacking in that respect," said Charles. "They all know that Marion is a first-class farmer who wants to put modern ideas into practice, and they all know that the old man thwarted her in every scheme she thought out. I've no doubt they all know that he wouldn't pay her a decent wage. If it hadn't been for those damned hens and ducks and geese Marion wouldn't have had a penny to call her own. It's the same with Malcolm: he can't do a full day's work, poor devil, he hasn't the physique for it, but the old man drove the boy till he nearly dropped at hay time—and then jeered at him in front of everybody because he writes poetry. My God! Do I want a drink? I ask you!"

"Yes. It must be pretty wearing," said Macdonald. "By the way, what pub do you want? Will the Green Dragon do? I'm staying there, by the way, but I don't think they've guessed who I am."

"Oh, haven't they! I bet every one knows who you are from Lancaster to Kirby. Yes, the Green Dragon's where I was making for."

He was silent for a moment and then broke out: "I'm in the deuce of a quandary, you know. You've been very decent to us—not rubbing things in. It'd be a relief to get a few things off my chest—knowing you're not likely to jump to wild conclusions."

"I take a conservative view of what I'm told," said Macdonald. "If a statement is relevant, I follow it up; if not, it's as though it hadn't been made."

"Good—then I can go ahead. I told you just now that some folk hereabouts are suggesting that Marion shot the old man. It's damned rot and it makes me livid, but I know the real trouble is that there's no proof. See here: you've got four of us, Richard and Marion and Malcolm and self. None of us has an alibi, I know that. You seem to have been putting your money on Richard. I can see your reasoning, but I don't believe it. Neither do I believe Marion did it, though I was bothered about that business of her gun going off in the office that day."

He broke off, and Macdonald, who had been driving slowly, pulled the car up, saying, "Sorry to delay your drink—but would you like to enlarge on that topic?"

"Well, it's like this," said Charles slowly. "Marion's a sensible, methodical creature. She didn't leave a loaded gun balanced against a table by mistake. Neither did she arrange a Heath Robinson pot-shot at the old man just when they were having a row the whole household could hear—cursing one another to high heaven. No. Whoever arranged that little incident, it was *not* Marion."

"Then who was it?"

"My God! You may well ask. There's one reason, and one only, why I'm telling you all this—because I won't have it said that Marion's the culprit. She's quixotic, you know. Did you notice that she said 'I was worried because I'd left my gun in the office'? She's willing to shoulder that now... Yet when she came out of the office that day, after all the shindy, she was livid because she knew someone else had left that loaded gun there... However, I'd better get my bit said and done with it. It's revolting enough in all conscience. You remember you asked if there was a vantage point whence one could see over the fields to Lawson's Wood?"

"Yes—and there is."

"You found a peep-hole in the hay loft. I thought of something else. There's an old lumber room over the dairy. Malcolm uses it for his bee-hive junk. I reckoned the window in there would give a view up the river, so I went up and had a look. There was a lot of stuff piled up in a corner, and I knocked some of it over when I tried to get at the window... I picked an old crate up—as I did

so I got hold of some filthy rag... which had been used for cleaning a gun barrel..." Charles Garth brought his fist down on his
open palm. "Lord, I feel a skunk telling you this!" he groaned. "I
went and told Marion... She just went up to the loft and took that
rag away. I tell you she'd let herself be hanged rather than... see
Malcolm suspected."

"Steady on," said Macdonald quietly. "Evidence can be inter-
preted in more ways than one. If one of the guns in your gun-room
was used for this job, it had to be cleaned before it was put away.
That lumber room isn't locked, I take it?"

"No. Nothing's locked in that house, barring the old man's desk
and chest. My God! This is a rotten business!"

"A rotten business it is," agreed Macdonald. "The only way of
clearing it up is to get at the truth. I'll tell you one thing, though
I'm chary of making such assertions as a rule—it's too easy to
make mistakes—but I don't believe your sister had anything to do
with the crime."

"Thank God for that," replied Charles, and then added: "By
way of anti-climax, I said I wanted a drink. I want one more than
ever now."

"All right. I'll drive you to it," replied Macdonald, feeling
for his gear handle. "There's one thing I should like to ask—
although you needn't answer it if you don't want to. You said to
the Superintendent, 'It doesn't make sense,' and you repeated it
more than once. Do you mean to imply that there's more than one
unbalanced person in this case—Jock being the one?"

"The Lord knows. Can you wonder that I've asked myself the
same question?" groaned Charles.

Macdonald drove Charles Garth up to the Green Dragon, but
he did not then seek to garage his car in the stable used for that

purpose. He drove on to Carnton to Layng's headquarters, and found the Superintendent waiting for him.

"Well, I reckon it's simply a matter of running the fellow to earth," said Layng. "There's a message for you from the Merseyside authorities. Richard Garth, seaman and ack-ack gunner, did not rejoin his ship before she put to sea this morning. Seems silly to me—but I suppose he knew we'd get on his tracks before he reached New York. A ship's as good as a rat-trap to a criminal these days."

Macdonald nodded. "A very fair analogy. Did you get on to the Ingleborough Ramblers, or whatever they call themselves?"

"Yes. They're the Pot Hole enthusiasts. Ever heard of those pot-holes—Gaping Ghyll and the rest?"

"Yes. I've heard of them."

Layng stared at Macdonald's non-committal countenance.

"Well, these lads are game to do their stuff for you, tomorrow being Sunday. They'll beat the whole hillside between them—and bring you anything they find, from a bus-ticket to a shotgun."

"Very kind of them. I shall probably go over to have a look-see. How long does it take to walk to Panstone from Garthmere?"

"Walk? Rather you than me. A matter of three and a half to four hours."

"Thanks—and you can get a bus from Ingleton to Lancaster?"

"On week days you can."

"Right. Now let me use your phone—and after that I'll tell you my own ideas of this case according to the evidence, strictly in camera—and if I'm wrong you'll have one good story to laugh over for the rest of your days."

"Story? Well, it's plain enough, isn't it?" said Layng indignantly. "Even a blockhead like me would have cleared it up if I'd been given the chance—though I'll admit you've been pretty snappy."

"Keep the bouquets until they're duly earned," said Macdonald, lifting the receiver. "Garthmere, 92," he demanded.

Layng sat and listened to Macdonald phoning. "Decent chap," he thought. "More considerate than I am by a long chalk."

Macdonald was saying, "Is that Miss Garth? This is Macdonald speaking. I'm a bit worried over that boy, Malcolm." There was a slight pause while Marion answered and then Macdonald went on: "I'm glad he's better, but all the same I think he's over excitable and capable of doing himself an injury. Will you undertake to stay with him to-night? If you feel you'd rather not, I can send a nurse."

There was another interval, during which Layng could just hear the murmur of Marion Garth's voice in the receiver. Layng murmured, "All very nice—and where the deuce do you think you're going to get a nurse? I haven't got one up my sleeve."

"As you will," said Macdonald at the phone. "I don't want to worry you, but I do think it's important that the boy shouldn't be left. I wouldn't stress it if I didn't think it was essential. If you'll undertake to do it, I'm perfectly satisfied."

"Doing the bed-side manner?" inquired Layng with a grin as Macdonald hung up the receiver. "We don't handle 'em quite so gently up here as a rule."

"I don't like making more trouble in the world than I can help," replied Macdonald, "and that boy went off slap into a fainting fit when I was questioning him. He's a neurotic type. However, you want to hear what I've been doing—and thinking, so here goes."

II

After Macdonald had rung off, Marion Garth went back into the
kitchen where Elizabeth was just making a pot of tea; Marion stood
and watched the girl as she set the teapot and milk and sugar on
the table, and poured out the tea.

"It's a good brew," said Elizabeth. "Why not have a spot of rum
in yours? It'd do you good."

"The rum's finished—or else it's evaporated," replied Marion.
"That was the Chief Inspector, Elizabeth. He rang up to say that
he was worried about Malcolm. He wants me to sit with him
to-night."

Elizabeth put the teapot down and then looked up at Marion.
Their eyes met and they stood in silence, each troubled but perfectly
self-controlled. At last Elizabeth said:

"If you do that Malcolm will get frantic. He's all right now—but
if you insist on stopping with him, he'll... imagine things."

"I know—but what can I do? Macdonald said that he would
send a nurse, and I promised that I would sit with Malcolm myself.
I couldn't bear the idea of a nurse. Anyway, I've promised, so I've
got to do it."

Elizabeth nodded. "Yes. I see. I do hate it though. I tell you
what we might do. I've got some Thalmane tablets upstairs. I'll
take him up a weak cup of tea and two of the tablets. They'll make
him sleep, because he's not used to taking them. Then you can go
in quietly when he's asleep."

Marion sat in silence, without replying, her face brooding, and
at last Elizabeth could bear her silence no longer.

"Oh, Marion, do say something!" she cried. "You know I
wouldn't hurt Malcolm. I'd do anything for him."

"I know you would—but I'm all at sea, Elizabeth. I just don't understand. Am I to sit with Malcolm as a gaoler—in case he runs away—or is it because he may try to kill himself, or because somebody might try to hurt him? It must be one of those things; it's not because he's ill."

"I don't know." Elizabeth's voice was quivering. "If you've promised you'll have to do it. I'll go and get that packet of Thalmane. It's a new packet, unopened—so you needn't be afraid. Heaps of people take it. An aunt sent it to me when I had that go of toothache, but I never opened it."

She hurried out of the room, and still Marion stood by the table, staring down at her cup of tea. Elizabeth came back and gave Marion the packet of tablets, saying:

"I'll pour out some tea for him. Will you take it up, or shall I?"

"You can. Malcolm trusts you."

Elizabeth's usually steady hands were shaking, so that the teacups rattled against the saucer.

"Marion, this is just the most ghastly thing that ever happened... What do you *mean*?"

"Just what I say. Pull yourself together, Liz. If I told Malcolm to take those tablets he wouldn't do it. He will if you give them to him. I'll come up after you quietly and wait outside the door. Leave it open and I'll slip in later. It's the kindest thing we can do."

III

Elizabeth Meldon came downstairs again and sat in the kitchen. She couldn't bear the thought of going to bed. To keep her hands occupied she found a jumper which she had meant to reknit and she sat unravelling it, glad of the mechanical occupation. It was nearly midnight when she heard footsteps on the flags and her heart jumped with a sickening apprehension. When the door opened and Charles Garth appeared, she nearly laughed aloud in a hysterical sense of relief.

"Good lord! What on earth are you doing at this hour?" he demanded. "Do you mean to make a new jumper before morning?"

"Yes," replied Elizabeth. "I sometimes get a fit of industry, you know." She was surprised that her voice was so normal. "As a matter of fact, Malcolm's rather poorly and Marion's sitting with him for a bit, so do be quiet as you go upstairs."

"Is that it?" said Charles. "Poor devil… he was always a nervy kid. I'll go up and tell Marion I'll take over for her. She's had enough to put up with lately, without sitting up all night."

"Don't do that, you'll only wake him up," replied Elizabeth. "I offered to do it, but Marion said she would. If you interfere she'll be furious. Malcolm needs a good long sleep, and he won't get that if *you* start arguing."

" 'A good long sleep,'" Charles quoted her quietly. "Well—one needn't grudge him that, poor kid. It's a bad show, Lisa. I met the Chief Inspector this evening."

She looked at him steadily. "Did you. I don't want to hear about it, Charles Garth. Things are quite bad enough without talking about them. Go to bed and leave me in peace."

"Well, well! Whose kitchen is this, my dear?"

Elizabeth got up and took a step backwards, still with her eyes fixed on him. "It's Richard Garth's kitchen," she said, "and when he tells me to clear out of it, I shall. Do you think he's likely to?—because I don't."

"I can't tell," replied Charles. "Has he a soft spot in his heart for you too?"

"Listen to me," said Elizabeth quietly. "I give you half a minute to get out of this room. I don't like you, and I don't like the smell of whisky. If you stay here any longer you're going to get exactly one gallon of cold water thrown right over you. I'm very strong, you know, and the pail's just handy."

Charles studied her thoughtfully. "God save us! Farming does coarsen a woman, doesn't it? Good-night, Lisa. We don't want any more rough stuff here. We've had too much already."

He went out of the room quite quietly, and Elizabeth sat down to her unravelling again, conscious that her eyes were smarting with tears.

CHAPTER FIFTEEN

I

Elizabeth had just finished her share of milking on the following morning—Sunday—when she heard the telephone ring, and she ran indoors to answer it, but Marion reached the phone first. A moment later she called to Elizabeth to join her in the parlour, and Charles Garth went to the phone in her place.

Marion's face looked less troubled. "That was Macdonald. He asked after Malcolm—quite gently and pleasantly—and I told him I thought he'd slept all night, and that he's still drowsy this morning and in no hurry to get up. Macdonald says he's sending a doctor over to see him. I said, 'Do you really mean a doctor?' and he said, 'Yes. Quite honestly, I think the lad's in a poor way, and I feel a bit responsible.' He sounds so decent, Lisa. Oh, and he wanted to talk to Charles—something about driving to Liverpool to identify a photograph of Richard, and to look through some things he'd left on board. Apparently he didn't rejoin his ship before she sailed."

A moment later Charles Garth came in. "Seems I've got to go to Liverpool with some police-wallah," he said. "Buck up and get some tea made, Elizabeth. They're bringing a car round for me. The Chief Inspector said they'd bring me back here before dusk. Quite a change to have a drive again."

Elizabeth went out to expedite the tea making, and Charles added: "It's a matter of looking at some of Richard's things. They've found his ship, so I suppose it's only a matter of time until they get him. It's a formality really. I don't think Macdonald himself believes now that Richard was responsible."

"Then why didn't he rejoin his ship?"

"G.O.K. More reasons than one for leaving a ship."

Half an hour later Charles Garth was driven away in a very smart police car, and Elizabeth turned impulsively to Marion.

"It's a gorgeous day, Marion, and we've got nothing important to do. Let's pick apples and play around in the orchard, and forget everything for a bit. Malcolm's all right. He's got piles of books if he wants to read, and he loves the idea of a day in bed. How long is it since any one had a day in bed in this place?"

"Not since Malcolm had pneumonia… Oh, all right, let's laze over breakfast and then go into the orchard."

"Good—and if you've any common sense, you'll take some cushions out and go to sleep in the sun to make up for last night. Things always look better in the morning."

Marion slipped her hand under Elizabeth's arm—a rare gesture from one of her reticence. "You are a brick, Lisa. Things would have been much worse if you hadn't been here."

Elizabeth smiled back—she had no intention of discussing "things" just now. "We'll make some coffee and put lashings of cream in it," she said. "There's still something to be said for living on a farm."

II

It was nearly dusk when Charles Garth returned. It had been a peaceful day at Garthmere. A doctor had come to see Malcolm— much to his surprise—and had told him to stay in bed for another twenty-four hours. Marion had asked if there were any cause for anxiety about the boy and Dr. Boyce had replied:

"No. Not anxiety—but he needs to go slow for a bit. He's too thin, his temperature's sub-normal and his heart is tired. Encourage him to laze and eat all that he can. What's the use of producing milk if you don't see that some of it goes down that fellow's throat? He could do with it."

Marion had felt comforted—prescribing milk for a lanky lad (who incidentally loathed milk) seemed a reassuring proceeding after the dark fears of last night's vigil.

Charles had only been in the house a few minutes when Chief Inspector Macdonald followed him. His face was grave, and he said to Marion.

"Can I talk to you and your brother for a minute? I have bad news for you, I am afraid."

Marion's heart gave another sickening thump; she said nothing, but led Macdonald to the parlour, where Charles was starting on his supper. Macdonald stated his news without further preamble.

"The body of your brother, Richard Garth, has been found to-day in one of the Pot Holes on Ingleborough. It was found by one of the associations which explore the Pot Holes."

There was dead silence for a few seconds when Macdonald had finished his sentence. Then Marion said: "What does this mean, Chief Inspector? Do you suppose now that Richard shot father— and then killed himself?"

"I don't know, Miss Garth. The matter will have to be investigated closely. I can't tell you anything more until after the inquest. I am sorry to distress you with this further burden."

"If only I knew," she said slowly. "I don't pretend that Richard's death means anything to me—he has been away so long. It's the horror of the whole thing, and not knowing what happened... or who did it."

"I know. I'm sorry," said Macdonald.

Charles said slowly, "I think your guess is probably right, Moll. If Richard *did* do the shooting, I think the rest is comprehensible."

He got up and followed Macdonald to the door, and accompanied him to his car. Charles then asked in a low voice:

"Was Richard killed by the fall down one of those infernal holes?"

"I can't tell you. The post-mortem has not yet been performed."

"Does this let Malcolm out?"

"Again—I can't say. That last piece of evidence you told me about the rag used for cleaning a gun will take some explaining." Macdonald stopped, as though he had suddenly remembered something and then said: "I meant to have spoken to your sister about that. We always like to have evidence corroborated. Do you mind staying outside for a while and I'll go back and speak to her."

"If you must, you must—but don't you think she's had enough to put up with for one evening? Let her forget Malcolm for to-night."

"I wish I could." Macdonald spoke very gravely. "Unfortunately I can't fall in with such comfortable counsel. There can be no forgetting until this case is settled."

"All right. I can't stop you." Charles spoke wearily. "I'll stay out here until I see you come back."

Macdonald went back by the now familiar fold yard gate; as he passed the smaller shippon two small calves mooed to him in thin little voices, and he wished again that he could turn farmer.

It was about ten minutes later that he returned to his car and found Charles sitting dejectedly on the running-board.

"Did she admit she'd seen that rag?" asked Charles.

Macdonald nodded. "Yes. She said that she had seen it, as you said, and destroyed it—because no one but Malcolm ever used that loft."

"Poor old Moll!" said Charles.

CHAPTER SIXTEEN

I

BY COMMON CONSENT, EVERY ONE IN GARTHMERE HALL WENT to bed early that night. Marion was heavy-eyed and silent, Charles moved about restlessly as though he were unable to keep still, and Elizabeth Meldon knitted with grim determination. She hated knitting, but anything was better than sitting with her hands in her lap. At nine o'clock Marion got up and said: "I'm going to bed. Charles, will you go up quietly. I think Malcolm's settled down, and I don't want him to be woken up."

"All right. I'll go up now. I'm sleepy after all that driving. Good-night, Moll."

He went yawning out of the room, and Marion and Elizabeth went their usual round of seeing that the doors were shut and bolted. Just before they went upstairs Marion said in a low voice, "If you hear anything outside, don't worry. There are police out there now. I saw one of them when I went to shut the ducks up."

Elizabeth squeezed Marion's arm. She did not know what to say.

Silence settled on the vast house: a stillness only broken by the occasional crack of an old board or the scurry of mice in the wainscot. Once or twice one of the cattle lowed, as though they were aware of strange human beings abroad. One of the constables who was on duty outside observed the faint beams of light which shone through chinks in the shutters. "Black-out not too good," he observed. The last light to be extinguished was in a window in the west wing—Malcolm Garth's room. He did not put his light out until nearly two hours after the other lights were extinguished. The lamplight in Malcolm's room shone out beneath his bedroom door and made a sharp line of yellow light which shone startlingly bright down the long passage outside. A watcher had been observing that light for more than an hour before darkness settled down on the passage—absolute darkness, which baffled the senses. The watcher in the passage kept very still. A listener might have heard the sound of breathing, but apart from that not a sound indicated the presence of the patient being who waited there. Downstairs, very far away, a grandfather clock chimed midnight and the watcher stirred at last. Boards creaked—that was all—but the boards creaked from different directions as the watcher advanced step by cautious step towards the bedroom door. There was silence again: the door handle was being turned, but the handle did not creak and complain as did most of the latches in Garthmere Hall. It was well oiled, as were the hinges of the old door: it opened with only the tiniest sound as it was moved inch by inch, and then silence fell again. The watcher at the door held his breath for a few seconds; the sound of Malcolm's breathing was audible now the door was open. The boy was sleeping soundly, breathing rather heavily in the darkness.

The watcher stirred again, and the blackness was relieved by the tiniest blur of light. An electric torch, muffled until it showed but the faintest of faint beams, was throwing that tiny uncanny glow on the floor. To one whose eyes were conditioned by the previous blackness the light was enough to show any obstacles and to pre-vent a collision with chair or chest which would have resounded throughout the silent house with an effect like a thunder clap. Step by step the watcher advanced towards the bed, and it was just as he reached within a yard of it that another beam of light slashed the darkness from the door and a low voice whispered, "Stop! Stop... don't make a sound... there's another way."

As though paralysed the man near the bed stood rigid. The pencil of light from the door gleamed on the pistol he held in his hand, and his first movement was to put the ugly weapon in his pocket.

"Don't make a sound... you'll wake him," whispered the voice. "Come out here..."

As though hypnotised the man by the bed turned and crept towards the eye of light and the unknown whispering voice. "Come!" it repeated.

The boy on the bed breathed more heavily and turned in his sleep, and the watcher who had crept up to the bed groped towards the light.

"Who are you?" he breathed, and there was terror in his voice.

The beam of light retreated a little, and in a panic the other leapt towards it, lost to all reason, overcome by the one mad desire to reach the whispering voice behind the beam of light. He sprang into the passage and the bedroom door swung to, shutting in the sleeping boy. The tiny swathe of light was still shining full on the watcher's face, bewildering him, as that other voice whispered, "Come! Come quickly!"

There was a sound of running footsteps along the passage as the watcher flung himself in pursuit and then a light was switched on which seemed to have the glare of a searchlight after the tiny beam which had preceded it. In that glare two men stood face to face and recognised each other. Charles Garth saw Macdonald only a yard away from him.

"God! It's you!" he gasped, and the silence of the house was rent by a report which echoed madly along the empty corridors, followed by the thud of a falling body.

II

Marion Garth had not slept since she went to bed that evening. She still did not fully understand what was in Macdonald's mind, but she instinctively trusted him. He had told her to go to bed or to stay quietly in her room, for he was coming back to the house to keep watch himself that night.

"I have trusted my own judgment in telling you that," he had said, "because I know you won't repeat what I say. Don't tell anybody that I shall be here."

"Very well. I won't tell any one," she had replied, and then asked, "And Malcolm?"

"I'll look after him," Macdonald had replied.

Hour after hour she had lain on her bed in the darkness, listening for she knew not what. She heard the strike of the grandfather clock, each hour seeming more interminable—and then she drowsed a little. She was awakened by the crash of a shot—a report which seemed like a bomb exploding in the echoing house, and she leapt up and ran outside along the passages, towards a beam of light at the stair head. "Malcolm!" she cried. "Malcolm!"

Macdonald's steady voice answered her.

"Malcolm's all right. Go to his room and tell him there's been an accident. He will probably think he's been dreaming."

Elizabeth Meldon appeared at that instant, and Macdonald said:

"Go and tell the Moffats there's no cause for alarm now—try to get them back to their rooms quietly. I've got a job to do."

"Malcolm?" She asked the one word, and Macdonald replied:

"He's all right… Charles shot himself. I'll tell you about it later."

She stood still for a few seconds and said, "I'll never forgive him for trying to put it on to Malcolm." And then she turned and ran down the echoing corridor calling softly: "It's all right, Mrs. Moffat. I'm coming. There's no need to be frightened any longer."

III

Long before daylight that same morning, Macdonald went into the kitchen and found Marion and Elizabeth drinking tea. Marion said, "We always make tea here when things are difficult. Won't you have a cup?"

"Thank you very much, there's nothing I should like better," replied Macdonald. "Is that lad all right?"

"Yes. I told him he was having a nightmare. He went to sleep again quite quickly. He was still a bit dopey after those sleeping tablets."

"Good. I was afraid of the effect of a shock on him. He's a nervy lad—but the doctor who saw him yesterday told me he wasn't likely to get unbalanced, he's quite tough in his own way."

Marion looked across at him, her eyes tired but very bright. "Can't you tell us what really happened, and get it over? I'm so sick and weary of this awful 'I wonder' feeling."

"Very well. If you'd rather hear it now, you've a right to," said Macdonald. "You've had a grim time, I realise that—and I'm sorry, but since things were as they were, it's better that it's all over, and that you haven't the misery of giving evidence at a criminal trial." He paused, and offered a cigarette to the others before he started his statement.

"I told you that Superintendent Layng gave me an excellent detailed statement, in which he included some shrewd comments on the various persons in the case, as well as a full report of the evidence you gave him. In addition to this, John Staple talked to me. I liked Staple, and I regarded him as a trustworthy judge of the folk he knew. He was certain that Ashthwaite had had nothing to do with the actual shooting, and he absolutely refused to consider for a moment that Richard Garth was responsible. Of course there was always the possibility that Jock had hidden in the hull—but I didn't believe that Ashthwaite would have risked letting Jock have his gun. Thinking the thing over after I had studied Layng's report, I considered who had a potent motive for shooting Mr. Garth. Motives can be reduced to a few elementary characters: hatred, jealousy, and desire to profit are the most usual. Take the first—hatred. Ashthwaite hated Mr. Garth, but, as Staple said, it didn't seem to make sense that he had waited so long to pay off his grudge, and had then done it when it was obvious to all the world that he had the opportunity. Ashthwaite is cautious, and he's also canny."

Marion nodded. "Yes. I always thought that. He isn't the type to take a risk."

"And if it was improbable on those grounds that he shot Mr. Garth, I thought it still more improbable that he gave Jock a gun and trusted him to do it. Jock might have shot anything or any-body, including himself," continued Macdonald. "Of necessity, I had to regard everybody here as suspect," he went on, "and I included Richard among those here. Yet I didn't believe that a son would wait for twenty-five years to shoot his father—and in any case Richard was heir to Garthmere. He had waited a long time for his heritage, but in the nature of things it wasn't likely that he would have to wait much longer. However—he had to be included as a Class A suspect. Then came Malcolm. He did not stand to gain much in the way of profit, if anything, but because he was a nervy, highly-strung lad, it was possible that he might have done such a thing in a fit of fury. Now as to Charles—and I pondered a lot over Charles. He had lost everything in Malaya. He was living a life he hated here, and he had very few prospects. It was plain enough that little profit would accrue to him on his father's death while Richard was alive—but if Richard were dead, then Charles was heir to the land, and Charles would have rather fancied himself as a landowner, or so it seemed to me."

"That's all true," said Marion slowly, "but I just didn't think it out."

"Well, now let us get down to the possibilities as I saw them last night," said Macdonald. "Richard Garth had been seen by Malcolm, and Malcolm told Miss Meldon about it in the orchard. Where was Charles at that moment? He had had tea with you, and grumbled bitterly about having to do more harvesting. Miss Garth went to telephone to Staple, Miss Meldon and Malcolm talked in the orchard—until Charles called them in. They hadn't noticed Charles while they were talking, but it seemed quite possible that he could have eavesdropped."

Marion nodded sombrely. "Again, I didn't think of that, but it was just like Charles. He *did* listen in, and I knew it, though I never said so to anybody else."

"The situation could have been reconstructed thus," went on Macdonald. "Charles saw, in one of those flashes that come over an unstable mind, that here was an opportunity. Richard was *known* to have been in the district. If he could eliminate Richard, and then kill his father, it was about a hundred to one that the blame for his father's death would be put on Richard. Now go back to that evening when you carted John Staple's oats—Miss Meldon remembers it."

"Yes," said Elizabeth, turning to Marion. "You and Malcolm and I all came in here for a hot toddy. We supposed that Charles had gone to bed—but none of us saw him. Next morning at breakfast Charles wasn't there. We supposed he'd gone into Lancaster by the early lorry."

Marion looked puzzled, and Macdonald went on: "Charles knew from overhearing Malcolm, that Richard was going to stay at the Wheatsheaf at Panstone. I haven't actual proof of the following points, but I expect to get it. I think Charles walked over to Panstone, spent the night in a barn, and watched early next morning to see if Richard would leave the Wheatsheaf and what he would do. Richard left after an early breakfast, and set out over Ingleborough. His body was found at the bottom of one of the deepest pot holes in the limestone, but he had been shot through the head. When the bullet that killed him is examined, I expect it will show the same breech markings as the bullet with which Charles shot himself a few hours ago." He paused here, and said to Marion, "I told you it was a grim story, but you wanted to know."

"Yes," she said resolutely, "I wanted to know."

"The actual facts otherwise are all at your disposal," said Macdonald. "I believed that the person who shot your father had reason to believe that he would go to the hull after the fox hunt, in order to get a post and mall to mend a fence. Probably Charles broke that fence deliberately. He had what must have seemed a marvellous opportunity with that fox hunt. Everybody was out with a gun—it would obviously be difficult to determine who did the shooting. Charles, on his own admission, went to Lawson's Wood and saw how the guns were placed. After that he came home and watched for his chance. He could overlook the fields from the ladder in the barn, and he went to the hull with his gun and shot

Mr. Garth when he appeared at the door of the hull. He then hurried back—knowing exactly what everybody in the household was
doing—cleaned the gun and replaced it in the rack. The gun he
used was one he had often complained of—it was covered with his
own fingerprints, and he was sensible enough to see that he ran no
risk there. That's a general outline. I may have missed a few points.
For instance it was Charles who put the twenty-five cent piece in
the hull—to incriminate Richard, and Charles, doubtless, who put
Miss Garth's loaded gun in the office—to incriminate everybody
else. He believed in confusing the issue."

"But *why* did he try to put it on to Malcolm?" demanded
Elizabeth indignantly, and Macdonald replied:

"Throughout the case he sought to confuse the issue: the
more suspects the better, though he was convinced, I am certain,
that a verdict would be brought in against Richard. It was for that
reason that Charles felt he could afford to be so magnanimous
about Richard. No one would have appeared more surprised than
Charles had it been proved that Richard was guilty. Malcolm was
only a second string—up to last night. I deliberately told Charles
that Richard's body had been found, but that the post-mortem had
not yet been held. Charles knew that the post-mortem would prove
that Richard had been shot through the back of his head—and the
situation looked desperate. I was convinced that if Charles were
guilty—as I believed him to be, he would make a desperate bid to
remedy the situation, either by bolting himself, or by a last effort
to weigh the evidence against Malcolm. That was what he did. He
meant to shoot Malcolm and fake a suicide by leaving the pistol
in his hand. That last tragedy, at least, was prevented. I suppose I
could have prevented Charles shooting himself—but I'm not sorry.
A murder trial in which the conclusion is foregone, is a horrible

business for those who have to give evidence." He turned again to Marion: "Don't think I don't realise what this recital has meant to you, Miss Garth. Again, I'm deeply sorry."

Marion stood up and took a deep breath, a tall dignified woman with a worn face.

"There's something else to be remembered," she said. "If it hadn't been for you, Mr. Macdonald, it might have happened that Malcolm was killed, too, and a verdict of murder and suicide given against him. In which case Charles would have inherited Garthmere. Oh, I know it's been horrible—but at least it's a nightmare from which there is an awakening. It might have been an endless nightmare—believe me, I'm not ungrateful."

She walked quietly out of the room, and Macdonald turned to Elizabeth. "Before I go I should like to thank you for all the things you remembered to tell me when you talked to me last night. They all helped."

"I never liked Charles," she said slowly, "and I liked him less when he began to be so nice to Marion after Mr. Garth was shot. It didn't ring true. The only queer thing I noticed at first was that Charles—who never had any money unless we lent him some, suddenly produced his own cigarettes in plenty, and took to going to the pub. Whisky costs money these days. I felt awful when I found myself wondering if he'd taken the money... from a dead man's pocket."

"Yes," said Macdonald. "It's an ugly thought—but I'm afraid it was true."

Elizabeth walked with him to the door, and as she opened it she gave a cry of relief. Above the stark blue line of the fells the sky was flushing to dawn, and the white mists of the valley were opalescent and luminous.

"Thank goodness for the beasts and the land!" she cried. "Presently Marion will come and help milk the cows and feed the calves and count the eggs, and do all the decent commonplace things which make life good... Listen! That's the calves calling already—they can hear our voices. Doesn't it smell good out here?"

"It smells very good," said Macdonald. He held out his hand to her. "Good-bye and good luck. I've liked this place so much... I wish I'd learnt to milk a cow..."

She laughed at that. "Come back again one day and try! If I possess a cow of my own by then I'll let you learn to milk her. Do you know the motto of Lancaster, by the way?"

"No. What is it?"

"Luck to Loyne. You wished me luck, you know."

"I repeat the wish," said Macdonald, "and—Luck to Loyne!"

THE END

THE LIVE WIRE

"NOW YOU THINK IT OVER, LORIMER. IT'S NOT AS THOUGH you hadn't any brains. You have. Use them to advantage. You can if you try."

Jeff Lorimer pondered over the Prison Visitor's well-meant words, applying them in his own manner, but in a sense very different from that implied by his mentor. Jeff had just served a three-month sentence, and he had had plenty of time to think while he was 'inside.'

The final talk with the official visitor had, to Jeff's way of thinking, 'just put the cap on it.' Wasn't he always thinking—thinking hard? He had been using his wits ever since he was a small boy.

"Our Jeff, he's a live wire, he is! You'd never believe a nipper could be so smart!"

Jeff's father had been full of pride in his offspring once, and yet now, at the age of fifty, Jeff Lorimer was leaving prison to start again at scratch, in his mind a sense of grievance that his abilities had brought him no reward.

"Use your brains…"

Jeff Lorimer fairly laughed when he remembered the words. "Not half I won't!" he chuckled to himself. "If only they're still at the same old game, I reckon I've got them bending!"

Jeff had plenty of friends. He used his first days of liberty to get into touch with them again, and to inform them about the results of his 'thinking' while he had been absent from them. Bill Higgins, an out-of-work navvy, and Bert Simpson, a powerful

ex-stevedore, were old allies of Jeff. Truly, their association had
brought them little profit so far, but, as Jeff said, "Luck had gone
against 'em."

"It'll be all right this time, mates," he declared, with the optimism
which had earned him the sobriquet of 'Sunny Jeff.'

"That beats the band! Cripes! How you think of it I don't know.
That's what I calls brains!" gasped Higgins. "I should never 'a
thought o' that if I'd tried till I was pink!"

"Now don't you bother with thinking, mate. Leave that to me,"
said Jeff. "You just do what I says—and then we'll see!"

Having organised the necessary assistance, Jeff Lorimer spent
some days in observing the scene of his objective. He was much
too intelligent to try to bring off a coup until he had studied the
conditions under which he would have to work.

Jeff spent a long time pondering over the time-tables so generously supplied by the railway company of his choice at its London
terminus.

He put some of the funds supplied by Higgins and Simpson to
the unaccustomed eccentricity of paying railway fares to various
places within a short distance of London. Jeff did not habitually
pay railway fares. He knew a few tricks which rendered such an
extravagance redundant, but on these occasions Jeff was full of
virtue. He was thinking.

Money had also to be expended on essential apparatus. Jeff
bought some yards of strong steel chain. He knew just where
to get what he wanted, and he bought the best. Higgins and
Simpson tested the strength of that chain, and pronounced it
"O Kay."

★

Finally Jeff bought a steel grapnel—a well-made gadget, whose jaws gripped tight with the simple law of the lever when the chain attached to it narrowed the compass of its business ends.

During several evenings Jeff sat with his chain and grapnel practising pitch and toss. He had a good eye and threw unerringly, with the skill of a lassoist—an art he had learned in a circus in his younger days.

"Funny how things comes in useful when you *thinks*," pondered Jeff darkly, harking back to the prison visitor. He remembered, too, the thrashings he had received from the circus owner while he fumbled with a lasso, years ago.

"Just shows—you never know when a chap's doing you a good turn," he said to his friend Bill, speaking with the optimism which had never quite left him. "I reckon I got this turn just so, mates!"

"Beautiful I call it!" agreed Higgins. "Seems you can't miss. 'And and eye workin' together. Oh, pretty!"

Zero hour was fixed for nine o'clock the following Monday morning at the London station. The departure platform for West Wensley suburban trains (non-corridor) was the rendezvous for Bill and Jeff. Bert was given his own post on the permanent way a couple of miles down the line (down side), having previously worked out a means of arrival and departure in which the railway regulations were not consulted.

Shortly before zero hour, Constable Jones, of the railway police, was standing by the carriage-way, on duty beside the vans of a long-distance train. The van was being unloaded, and Jones was keeping his eye on the packages which were being lifted from the train.

These packages were square wooden boxes, about twelve inches long by eight inches deep—very uninteresting objects to the casual observer.

They were uninteresting to Constable Jones, too. He had seen dozens of them: sometimes they were being brought in from abroad, sometimes being sent from England overseas, sometimes to destinations inside England.

In his own slow, rather dull way, the constable connected those prosaic-looking boxes with a newspaper phrase of some years back, 'The Gold Standard.'

The boxes contained bullion; they were packed with gold ingots—that strange, incalculable, precious metal, the possession of which had been likened to the Army by some wit. "You must have it, just so that you need never employ it."

Such witticisms were alien to the slow-moving minds of Constable Jones and his mates. He just thought of the boxes as the cause which brought him to the easy duty of standing by at the station. An easy job, but dull. Not any hope of advancement in it. Nobody had ever tried any liberties with those boxes at the station. They were too well guarded.

It was those same boxes which had been the basis of Jeff Lorimer's thinking while he was in prison. It irritated his nimble wits to think of gold—real solid, hundred per cent, indisputable gold—lying about on a station platform almost within reach of his fingers.

There *must* be a way of getting hold of it, Jeff had argued to himself, if you only figured it out, just thought a bit.

Jeff had thought, good and hard. He knew that the railway vans in which the boxes travelled were locked and guarded. He knew that the boxes were transferred to lorries for transit to the vaults of the various banks. No hope of getting hold of them *en route*.

The only time the boxes could be touched was during the short period when they were being transferred from train to motor van. Then, Jeff had observed, some of them lay on the platform for a bit. That was the crucial point on which Jeff's thinking had turned.

On the Monday morning Constable Jones watched the boxes of bullion being unloaded. There were bank officials standing by, to check the unloading and loading. The railway men who moved the boxes were all trusty fellows of known character. Jones felt a little morose. He wanted a chance to do a bit of smart work which would bring him to the notice of the authorities so that he could get his transfer to the plainclothes branch.

He looked around the platform and sighed. The train which was being unloaded was standing towards the end of the platform; the motor van, ready to receive the gold, was backed up conveniently by the train. There was no one within twenty yards of them.

Across the carriage-way which divided the two platforms, a little distance nearer the booking hall, the usual local train was standing. It had disgorged its crowded complement of passengers some minutes ago.

The driver had come forward to his cab, the guard was standing with his flag at the rear. One minute to nine. Jones nearly yawned. He knew a girl living in West Wensley. Pity he couldn't get into that train…

The guard's whistle blew. Jones turned his eyes resolutely back to his inanimate charges, and the local train began to draw out.

★

The first thing that Jones knew about any departure from the normal was a metallic rattle just behind him, and then a yell from one of the porters close by.

His slow wits galvanised into activity, the constable jumped round and saw with unbelieving eyes one of the boxes moving past him, attached to a chain and grapnel which issued from one of the windows of the local train which was accelerating on its non-stop journey to West Wensley.

The porter—Walter Bream—was the only witness to Jeff's skill in casting his grapnel. It was a beautifully calculated throw, made just as the train drew level with the boxes. In a graceful parabola the grapnel fell dead over the box and gripped it, a triumph of skill and thinking on the part of Jeff.

Jeff, crouching alone in an empty compartment, had his thrill of triumph at last. 'Use your brains!' he thought delightedly.

His hands still gripped his chain, but its end was made fast to the radiator under the seat. At its other end the grapnel bit the box good and true, and those solid ingots of gold were being drawn down the platform with all the power of the local electric train to motivate them. It was the triumph of mind over matter—Jeff's mind.

"By gosh, it's jam!" he chortled.

Constable Jones felt as though an electric shock had run through him, too. He had no time to think, but as the box drew past his feet he flung himself on it. His action was instinctive. The box was going.

"Stop it!"

Gripping it like a bulldog with his powerful hands he was pulled off his feet in a trice, and was dragged along the platform.

Walter Bream flung himself on to Jones's back; two bank officials followed suit, and the box with its human convoy went down
the platform like an electric hare. The chain was a good chain (Bill
Higgins and Bert Simpson had 'O-kayed' it, and they knew a bit
about chains).

Old Tom Harris, platform man for twenty years, blew his whistle and yelled "Guard!" as the guard's van of the local went by. All
to no avail. Jeff had thought of the guard and of the emergency
brakes in the guard's van.

Bill Higgins was sitting on the guard's head in the darkest recess
of the van. Bill had hidden himself there when driver and guard
changed ends. Jeff had been very thorough in his observation.

Constable Jones never knew how long he had held on to that
box. The few seconds which passed while he was dragged ever
more swiftly down the platform seemed an eternity.

Walter Bream was clutching the stout uniform collar and
unknowingly choking the senses out of the unhappy policeman.
Two bank officials were gamely gripping Bream. The combined
weight of four unofficial passengers attached to the nine o'clock
local were no odds to the power of the electric train.

The end came when Jones bumped from the end of the platform on to the metals. He was half-throttled; his grip gave; and he
bounced hurtfully on to the permanent way. For a brief second
there was a tangle of humanity, four guardians of the country's
gold, using their own peculiar idioms, as dynamic force flung them
into painful contact with the metals and sleepers and clinkers of
the permanent way.

Jeff saw them bounce. He saw them break apart, a whirl of arms
and legs, and he saw his box still safe at the end of the chain. Small
wonder he laughed! It was a good laugh, if his last.

He laughed so much that he forgot to draw in the slack of the chain when the human weight was released from it, and the box bounced merrily forward. Still laughing, Jeff felt a terrific blow as his chain fouled the live rail, and the current ran through him. Just a blow, he knew not from whence—nor had time to concern himself about it.

It was Walter Bream who saw the flash, when the chain contacted the conductor rail. It was the biggest fuse he had ever seen, and he thought for a moment he was dead, too. An intense blue light flashed across his vision, something crackled—and the train ahead began to slow down at last.

The signalman in the boxes said: "Blazes! Down line's dead…"

With the failure of power over the whole of that circuit the railway slowed down, stopped—as a man's pulse stops beating.

At his post two miles down the line, Bert Simpson waited in worried uncertainty. He knew to a minute the time the nine o'clock train ought to come in sight. He knew what his job was to be—salvaging the box when Jeff should release the chain and leave the loot to be gathered in by the powerful ex-stevedore.

Jeff himself was to drop off the train when it slowed down for the junction signals.

The whole thing had been worked out in detail by Jeff's calculating mind—but something had gone wrong. The trains which should have passed Bert did not pass. The whole section was dead. Uncertainty grew to fear, fear to panic.

"Cripes! I'm getting out of this. Something wrong somewhere," said Bert. "Time for me to git."

He got—just in time.

It was poor Bill Higgins who had to stand the racket. Jeff was no longer there to think for him. When the train drew to a standstill, Bill still straddled the inert form of the unconscious guard. True to his record for bad luck, Bill climbed out on to the permanent way just as the panting railway men drew level with him.

Bill gave them best. Six to one. He knew when he was beaten. Puzzled and unhappy, he saw Jeff being lifted from the train.

"Pore ole Jeff! He was a live wire, he was," said Bill sorrowfully, when he realised that Jeff was not playing possum.

"You've said it," said one of the railway men, not unkindly. "That's just what he was—a live wire. He forgot the current, mate."

When the Prison Visitor heard the story he was quite upset.

"He was a clever fellow," protested the bespectacled philanthropist sadly. "No end of ability if he'd only used it properly. I did my best for him. These men just *won't think*."

Bill Higgins, working out his own sentence, came to a contrary conclusion.

"It was all that thinkin' did for 'im," he concluded sadly. "If he hadn't thought so much, 'e'd still have been 'ere. Pore ole Jeff. A live wire, he was."

MURDER BY MATCHLIGHT

E.C.R. Lorac

'A man who played about on the fringes of the Black Market, who had fought for Sinn Féin, who lived by his wits – and who finally became dangerous to somebody and was knocked over the head in the blackout. It may prove to be a sordid story, but I certainly find it an interesting one.'

.　　　.　　　.

London, 1945. The capital is shrouded in the darkness of the blackout, and mystery abounds in the parks after dusk.

During a stroll through Regent's Park, Bruce Mallaig witnesses two men acting suspiciously around a footbridge. In a matter of moments, one of them has been murdered; Mallaig's view of the assailant is but a brief glimpse of a ghastly face in the glow of a struck match. The murderer's noiseless approach and escape seems to defy all logic, and even the victim's identity is quickly thrown into uncertainty. Lorac's shrewd yet personable C.I.D. man Macdonald must set to work once again to unravel this near-impossible mystery.

Includes the E.C.R. Lorac short story 'Permanent Policeman'.

MURDER IN THE MILL-RACE
E.C.R. Lorac

'"Never make trouble in the village" is an unspoken law, but it's a binding law. You may know about your neighbours' sins and shortcomings, but you must never name them aloud. It'd make trouble, and small societies want to avoid trouble.'

·   ·   ·

When Dr Raymond Ferens moves to a practice at Milham in the Moor in North Devon, he and his wife are enchanted with the beautiful hilltop village lying so close to moor and sky. At first they see only its charm, but soon they begin to uncover its secrets – envy, hatred and malice.

A few months after the Ferens' arrival, the body of Sister Monica, warden of the local children's home, is found floating in the mill-race. Chief Inspector Macdonald faces one of his most difficult cases in a village determined not to betray its dark secrets to a stranger.

BRITISH LIBRARY CRIME CLASSICS

ALSO AVAILABLE

Many of our titles are also available in eBook and audio editions